Kian

Kian

AN **UNDERCOVER BILLIONAIRE** NOVEL

MELODY ANNE

Montlake
Romance

Published by Montlake Romance, Seattle

www.apub.com

Amazon, the Amazon logo, and Montlake Romance are trademarks of Amazon.com, Inc., or its affiliates.

ISBN-13: 9781542046046
ISBN-10: 1542046041

Cover design by Letitia Hasser

This one is for Chris. Very rarely do people enter our lives who we truly don't want to live without. From the moment you stepped into my life, I knew you were that person. I adore you, Christopher. My world is a better place with you in it—always has been and always will be.

Chapter One

"Dr. Forbes to ER STAT."

The voice boomed over the hospital speaker system at the same time his pager buzzed. It was a Friday night in Edmonds, Washington, and there was no time for rest, with traumas pouring in through the double doors.

Kian was a trauma surgeon, and he loved the knowledge that he was capable of saving a life other doctors couldn't. And when it came to the kids, he had an extrawide soft spot. Yes, he'd seen enough trauma to last a lifetime, but the hope that he could save one more child kept him moving forward.

Kian swept through the corridors of the hospital as he thought about the fact that he was grateful to only work the night shift once a month. He'd paid his dues on nights and now enjoyed only being called in for special cases, but there was nothing that got his blood pumping more than a code-three ambulance coming through the doors. It wasn't uncommon for the ER physician to consult with the surgeons, especially in cases of trauma.

Kian screeched to a halt in the entrance to the busy ER as he glanced at the heavy commotion of hospital staff scurrying to and fro as patients rushed through the hospital doors. For a weekend night in suburban Seattle, this was nothing new. When he scanned the trauma bay, his heart lodged in his throat. Kian found a very pregnant woman lying on a stretcher covered in red as a highly capable staff did all they could to help her. Her clothes had been cut off, and it was difficult to see any area of her body that wasn't blood soaked, making it impossible to identify her.

A crime scene would have been less gory than what was before Kian. He quickly assessed the room. Detectives? Check. Gore? Check. Cries of pain? Double check.

On a stretcher next to the pregnant woman was a young girl—three, maybe four. Her eyes were wide with fear, and her frail body was covered in blood. Nurses worked efficiently to place her on the monitors and assess her for life-threatening wounds.

"We have a twenty-eight-year-old female, seven months pregnant, with approximately fifteen to eighteen stab wounds in the chest, neck, and abdomen. Blood pressure is 76/52, heart rate is 133, oxygen saturation is 82 percent, and we are bagging her while we prepare for intubation," a nurse called out. Kian nodded.

"Also, her three-year-old daughter, multiple stab wounds in the arm, back, and head, bleeding is controlled and her vitals are stable." The last part of her words came out slightly choked, and she had to clear her throat before she continued.

"The baby's heartbeat is one hundred and dropping, and we're having a hard time controlling mom's bleeding. We are transfusing blood now, but it may not be enough. We need to get her into the OR ASAP."

Without conscious thought, Kian was already getting to work, grabbing gloves and continuing to assess the progress the team was making. He noticed the new ER physician trying to maintain a grasp on the situation, but the man seemed overwhelmed. It was understandable.

"We need the NICU team and the neonatologist in the OR now in case this baby is viable," Kian said with sharpened focus.

"We did a fast scan that shows significant internal bleeding including lacerated liver, right hemothorax, and possible cardiac tamponade. We're also putting pressure on her left carotid artery, which has been lacerated. She has two sixteen-gauge IVs and an IO in place. We have two units of blood infusing now, and she's on her third liter of fluid," the ER doctor said, sounding exhausted as he prepared for intubation.

"It's not enough, we need to get her into the OR and open her up," Kian replied. The ER doctor nodded as Kian turned toward the OR to prep for surgery.

Just then, the woman gasped, and he felt her fingers gripping his arm. He stopped, tuning out all the sounds around him as he looked into the woman's face. She was staring at him, and there was something so familiar about her eyes. He was trying to put it all together, but it was just on the edges of his memory.

"Kian . . ." The word came from her mouth in a gurgle of blood, a mere whisper that might as well have been a shout.

He leaned down. His brows furrowed as he tried to recognize this battered woman. Why did it feel as if he were suddenly in a tunnel? The world felt as if it was slowly shrinking in on him, and he didn't know why.

"Kian," she said again, and he leaned in even farther as a nurse tried to stop him. He wasn't wearing enough protective gear, and she was openly bleeding. He didn't care. For some reason he didn't understand, he needed to hear whatever it was she needed to say.

As he drew nearer, he realized he recognized this woman. Pamela. She was Roxie's sister, and he'd foolishly spent one night with her when he was at an all-time low in his life. He'd regretted it instantly and had avoided her ever since. But now that she was on his table, guilt filled him at his behavior.

"I'm here," he told her, coming out of his own head to focus on her instead.

"She's your daughter, Kian. I'm sorry. I'm so sorry I didn't tell you sooner. I messed up in a real bad way this time," she said, her words so quiet no one else in the room could have possibly heard her.

Kian felt as if his heart had lodged in his throat as her stilted, pained words processed in his brain.

"My child?" he questioned as he looked down at her stomach. They'd been together four years ago. A pregnancy certainly didn't last that long.

"No. Lily," the woman gasped. Kian could see she was fading quickly, and she had just stated words that could literally change his life forever. This had to be a mistake. Still, he found his head swiveling for just a moment toward the small child across the room whom the staff were frantically working on.

"Pam . . ." he said on a sigh. He was desperate as he gripped her hand, her fingers slowly loosening on him. She was letting go, and he wanted to shake her.

"You and Roxie need to raise her. She's yours now, and this baby, too, if she makes it."

Kian opened his mouth to speak when her fingers went limp and her eyes rolled back in her head. He was in such shock, he froze for what had to be only a fraction of a second. At least the nursing staff was more alert than he was.

"We're losing her. Asystole. Start compressions." Kian needed to save this woman. He needed to get more answers and know if she was telling him the truth about Lily being his daughter. He couldn't think about that, though, as he tried to save her. He had to be in doctor mode.

"We need to do a pericardiocentesis now, get me the supplies." He began moving again, more determined than ever to save Pam, to figure out exactly what was happening. He was almost afraid to look back over at the young child he'd just been told was his.

Could it be true? Sadly, he realized, there was a possibility. He had slept with Pam, even though he should never have opened that door. But how could she have possibly hidden a child from him?

He was filled with shame when he realized how easy it would be to do just that. He hadn't thought of her once since their night together.

Instead of dwelling on that, he focused on trying to save her so she could talk to him more.

As Kian finished his procedure, he expected her to regain her heartbeat, but it was fruitless, even though the tireless staff continued the chest compressions.

"We can't pick up the baby's heartbeat. If we can't save Mom, then at least let's try to save the baby," Nurse Ridgley said in a moment of clarity.

Kian didn't want to admit she was right, not at all, but he knew Pamela wasn't savable, not with her injuries. They were pumping her heart, but she was already gone. He had to shake off the almost-inconsolable grief and try to save her unborn child.

The focus in the trauma bay changed immediately as they prepped for an emergency C-section. Kian placed the scalpel to Pamela's belly and made an incision that he could have done with his eyes closed. Intently focused, he reached in and pulled out a lifeless newborn. The background noise of the trauma bay seemed to dim to a hush. Kian placed the baby on the table and attempted futile resuscitation for what seemed like an eternity.

Pamela lay still on the stretcher, her eyes shut, and Kian cradled her three-pound infant in his arms for just a moment before laying her against Pam's chest, both of them completely motionless.

"Please cover them," Kian said as he turned away. Nurse Ridgley quickly did as he asked. This was the part of his job he couldn't stand. It didn't matter how many times he lost a patient, even if that patient hadn't started out as his, he would always question himself, always wonder if there was more he could have done. And in this case, he had a feeling he'd be doing a lot of soul-searching, and hitting the books on any procedure that could have saved this family—his possible family. He looked over to where his only surviving patient lay still on her stretcher. The detectives had confirmed that the child's name was indeed Lily, and said they'd called her only surviving relative—her aunt, Roxie.

In the past few minutes, he'd heard her name twice. Once from Pam's lips and once from the detectives. It had sent a pang through him both times. Roxie. The only woman he'd ever loved. And now he'd see her again. He wasn't ready for any of this. So, he shook his head and pushed her from his mind.

Though he wanted to run and hide, wanted to think Pamela's last words had been delivered in a delirious uttering of nonsensical sentences, as he gazed at the young girl, he knew she was his. He just didn't know how to process that, or how to understand what he was going to do about it. For now, though, he knew he had to help her, had to be at her side.

Finally, he moved, stepping up to the stretcher as he ran his fingers through her soft brown hair. She was still as he held in the tears desperately wanting to escape in a show of the powerful emotion he was feeling.

"Lily, I'm so sorry," he softly whispered.

Kian was startled when her eyes flew open. She'd been given enough meds to keep her asleep for a long while, but obviously she had the endurance of her mother and aunt. Her injuries could have easily taken her life. He had always loved a fighter.

Kian reached for her small fingers, and she grasped on to him and held on tightly. Her grip made him happy. He didn't know how to tell this child what had occurred on this horrible night. He didn't want to be the one to utter those fateful words. Where in the hell was the social worker?

"We need to get you to your room so you'll start feeling better," Kian said quietly as he raised his free hand and again pushed back her delicate brown hair. She blinked at him but didn't say anything.

Kian tried pulling his hand from Lily's, but she let out a heartbreaking sob and held on tighter, her eyes growing wider. His heart stopped beating at the pain of that sound.

"Dr. Forbes, we need to move her now," his favorite nurse, Stephanie, said.

"I'll go with her," he told the nurse. She nodded and smiled. The entire staff knew his job meant more to him than stitching someone up and forgetting them. He'd have moved a lot farther up the evolutionary chain of medicine if that had been his main focus. But Kian didn't have to worry about that. He wasn't interested in titles.

Carefully easing himself onto the edge of the bed, he kept his hand entwined in Lily's, and the nurse pushed the stretcher out of the surgical suite and down the hall to the elevators. Lily didn't take her eyes off him until they came into the children's ICU.

Lily still didn't let him go as she was transferred to a bed and set up for the night. Someone offered to take Kian's place, but when Lily whimpered again, Kian knew he wasn't going anywhere.

She was his daughter. The thought was both terrifying and humbling. She was his daughter, and he'd already lost three precious years with her. He was too broken in this moment to feel anger over the situation. All he felt was a heartbreaking sorrow that he wasn't sure would ever go away.

"Lily," he whispered as he finally allowed a tear to escape his burning eye. One fell, and then he firmed his face, never looking away from his sleeping daughter. He wasn't a weak man and wouldn't allow himself to break now. This child needed him. She needed him and Roxie. He just wasn't sure how well that was going to go for either of them.

A lot had happened, and it seemed that before this night was over, a storm would brew and burst open. He might need to rest before Roxie Gilbert walked back into his life. He wondered if she was aware of what had happened, of the fact that Lily was his daughter. He somehow doubted it.

Kian laid his head down on the bed next to hers, his fingers still lightly clasped in her small hand, and he closed his eyes. He blanked his mind of all thoughts, something he'd learned to do when he'd only been able to manage two-hour naps after thirty-six hours straight of school and work. He couldn't do his best if he couldn't refresh his body. Hopefully when he woke, this would have all been nothing but a nightmare.

It was a thought that put a small smile on his lips as he drifted to sleep beside his daughter.

Chapter Two

No one ever wants to receive the call that Roxie Gilbert had. A far-too-efficient nurse had told Roxie that her sister had been admitted with life-threatening injuries and then wasn't saying anything more.

Roxie was well aware of this routine, as she'd been a nurse for the past six years. They weren't telling her anything because they needed a doctor to pass along the information. She was left with no choice but to pace the worn floor as she waited for answers. She was left with nothing to do but think of the past.

Roxie had run away from her small town of Edmonds to Portland four years ago—she'd run from her sister and from a life she'd once thought she'd wanted. She'd run from Kian Forbes. What had she done? What kind of person fled her only family? Roxie was afraid she'd never again be able to look at herself in the mirror, with all the guilt flooding through her.

Tears continued to flow as she fought down nausea, fatigue, and anguish too great to describe. So, she paced and she waited.

"Ms. Gilbert?" A doctor was standing in the doorway to the waiting room, his face not necessarily giving anything away, but she could see the detachment in his eyes. He was going to tell her something she didn't want to hear. He was preparing for her to fall apart.

She knew that look all too well. She'd carried that same message in her own eyes. It couldn't be too late. She couldn't have messed up so badly in her life that she wouldn't have a chance to make things right with her only sibling, her only family.

"Yes," she said. Slowly, she moved up to the doctor. Her entire body was trembling. This couldn't be happening. Right now, she wanted nothing more than to run away again, something she was good at, wanted to deny what she was about to hear.

"I'm Dr. Peters and was in the room when your sister came in. Can you come with me?" he asked. Yeah, things were about to fall apart. He didn't want to tell her in the public waiting room. She almost refused to follow him. If he didn't take her somewhere private, then he couldn't shatter her. Somehow her feet carried her across the busy emergency room floor, and she passed through the doors with the doctor at her side. The sound of crying and muted voices quieted as soon as the door closed.

"Take a seat," Dr. Peters told her.

"I don't want to sit down. Just tell me," she said. "I'm a nurse. I know how this goes."

His eyes flashed to hers with sympathy pouring from him. She wanted to turn away, wanted to demand he not drag this out. But, somehow, she kept from yelling at the man who was only trying to do his job. Somehow, she stood there holding herself in one piece.

"Do you have anyone else who can be here with you?" he asked. If she'd had even a glimmer of hope before this moment, it was now dashed. The news was very bad, indeed, because they didn't want her to be alone.

"No. There's no one left. It was just down to me and my sister in our family tree," she said quietly. Tears were burning her eyes, but she refused to let them go. She couldn't fall apart. Not yet.

"Your sister and niece were brought in tonight with multiple stab wounds," he said.

Now the tears began falling. Who would stab a child? Who could be that monstrous? Roxie had seen some evil things in her years in the medical profession, but she was still in disbelief when she saw something this horrendous. She nodded. There was no way she'd be able to get words out at this point. She was hurting far too badly.

"I want to tell you, first of all, that your niece is in stable condition. Barring any complications, she should make a full recovery."

It took a moment for the doctor's words to sink in. Roxie hadn't been expecting any good news on this dreadful night. Maybe she'd been misreading the situation. Maybe it was just a traumatic accident, and no one would die. There was a glimmer of hope inside her. Lily was okay. Her niece was going to be okay. She knew complications could happen, but Roxie would monitor Lily like a hawk. She looked at the doctor with renewed energy.

"Unfortunately, Ms. Gilbert, your sister and her premature baby haven't made it. We tried all we could, but the injuries were too great, and they succumbed a couple of hours ago," he told her.

Once again it took a few moments to process his words. Her sister was gone. Murdered. Someone had stolen her sister's life. Roxie's body trembled, and she rocked back and forth on her heels as she absorbed the impact of the situation. Pamela was gone.

She'd suffered at the hands of some criminal, and now she was gone. If Roxie had been there, then maybe she could have helped; maybe none of this would be happening now. She was too trained to ask silly questions. The doctors could tell her that her sister hadn't suffered, but she wouldn't believe them. Roxie wanted to scream, to demand answers, to get the person who had done this. Her emotions were fried, and she felt herself spiraling.

"Ms. Gilbert, your niece needs you right now," the doctor said, his voice gentle, pulling her out of the whirlwind of thoughts rushing through her brain. "She's been through a terrible ordeal. Would you like me to take you to her room?"

Roxie looked at him as if she'd just realized he was there. She shook her head to try to clear it. She wasn't sure what to do or say right now.

But then she saw that flash of light at the end of the tunnel. Her sister might be gone, but Lily was alive, and Lily only had Roxie left.

"Yes, please take me to my niece," she told him.

Renewed determination filled Roxie. She'd left her sister, but she would never walk away from her niece, never let someone hurt her again. It was just the two of them, and they would heal together. They would make sure their family's mistakes would never be repeated again. They'd start fresh and they'd heal over time.

"Take me to Lily," she said, her voice stronger.

The doctor nodded, but he'd said all he needed to say, and the walk down the long hallways was made in silence. Roxie appreciated that.

Roxie barely managed to keep it together as she placed one foot in front of the other on her journey to her niece. Thoughts of finding the murderer helped her somewhat, but not enough. Whoever had done this evil deed to Pamela and her unborn child would most certainly pay.

And from this moment on, Roxie realized her life was no longer about just her. She had a beautiful child to take care of, and Lily would never know a day without love and security. Roxie just prayed she wouldn't let Lily down. She prayed she had what it took to be the parent Lily needed. Growing up with an abusive alcoholic for a father hadn't left Roxie—or Pamela—with great parental role models, but Roxie was a fast learner, and failing wasn't an option.

"I'll leave you here," the doctor informed her before he slipped away.

When she finally stepped into the dim room, Roxie's eyes were drawn to her niece, who looked so small as she lay in the giant hospital bed. It took her a moment to realize her niece wasn't alone. There was a man in a doctor's coat with his head lying facedown on the pillow next to Lily's. Roxie was so grateful to the man for not leaving her niece alone. She would thank him profusely when she wasn't so overwhelmed.

Roxie didn't want to disturb her niece, or the doctor who'd chosen to stay by her side, so she slowly stepped forward and gently sat in the chair next to the bed. She reached over to grip her niece's tiny fingers. Roxie focused on Lily as she allowed more tears to fall. She was quiet as she spoke, but she needed to say the words that were trying to rip themselves from her throat.

"It's you and me now, kiddo, and I will never leave you," Roxie promised. Her niece squeezed her fingers in sleep. Roxie held on tightly.

The man stirred and finally lifted his head, giving Roxie a full view of his face.

Fresh panic invaded Roxie as she stared into the eyes of the first and only man she'd ever been in love with. With all the trauma of the call she'd received and her rush to get to her sister in time, Roxie hadn't really had time to think about the possibility of seeing Dr. Kian Forbes again.

There were a million questions blazing to life in Kian's gaze, but his lips didn't move as he continued to stare at her. He swallowed, all without uttering a single syllable, which made her rip her gaze away from his eyes and focus on his throat instead while she tried to quiet the thundering in her heart. That turned out to be an utter mistake, as it made her think of the times her lips had caressed his salty skin in just that particular spot.

She forced herself to look completely away, fixing her gaze on the worn hospital badge he was wearing. He looked tired and a little bit broken, which she didn't understand.

Four years. It had been four years since she'd sat across from him, looked at his beautiful face, felt his nearly magical touch. It felt as if it had been an eternity.

That panic Roxie had been feeling all night rose inside her like a volcano about to erupt, and she tried desperately to focus on the breathing techniques she'd read about. They weren't helping her at the moment. She wasn't sure anything could. Kian wasn't supposed to be here.

Kian had shattered her, had broken her into mere fragments of the person she'd once been. It didn't matter that he hadn't intended to do it; it only mattered that she'd felt so broken, she'd had to run to save herself. He had also been in the category of those she hadn't said goodbye to. One night they'd been making love; the next night she'd been gone with very little explanation.

She wanted to hate him for her own loss of identity, but she didn't. It wasn't his fault; it was hers. All her problems were her own. She'd hoped to never face this man again, because she feared herself when she was around him. But fate had a funny way of putting in front of you what you tried your hardest to avoid. Maybe fate got bored, or maybe it just liked to torture people. She couldn't even begin to think she had any answers about life, especially when it came to dealing with her own.

The worst part was that Roxie knew if she'd had the strength to understand herself better, she wouldn't have spiraled so far out of control. Kian had been a good man to her, loving and attentive, sweet and in love. They'd been young and he'd been out of her league, but he'd never treated her as if she were in any way less than he was. All of it had been in her own mind. And she had hated herself for that.

With him now sitting before her, Roxie felt all those uncertain emotions creeping back in, making her truly feel like a lesser person, making her feel shame and regret. Seeing him caused an ache unlike anything else she'd ever felt.

The instinct to run crept into her feet and made her fidget as she sat before him, not knowing what in the world she could possibly say. She wasn't owed his forgiveness. She hadn't earned it. And she didn't think it was possible for her to receive it. This was a mess unlike any of the other messes she'd ever been in, whether self-inflicted or beyond her control.

Seconds passed without sound beyond that of their breathing. He seemed to be recovering a lot faster at the sight of her than she was at seeing him. Kian had always been like that, though. He could control his emotions and expressions, where she couldn't. It was only one more thing for her to be angry with him about. Another irrational emotion she was feeling.

In four years, Kian had changed. Thirty-five looked good on him. His shoulders had always been broad, but now they seemed massive beneath the light-blue scrubs he was wearing that hinted at the beautiful muscle beneath. His jaw was square, shaved clean, and his dark eyes were now blank, not showing an ounce of the emotion that had flashed in them just seconds before. She could see where laugh lines wanted to emerge, but they certainly weren't showing at the moment.

The biggest change she noticed about him was that gaze. Kian had always been the first person to offer a smile and reassuring words. Now, this man before her was gazing at her with icy coolness that made her want to shiver.

When she'd rushed home tonight, she hadn't been worrying about running into Kian. And now that she was here, she couldn't afford to spiral into a pit of despair, not when she had Lily to take care of.

Kian slowly stood up and towered over her own respectable height of five foot five, and she suddenly felt smaller and more insignificant. If she'd ever allowed herself to think about her emotions regarding this man, then maybe she wouldn't be feeling the insane grief she was experiencing, sitting before him now. If she'd faced her feelings instead of running away from them, then maybe she'd be able to give him a polite hello and ask him to move on, and not have to worry about endless torment. She had enough to last her a lifetime as it was.

If was a word Roxie had always hated. Life wasn't about *if*s. It was about living without regret, though she failed in that so much because she *did* have regrets. But she'd tried to stop adding any more to her already-long list. Every decision a person made helped shape them into who they were truly meant to be. A person filled with regrets was a person who hadn't truly lived. But Roxie was failing miserably at the moment to practice what she so often preached.

"Hello, Roxie," Kian finally said, his rich baritone deep and sure. There was the slightest edge of gravel to his voice that had always melted her, and it seemed time hadn't changed that at all.

Her stomach quivered as her knees shook. She was grateful to be sitting, as she didn't think her wobbly legs would be able to hold her up right now. She was also grateful Lily was sleeping. This man had power in ways she was sure he didn't understand. Or maybe he did. How was she to know who he was anymore? He'd once been full of life and light that naturally drew people to him. Right now, he didn't seem to be full of anything except disgust. And he had a right to feel that way.

"Kian," she said, her voice coming out raspy and unsure. She was almost saying his name as a question. She wasn't sure what to say, think, or do. And she certainly didn't know what the question would be if she were to ask one.

Her niece stirred in the bed, and that caught Roxie's full attention as she looked down and saw Lily open her eyes. It had been a while since she'd Skyped with her niece. Those moments had mattered a lot to Roxie, but guilt consumed her that even with that, she still hadn't come back home to help raise the fragile child.

"Auntie," Lily said in a too-small voice as she tried to wipe the fog from her eyes.

"I'm right here, baby girl," Roxie assured Lily.

Her niece smiled a tiny bit before squeezing Roxie's fingers and closing her eyes again. This moment was one Roxie would forever hold in her heart. She could handle Kian because she had to be strong for Lily. There wasn't another option.

Roxie hadn't forgotten why she was at this hospital, but for a moment, she'd only been able to see Kian. It was sort of like when he was there, the rest of the world slowly faded. He seemed to have his own universe surrounding just him, and anyone in his presence surely would be sucked into it. Roxie flexed her fingers against Lily's as she tried to stay firmly planted on the ground.

Kian released Roxie's gaze as he looked down at Lily, his expression filled with something she couldn't quite interpret, but something that had a tight knot pinching her stomach. He flashed his gaze back up to hers, and some of the harshness of his expression was gone.

While his anger might have dimmed, resignation took its place as he looked from her to Lily and back again several times. She didn't understand this at all. Did he know Lily more than as a patient?

Roxie opened her mouth to say something to break up this tension, but she couldn't seem to form words. Nothing would come out. This was just one more thing to show her she was in no way prepared to be this traumatized little girl's mother. Here Roxie was being faced with the man she'd always been in love with, and Lily was lying so helpless in the bed between them.

Rubbing her thumb against the back of Lily's hand was enough to calm Roxie and allow her to draw in a couple of breaths before she looked at Kian once more. Though Roxie's body was still shaking a bit, she was strong enough to comfort her niece while she faced her past. If she ever planned on moving forward with life and the choices she had made, then she had to be able to handle adverse situations. That was all just part of being an adult.

"We have to talk about Lily," he said. She didn't understand how he knew her niece. It had to be nothing more than him being her niece's doctor. Maybe he'd grown attached after this tragic attack.

"How do you know Lily?" she asked.

Kian was quiet for several moments, and Roxie's heart raced so out of control, she didn't know what to do or say or think. She was close to falling apart, and if Lily didn't need her to be strong, she feared that's exactly what would happen.

Finally, he sighed. All the noise around them seemed to freeze. "I was in the ER with her tonight," he told her. There was more; she could feel it.

"And?" she questioned. She was rubbing her niece's back, trying not to throw up.

"I didn't know . . ." His voice trailed off.

Roxie's stomach heaved as she put together what she didn't want to. She'd only been gone from town a couple of months when Pamela had gotten pregnant with Lily. This couldn't be real. As he sat back down and reached for Lily's free hand, she somehow didn't need words to tell her what he needed to say.

Roxie felt as if she was going to faint. She knew she had to be stronger than this, especially right now. But in this moment, she wasn't sure there was much more she could take. This night had gone from tragic to unbelievable. Her world truly was spinning now. She wasn't sure she'd ever be able to stop it.

Chapter Three

Although Kian had never actually been hit in the face with a sledgehammer, that was the only equivalent he could think of to describe how he felt at this particular moment. It felt as if someone had come along and slammed a thick wedge of iron in his face, and now he was still reeling from it.

His chest hurt, his body ached, and his face was tingling. He felt a mixture of sadness, regret, and disbelief, but mostly red-hot rage. This woman, this person before him, had been the only girl he'd ever given his heart to. And she had taken that gift, smashed it on the ground, and thrown it back in his face.

His fingers twitched as he remembered the feel of the diamond he'd carried around in his pocket for months as he tried to come up with the perfect proposal. He'd known without the shadow of a doubt he'd make her his wife.

And then she'd disappeared.

At first, Kian had panicked. Something surely had happened to her. She wouldn't have left on her own. They were happy, in love, had the rest of their lives before them.

But, too quickly, he'd discovered the truth. After years of friendship and two years of dating, she'd left a note that simply read: *I can't do this anymore. Please let me go. Roxie.*

That was it. There had been no other explanation, no words to tell him what had gone wrong. Kian's first reaction to that note had been to hunt her down and force an explanation out of her. But then he'd found his pride, and he was furious.

"After our breakup, I made some bad decisions," he admitted. He didn't know why he was bothering to tell her this. "I drank a lot, partied even more, and yeah, I didn't care which women I was with. I just wanted to forget you."

He refused to allow himself to feel bad when she flinched. She'd been the one to leave him, not the other way around. If that wasn't something she wanted to hear, then too bad.

"I don't need to know any of this," Roxie said in an emotionally charged tone.

"I wasn't going to ever trust anyone again after what you'd done to me." He'd been smart to feel that way. And now he wasn't sure how he was feeling.

There were so many emotions filling Kian, he didn't know which to focus on. There was a sense of urgency to grab his child, to make sure Roxie knew Lily was his and that he wouldn't lose another moment in her life. But there was a need to protect Roxie as well.

She'd left him, and it had nearly destroyed him. Kian in no way thought of himself as a weak man. He was strong and capable, and this small woman had done her best to drop him to his knees. And yet he still couldn't turn away even now, not when she was in pain.

"Maybe you need to realize what your exit did to the people around you," he pointed out. "And maybe it's just that I never really knew you at all, because the girl I'd been in love with wouldn't have been capable of leaving like you did, wouldn't be capable of such a coldhearted act."

Finally, Roxie looked up at him, and there was now fire in her eyes. Kian felt an urge to take a step back, but there was no way he was going to retreat. She'd pushed him back enough in the past four years. If anyone was going to retreat, it would be her, he thought.

Though he had tried to push her from his mind, he hadn't been very successful. Every woman he'd dated, every night he'd laid his head down to sleep, every time he'd listened to classic country and "I Love the Way You Love Me" by John Michael Montgomery came on the radio, he was reminded of Roxie. She'd consumed him for years, and she'd continued doing so even after she was gone.

He hated her a little for that. He hated himself even more. Before Roxie, he'd always thought men who couldn't get over a relationship were a little pathetic. Sometimes things just weren't meant to be. Endings shouldn't be what defined a person.

"You were with Pamela," Roxie said, her voice filled with accusation. There was so much hurt and rage in her tone, he didn't know how to respond. He didn't owe Roxie a damn thing, but he found himself wanting to explain the situation to her. He shifted as he fought the urge—and lost.

"I was with her one time. I went to a bar with friends. She was there, and she made it clear she wanted to go home with me. I was drunk and she was available," he said as he shrugged, trying to act as if it didn't matter.

"I would have thought you'd at least use protection," she said.

"I *always* use protection. Obviously, it fails sometimes," he snapped. "This isn't a discussion we should be having in front of Lily," he added.

"She's only three, and even if she was awake, she wouldn't understand what we're talking about," she pointed out.

"You have no right to be mad. *You* left *me*," he reminded her.

"I'm not mad at you," she snapped. He watched as she closed her eyes and took a few calming breaths. He knew that was exactly what he should be doing as well. Snapping at each other wasn't solving any of their problems.

"Fate can be cruel," he said with a humorless laugh. "It looks like the two of us are now locked together for the rest of our lives."

There were equal parts of joy and apprehension at the thought of raising Lily with Roxie, which appeared to be what Pamela wanted for their child. At one point in his life, that was the ultimate dream, to raise children with Roxie. But then she'd left. And Kian hadn't truly had time for all this to sink in, and it would probably be far safer for the two of them if they both calmed down before saying some things that couldn't be taken back. He certainly didn't want Lily to see him as a monster.

What had she already been through? What kind of life had she led? He could've given her the world, and would have, if her mother would've only told him he was a father.

"We aren't doing anything together, Kian," Roxie was quick to point out, which made him angry all over again.

"You're not paying attention, Roxie," he said, not in the mood to stroke her ego. There was something deep down that made him still want to protect her, but he pushed that aside. "Maybe all your family knows is how to play games, how to deceive men. Maybe your sister loved holding one over on one of the Forbeses. I know there are many who are jealous of my family, thinking we hold too much power. But you used to know me better than any other person on this planet. You knew I never wanted to take advantage of my family name, that I wanted to make it on my own."

She sighed, and he saw that knowledge in her gaze. At least she wasn't going to sit there and lie to him or put him down. He wondered if that would hurt him.

"You always did work so much harder to prove yourself so people wouldn't say you were spoiled," she admitted.

Kian hadn't wanted to say he'd been given a silver spoon because of the way he'd been born. He'd studied hard, and now he was a doctor in extreme demand. He was often called to other places where only *he* could help. There was a lot of pride in knowing he was worthy of his family name.

It was almost odd to him that he'd been coasting through life without a lot of care in the world until he'd met Roxie. And then he'd been in love, willing to drop to his knees for her. Then she'd left, and he'd become a different man—harder. And now he was a father. This woman was responsible for all the major shifts in his life.

He was about to speak when she slapped him again with her words. "You didn't have to sleep with my sister for revenge, though."

"It wasn't revenge. I was doing what I had to do," he said with a shrug. "And that's all on my shoulders. But I wouldn't have been on the prowl for anyone else had you been at my side, where I thought you'd always be."

Roxie's eyes filled with tears before she looked down. He glanced at his daughter again, letting the knowledge of his fatherhood truly seep in.

"I missed her first word, first steps. I missed too much," Kian said.

Roxie looked afraid as she clung tighter to Lily's hand. His eyes narrowed. If she truly thought she'd keep him away from this child, she was sorely mistaken. Kian knew nothing about Roxie anymore. He didn't know if she had a husband, a boyfriend, a life outside of Lily. The thought of another man in her life sent a whole new burst of fire racing through him.

He had no claim on Roxie. But he certainly had a hell of a claim on Lily. He was sure Roxie had no other immediate family left. No one else would be trying to make a claim on his child. He also knew, with his power and influence, he could take his child from Roxie within days. She was *his*, after all. As soon as the blood tests came in, the courts would hand her over, no matter how much Roxie might try to fight it and no matter what it was that Pamela wanted. He didn't owe Pamela anything, either. She'd deceived him for more than four years. She would have known within two months she was pregnant, and not once had she come to him to do the right thing. Why he should consider her feelings now, he didn't know.

But Kian didn't want to go that route. He didn't understand why he would hesitate to do what had to be done, but he wanted to give Roxie more respect than that—certainly more respect than she'd given him.

Too much emotion and far too many thoughts were clouding up Kian's thinking. He wanted answers right now, but he wasn't sure he could remain calm enough to listen. This was a mess, and they would get to the bottom of it, but maybe he would give her a day or two to come to terms with the loss of her sister.

"Maybe my sister didn't know," Roxie finally said. It took a moment for Kian to hear her words. He was so stuck in his own head, it was difficult to come back out.

"She knew," he said with a sigh. "She confessed to me. That's how I know." This sentence was uttered with respect. He wouldn't continue to speak cruelly about her, not when she wasn't around to defend herself.

"Don't you think she would have come and asked for help if she'd known?" Roxie pointed out.

"No, because she would have known I could take my child," he said. He forced himself to calm. "But in the end, she did the right thing. That's what I want to remember and think about."

A shudder racked Roxie's body as she leaned away from him as if trying to protect herself. That enraged him all over again. She in no way needed protection from him. He'd never done anything to harm Roxie—not ever.

"Look, Kian, I know this is a lot to take in, and you're probably upset right now," Roxie said, her voice calm as he realized she was trying to placate him. He hated when people tried doing that. It only made his blood boil all that much more.

"Yeah, that's an understatement," he told her. What he needed to do was find a punching bag and destroy it, or maybe find some asshole in a bar and start a fight. What he *wanted* to do was take out his aggression in any form possible. But, instead, he was forcing himself to stand there calmly and look at the woman who'd betrayed him while she clutched his daughter's hand in hers.

"Were you going to even tell me you were here if you hadn't seen me?" he asked after several moments of silence. Maybe that shouldn't have been the question he asked, but he wanted to know if she was planning on hiding from him while here.

"I'm sorry about the way I left, but that was a long time ago, and I don't think it does either of us any good to dwell on the past," she said, not answering his question. If she thought he was that easily dissuaded, she hadn't really known him at all. Maybe she hadn't.

"You clearly think you have all the answers and know exactly how I might have felt or how I'm feeling right now," he said. This wasn't a question; it was a harsh assessment that, in his honest opinion, hit the nail on the head.

"I'm not saying that," she defended. Then they were both silent for several moments as the two of them tried to find their footing in this traumatic situation.

"I'm going to take a walk," he finally told her.

The relief on her face as he stood up was another shot to his ego, but he pushed it aside. This wasn't the time to keep thinking of himself—not with his daughter lying there so helplessly.

He left the room. This night was nowhere close to being over, and the best thing for both of them in this moment was to have a break. And he needed to call his parents. Though they'd be just as disappointed in missing out on the past three years of Lily's life as he was, he had zero doubt they'd embrace her with all the love they had to offer.

His family was so much more than the money in their accounts. Even if others didn't realize that, he was sure in that knowledge. It was the first thought all night that put the slightest of smiles on his lips.

Chapter Four

The circles beneath Roxie's eyes were growing deeper by the day, but she didn't care in the least. What she cared about was that her niece was finally getting released from the hospital. Two weeks of sleeping on an uncomfortable couch so she could be by her niece's side had been well worth the aches and pains in her body.

Two weeks of seeing Kian every single day was playing havoc with her nerves, but even that she could deal with. They hadn't discussed the two of them any further, and he hadn't threatened her with taking Lily away, but his very presence was letting her know he wasn't going anywhere.

She didn't want to even think about that at the moment. It was too much for her to process, and she wanted to feel a bit of joy that her niece would survive. But now it was time to tell Lily her mother wasn't coming back to her. How was Roxie going to do that?

Kian walked into the room and grinned as he sat down next to Roxie, far too close for her comfort. He easily reached out and clasped Lily's hand, and she looked at him with a bit of hero worship that had Roxie wanting to grind her teeth.

"How is my favorite little girl today?" Kian asked Lily.

"I want to go home," Lily told him with a bit of a stubborn tilt to her chin that clearly showed she was most certainly Kian's child.

"Guess what?" he said.

The hope in Lily's eyes had Roxie's heart breaking all over again for this precious child.

"What?" she said.

"You get to go home today," he told her.

She smiled as she reached out for him. He didn't hesitate as he gently pulled her into his arms and lightly squeezed. Roxie couldn't have spoken in that moment, even if her life were in danger.

"And I get to see my mommy?" she said as she looked around the room, her eyes connecting with Roxie's. Kian looked over at her, his smile quickly falling. There was a question in his eyes, and Roxie knew she had no choice but to talk to Lily about this.

"Sweetie," Roxie began, and Lily looked at her with sadness. "Remember how I told you your mommy couldn't be here right now?"

Lily nodded as her eyes filled with tears. There was a huge lump in Roxie's throat, making it impossible to continue speaking. Kian reached out with his free hand and rested it on Roxie's leg as he looked at Lily.

"Your mommy needed to go be with the angels," Kian said gently as he squeezed Roxie's leg. As much as she didn't want to lean on this man, she couldn't reject his comfort in this moment. She had no one else.

"But why?" Lily asked as her first tears fell.

"I don't know why," Kian told her. "Sometimes we don't get to know the reasons, but we do get to know she's watching out for you, and she misses you so much."

Lily was silent as she looked from Kian to Roxie, sadness in her expression. Roxie's heart was completely broken as she tried to figure out what else to add.

"No one can make you stop hurting, but we will be here for you always," Roxie told her.

Lily continued to cry as Roxie joined her. This moment was too much, and yet there was nothing that could be done to take the pain away from a child losing her parent, especially a child as young as Lily, who just couldn't possibly understand why her mommy didn't want to see her again.

"I want you both to come home with me for a few days," Kian said, and Roxie instantly tensed. This was something he should have discussed with her first, not just sprung on her, especially with Lily so vulnerable. His tone might have been calm and soothing, but that didn't help her at all.

"I . . . uh, don't know about that. I was thinking we'd just go to my sister's place," Roxie told him, keeping her own tone calm.

"It's not ready yet," he said, giving her a look. For a brief moment, Roxie had forgotten that's where the crime had happened, had forgotten that it might be a crime scene.

"I didn't even think about that," Roxie said slowly. "We can figure something out." It was more than obvious that Kian didn't like that idea at all.

"I'm off work now. Come home with me and get a shower and a decent night of sleep, and then we can go from there," he insisted. She didn't want to argue in front of Lily, but she in no way wanted to go to his place.

"I really think that's a bad idea," Roxie told him. Lily wasn't saying a word during this exchange.

"We need to talk about what happens next," he said, his voice firmer.

"I will be caring for Lily. There's not a lot to talk about," Roxie said, deciding there was no further discussion on the matter.

"Come home and speak with me tonight or . . ." He stopped. Maybe he was smart enough to realize ultimatums might not be the way to go at the moment. "The choice is yours," he finished.

"Is that a threat?" she whispered, not wanting Lily to feel the tension. Kian sighed before he shook his head.

"No," he finally said. "It's not, but we do need to talk," he told her.

Roxie gazed at him with suspicion, but exhaustion was making her not want to fight, and she really didn't know where else they were going to go for this night. Maybe after a solid night of sleep, she'd have a clearer frame of mind.

"Please, Roxie, we need to talk," he told her. It was more than obvious he wanted to monitor Lily as well. She'd been given the all clear, but that didn't fully abate their worry over the child.

"For tonight," she told him and looked at Lily.

"We get to leave now?" Lily asked.

"Yes, baby girl, we get to leave," Roxie told her.

Her tears dried up as Kian stood and walked from the room to finish the paperwork that would allow Lily to go home with them. Roxie just wasn't at all sure what was coming next. Was it a mistake to go to his place? Would she be able to take Lily away again once she stepped through those doors? She wasn't sure of anything anymore.

Chapter Five

Lily was fast asleep when the three of them pulled up to Kian's place, and Roxie was grateful. What had she been thinking? Maybe it had been a few years and she'd somewhat forgotten the wealth of the Forbes family. That had to be the only explanation for the awe she felt looking at the mansion Kian called home.

She didn't live in this world in any way. She was used to eating ramen and living on four hours of sleep so she could pick up extra shifts. Sure, she was a nurse, but that meant she had a lot of school debt to pay off, and she'd been on her own for a long time.

Maybe one of the reasons she'd left Kian had been resentment. Everything came so easily to him. It wasn't his fault he'd been born with money and respect, and it wasn't her fault she envied him a little for it. It was just how life worked out.

"Shit," Kian mumbled beneath his breath, startling Roxie.

"What?" she asked, afraid to wonder what he could possibly have to worry about.

"It looks like my brothers are here," he told her with a sigh.

"Why?" she asked. She in no way wanted to run into any of his family members, not with their past together, and certainly not with this newfound knowledge circling in her head. She never had been much of a liar.

"I've kept my family informed about what's happening, and they want to meet their niece," he told her. "It won't take long to get rid of them."

"Just take Lily and me somewhere else," she pleaded.

"Not gonna happen," he said as he opened the garage door and pulled inside.

Roxie looked around and felt herself growing sicker by the second. She counted twelve car bays—and all of them were filled. She didn't want to think about the price tag on each vehicle. Kian certainly didn't mind spending money. That was for dang sure.

Kian was out of the car and around to her door before she could undo her seat belt. He stood there waiting, as if he had all the time in the world. Roxie wished she could find the same confidence that had gotten her through college right about now. When she'd gone away for her education, she had left the pathetic Roxie behind. Somehow the second she'd crossed the city-limits sign, all her insecurities had come roaring back. She hated herself a little for feeling that way.

Doing her best to shake herself from her poor-me attitude, she climbed from the passenger seat and stood up, making sure to move a couple of feet away from Kian. Standing too close to him was like looking directly at the sun, and she feared her skin and eyes would be seared before too long.

After she was safely out of the vehicle, he moved to the back door and carefully undid Lily from her brand-new booster seat, then lifted her into his arms. She cuddled against him, and a look of awe settled over his features. He was already far too attached to Lily, and that was more terrifying than anything else to Roxie. She felt as if she was losing her a little more as each day passed.

"Come on," Kian said as he moved forward. Roxie didn't look at him again to try to decide how he was feeling. She felt as much a victim as he did. He'd slept with her sister and created a child. Both of them had kept that from her. She could forgive her sister since she'd made a mistake, but could she ever forgive Kian? She didn't think so. It was either that, or she just didn't want to face how he made her feel.

"Welcome home," a voice called as they stepped into a large kitchen.

Though Roxie had been nervous to see Kian's brothers, the moment she looked up and saw the pleasure on their faces, she couldn't help but give an answering grin. She'd always loved Kian's family, even if she had wanted to avoid them after what she'd done.

"Roxie, it's so good to see you. We wanted to come to the hospital, but Kian asked us to wait," Owen said as he took a few strides in her direction.

Before she had even a moment to say a word, he pulled her into his arms, her feet leaving the ground as he cut the air right out of her lungs in a bear hug that had her squeaking as she tried to breathe.

"Sorry," he said as he released her.

"I guess you forgot your own strength," she said, almost feeling as if she'd just run a marathon.

"Yeah, and I missed you," he said with a sheepish smile that had her heart leaping. He might be a beast of a man with shoulders almost too wide to fit through standard doorways, but he'd always been a giant teddy bear. She might even admit, if only in her head, that he was her favorite sibling of Kian's. Those shoulders were perfect, too, since he was a fireman who absolutely loved his job.

"I missed you, too," she admitted, her cheeks reddening just a little.

"What about me?" Arden asked with his own tamped-down grin as he approached next and hugged her with less force, but still hard enough to constrict her lungs.

"Yes, of course, Arden. It's great to see you," she assured him. Seeing these wonderful men was helping her push back the unbearable grief she'd been feeling for weeks. He smiled at her before flicking her hair away from her face. She shifted on her feet as she looked over at Declan.

Declan rarely wore any emotion on his face, and he'd been the hardest of Kian's siblings to get to know, and, if truth be told, he intimidated her a little. He'd never been anything other than kind to her, but there was an edge to him that kept her feeling as if she should confess every secret she had while holding out her hands so he could arrest her.

He stepped forward and gave her a light hug, quickly pulling back, and Roxie didn't quite know what to say.

"Um . . . good to see you, Declan," she said awkwardly.

"I'm sorry it's under these circumstances," Arden told her. And just like that, the pain was at the front of her mind. She flinched.

"We decided not to speak about that," Declan said with a growl.

"I'd rather not," Roxie admitted.

"Then we won't." They all turned and looked at Kian, who held Lily tightly against him. He hadn't said anything so far at this family reunion, but he finally sighed.

"How did you keep Mom and Dad from coming here?" Kian asked.

"We didn't want to overwhelm Roxie and Lily right when they're getting home from the hospital," Owen said.

"And you three being here isn't overwhelming?" Kian said with a raised brow.

"Okay, we didn't tell them you were coming home right now," Arden admitted.

"That's what I thought," Kian said. Roxie had a feeling he was going to catch hell for that one.

"Why don't you tell us what you've been doing since you've been gone?" Owen said as he tried to switch the subject. Roxie was grateful.

"She's been living in Portland," Declan said quietly.

Her gaze locked with his as his brothers turned and looked at him, all of them looking confused. Roxie didn't know what to think of Declan knowing exactly where she'd been. *Intimidated* would be a good first word, she thought.

"How in the hell do you know that?" Kian asked, glaring at his brother.

"I like to know things," Declan said with a shrug. Yep, he still intimidated her, she decided.

"Maybe you should mind your own business," Kian grumbled. Roxie had a feeling the brothers would be talking more later when she wasn't in hearing range. She kind of wished she could be a fly on the wall for that conversation.

"Never going to happen," Declan assured his sibling.

"We can gossip later. It looks like Lily needs a warm bed," Owen said, always the first of the brothers to break up tension. It was odd how nothing at all had changed in the four years since Roxie had left.

"I really could use some rest as well," Roxie said, hoping they'd allow her to escape.

Instant remorse flashed across all the brothers' faces, even Declan's, which surprised her.

"I'm really sorry," Owen said. The brothers instinctively moved a few inches closer to her, as if forming a protective circle.

Roxie's throat suddenly closed up, and she found herself incapable of speaking. This had to have been the worst couple of weeks of her life, and before this had happened, she would have thought leaving Kian had been the hardest. It wasn't going to get any easier, no matter how much time passed.

Kian moved closer to her side, and instead of feeling uncomfortable, she suddenly wanted to lean against him. He always had managed to carry her burdens for her. But wasn't that one of the things that had made her lose her identity in the first place? It was odd how easy it was to want that again.

The sympathy flashing across his face was too much for her, though. She didn't want to keep seeing that expression in everyone's eyes. She didn't want them feeling sorry for her. That wasn't going to help her process her grief.

"I'm going to be fine, but I really just need to be able to take care of Lily, and I can't do that if I keep dwelling on the loss of my sister," she assured the men circling her.

"It really is okay to take a little bit of time for yourself to grieve and pull yourself together so you can be strong for Lily," Kian assured her.

Arden moved over to a liquor cabinet and poured a stiff drink, then brought it over to her. She automatically took it when he held it out, then stood there not knowing what to do.

"Just drink it. You'll feel much better," he assured her.

She looked at Owen, who nodded. "You will, I promise," he quietly said.

Roxie didn't have the will to fight all of them, so she lifted the glass and actually enjoyed the sensation of the burn as the fine alcohol slid down her throat.

They were all right. She did need to pull herself together so she could be there for Lily when she woke up. The next weeks, and then months and years, for that matter, weren't going to be easy on either of them. They had to stick together, and that meant Roxie had to be strong. It felt good to let her strength recharge.

"Lily and I really should rest," she told the brothers as she glanced at Lily, who was shifting in Kian's arms.

"I agree," Kian said intensely as he captured her gaze.

Roxie suddenly forgot about Kian's brothers being in the room. The bolt of electricity sparking through her made her stress disappear, and her hormones light up. Maybe it was her wanting to forget her sorrow, and maybe it was the fact that she'd been refusing to think about her feelings for this man. She didn't know and didn't care. She suddenly wanted his lips on hers in a way she'd never thought she'd want again.

Lily stirred in his arms again, and that broke the spell between them. She looked away in relief, knowing there was certainly something wrong with her. Maybe more than she could ever possibly fix.

It was both with sadness and relief that she was led away from the Forbes brothers and into a room where the two of them tucked Lily into bed. She stood next to Kian, and all of the trauma from the past few weeks began to truly sink in. Her body trembled as she looked at

Lily, who let out a sigh as she turned over in bed, clutching her favorite stuffed pink horse.

"She's strong," Kian said, pure awe in his voice.

"Yes, she's been through far too much already," Roxie told him.

"We can do this," he assured her.

Tears dripped down Roxie's cheeks. He'd said "we" not "I"—not just him. She wanted it to be just her, or did she? She wasn't sure of anything right now but the need to clear her head. She didn't say anything more to him.

After another couple of minutes, he led her from the room. The two of them shared one more intense look before she shut her own bedroom door and leaned against it, letting a few more tears fall before she stood strong.

Tomorrow would be a new day. She'd be much stronger then, she assured herself.

Chapter Six

Dreams could be wonderful, or they could be terrifying. Because Roxie had always dreamed in color, which she was assured was a rare thing, hers were so much more real than the dreams of others. She also rarely tried to fight her dreams. She chose to go on the adventures her brain took her on.

Stirring in her unfamiliar bed, Roxie wanted to fight the dream she was currently having. She didn't want to face the reality her emotions were causing her to face when she needed a dose of fiction instead.

Tonight's dream was making her stir restlessly in bed. She tried pulling herself from the dream, but it was so real, so burdensome, she couldn't get away from it. Her sister was at the end of a dark road, reaching out to her, calling Roxie's name.

No matter how fast Roxie ran toward her, she couldn't catch her. Then, from a small opening in the wall, a huge man stepped out, a bloody knife in his hand. Roxie screamed at her sister to run as the man drew nearer, but Pam couldn't hear her, couldn't see the man coming up behind her.

Suddenly he reached out from behind her, one hand gripping Pam's throat as the other one—the hand with the sharp blade in it—lifted high before arcing down.

With a scream, Roxie ripped herself from sleep as she sat straight up in the bed, her heart thundering, her body trembling. She was in a panic as she called out Pam's name, her feet trapped within the blankets.

"Pam! Run!" Roxie was between sleep and wakefulness, and the panic wasn't fading.

When a light shone beneath her doorway, it only amplified her confusion. The door burst open and was filled with the shadow of a huge man, and Roxie screamed again. Pain and fear rolled through her as she searched for her sister.

"Run, Pam!" Roxie called again.

The man stepped into the room, and Roxie tried to untangle her feet and get away. She had to run, had to get away, had to save her sister and her niece.

"No!" she shouted as the man sat on the edge of her bed and reached for her.

"Roxie, it's okay, it's just a dream. Roxie, it's me," the man said. The calming timbre of his voice wasn't computing in her brain. When he reached for her, she clawed at him as she tried to scoot away.

"You need to wake up, Roxie. Wake up!" he said more forcefully as his hands grasped on to her shoulders and shook her.

"No!" Roxie cried again.

"Roxie!" His sharp word along with the hard shake of her body finally pulled her awake.

Roxie stopped moving as she focused on the hands holding on to her and the voice of Kian as he whispered soothing words. She began shaking as tears poured down her cheeks. She called out Pam's name, horrific sadness invading her.

Kian pulled her into his arms and continued comforting her, but Roxie felt as if she was beyond comfort. She should have been there for her sister, should have spent more time trying to get to know the woman she'd become. Now she would never have that chance.

"Roxie, it's okay, I'm here," Kian told her, his hands rubbing gently up and down her back. "I'm right here."

Roxie clung to Kian as she focused on the feel of his hands, on the sound of his voice. Something within her shifted as she felt the fogginess of her dream begin to fade. It had been so long since she'd been held, so long since she'd felt anything other than pain.

"Talk to me, darling," Kian said.

Roxie buried her head against his neck as she inhaled his tangy scent. Then, without much conscious thought, she kissed his throat, her tongue sweeping out and licking the pulse that suddenly began to beat faster.

"What are you doing?" he asked as his hands stilled.

"I need to forget for a while," Roxie told him as she sucked on his skin.

"Roxie, this isn't a good time," Kian warned. He didn't release her, but his entire body was still.

"I don't care. Make me forget," she said, feeling more tears in her throat. She was finished with crying, didn't want to cry one more tear. She knew that was unrealistic, but for this moment at least, she could get lost in her old lover's arms.

"Roxie, I don't have the willpower to resist," Kian warned.

"Good," she said as she kissed her way across his jaw. "Please make the darkness go away."

With all the trauma pushed to the back of her mind, she allowed herself to get lost in his embrace. For this one pause in time, she was alive and feeling something she hadn't allowed herself to feel in four years.

"We shouldn't do this," Kian whispered as his tongue traced the edge of her ear before he moved down the curve of her throat. "But I can't stop when you touch me like that." The low growl of his voice had her back arching.

"Don't stop, Kian. It's you, it's always been you," she moaned as his hand slid beneath her shirt and cupped her breast. He gave out a frustrated sigh, and then she felt the air touch her skin as he removed her shirt before his head descended and tasted her nipple. The ache consumed her, shooting down her body and pulsing at her ready core.

His strong grip squeezed her breasts as he tasted her, sucked her, and made her squirm beneath him as she reached for him, needing so much more than he was giving. He'd always lit her on fire, making her lose all sense of sanity within seconds. He was the sun, and she was drawn to him, even knowing she'd burn up before she got close enough.

Kian pulled himself over her body, and the sweet weight of his perfect muscles was almost more than she could possibly take. She reached around him, loving the feel of his heated skin beneath her fingers. It was so familiar, so right. The barrier of her pants was still between them, and she wiggled beneath him in frustration.

"Please," she begged. "I can't wait. Now!"

"You're mine," he said in a deep, guttural growl that had her pushing her hips up so she could feel the solid length of him against her core. He moved back and she complained, but stopped the moment she felt his hands on her pants, the material finally disappearing.

Her arms opened as she accepted him back into her embrace, finally feeling his naked length against her needy skin. She wrapped her legs around his back and tilted her chin, needing to feel his lips pressed to hers.

"Can't wait," she moaned. His thickness was right there at her hot opening, and she could barely take the separation. It was too much, and yet it wasn't nearly enough. Her body was on fire, and the longer he took to give her what she wanted, the more she felt as if she were going to be lost forever.

Finally, with one last groan, he leaned down and captured her lips in a scorching, deep kiss that took the last of her breath away. The heat in her body increased to levels so high she didn't understand how they weren't both going up in flames.

She felt alive again for the first time in four years, felt her body and soul immediately open to him. She was home; she was right where she'd needed to be all along. Why she'd fought it, she had no idea.

In the back of her mind, she knew this was wrong, but she immediately pushed those thoughts aside. There was no room for negativity right now. This was only about desire and want. It wasn't about what was good for her.

Kian pulled back only long enough to allow them both to catch their breaths, and then his mouth was consuming hers again. His hand trailed down her body at the same time, and she easily opened to him as he slipped two fingers inside her. Oh yes, this was what she needed, wanted with a burning desperation. She was more than ready for him, and she thrust her hips upward to indicate just that.

"Look at me, Roxie," he growled. "I want to see your eyes when I bury myself inside you again for the first time in too long." The utter command of his voice made her want to obey him.

No. She shook her head and nearly cried as she thrust her hips up again, feeling the tip of him sliding into her opening. So close. He was so close. She pulled back and thrust up again, taking him an inch deeper. He growled at her as his tongue slid from her throat, up her chin, and around her lips. She sucked it inside her mouth and gently bit down on it, making his erection twitch against her.

"I can't resist," he growled. And then the teasing ended. His hips surged forward, and finally he filled her, making her scream out her pleasure. Kian's body covered hers, his thick, hot steel buried deep inside her, and she knew she wanted more. The fire of their passion might kill them both—and she didn't care.

The man she'd always loved and desired was exactly where she needed him to be, and instead of pulling away from him, her legs wrapped more tightly around his hips as she thought about how amazing he felt. It had been so long since she'd had a man inside her, she felt the smallest hint of discomfort, but that quickly fled as he flexed his hips and made a subtle movement inside her, stoking the flames of her desire even higher.

"Please make love to me," she said when he rested too long within her. She needed movement, needed completion.

The light was minimal, but enough that Roxie could look into his beautiful face. She wanted to close her eyes, but he didn't allow it. He gazed down at her as he began making long, deep strokes within her folds.

She felt herself open to him, felt her body mold perfectly to his solidness. They'd always fit together as if they were made only for each other. Nothing had changed over the years, and that should have scared her, but for now, it made her grateful.

Roxie let go of all reservations as he pushed in and out of her, their eyes never straying from each other. Tremors shot through her as her orgasm drew closer. She could feel the sweat beading on his back as his own body tensed with the sweet brushing of their bodies.

Kian broke the connection of their gaze as he leaned down and took her mouth, tugging on her bottom lip and sucking as his thrusts sped up and he pushed hard into her. It was exactly what she wanted—the nightmare was long gone, and Kian was right where she needed him.

She met him with each thrust, silently commanding him to go harder and faster. He gripped her hip and held her in place as he sped up even more, their groans mingling in the air as they sought release.

Without warning, Roxie felt herself explode, her body shattering into what felt like a million pieces. She gripped him tightly as he continued to thrust, drawing out her pleasure for an endless moment in time.

And then he shouted as she felt his hot pleasure shoot inside her, revving up her own pleasure as he found his, both of them shaking from the intensity of the moment. It might have been seconds, maybe hours, but finally the last shudders ran through them as they collapsed into the bed.

Kian turned them, keeping their bodies connected as he continued holding her tightly while taking his weight off her pleasantly used body. She wasn't quite ready to let him go, so she clung on as she felt darkness trying to pull her under.

She wasn't sure she'd survive another nightmare like the one she'd had, but as she drifted, her lips were turned up, because with Kian holding her, the nightmare would turn into fantasy.

In a dream world there was no sorrow, she assured herself. And with that thought, she let go and fell asleep with Kian still pressed tightly to her.

Chapter Seven

Roxie was unable to move. Panic began invading her senses as she realized she was trapped. Her heart thundered, and she snapped awake with a less-than-pleasurable entry into reality. Her eyes opening, the fogginess of her dream world was instantly snatched away as she found her gaze captured by Kian, who looked entirely too smug.

"Morning," he told her with a low growl that had her stomach doing tiny flips.

Uh-oh. She instantly recalled her nightmare, and her rescue. Though she'd needed Kian with a desperation she wasn't even remotely able to explain to him or herself, she also knew instantly it had been a mistake to fall back into Kian's arms. It was going to mess with her head too much when she needed a clear mind. What in the hell was wrong with her?

"That was a mistake," she said, her voice raspy. She chose to believe it was raspy from sleeping so soundly and not from crying out in pleasure.

"Whenever I have a night like last night, I don't *ever* think of it as a mistake," Kian told her as he pressed closer, clearly pushing his morning arousal against her suddenly aching body.

Though it took all the willpower she had left within her, Roxie pulled away from Kian, and even though there was disappointment in his gaze, he let her go. She assured herself that was what she not only needed, but wanted as well.

"I'm a horrible person, Kian. I can't believe I allowed myself to forget what was happening for even a few minutes, let alone hours," she said as she climbed from the bed, wishing she wasn't naked, but reminding herself he'd seen her unclothed body too many times to count. Still, the vulnerability of being naked wasn't what she needed right now.

"You have gone through a lot these past few weeks. Letting your mind and body go doesn't make you a bad person," he told her.

The sight of him lying there, looking so handsome with stubble on his cheeks and a spark in his eyes, almost made her want to turn back to him, made her want to climb on top of him. But she wasn't that same girl she'd been when she was his. She was stronger now, and she'd made a mistake coming to his place.

"I had a nightmare, and then you were there, and I needed to forget," she admitted.

He frowned for only a moment before his lips turned up in a grin that made her forget she was still standing in the middle of the room naked.

"You needed me," he told her as he licked his lips. "And, admit it or not, you haven't forgotten anything about us because you responded perfectly to my touch."

"I'm not having this discussion with you," she said as she turned away from him and began making her way toward his bathroom. Escape was all that was on her mind right now.

She practically ran to his bathroom, then drooled at the size of his massive shower with four different nozzles. She wasn't sure if they all did the same thing or not, so she simply began turning them.

When hot steam began filling the gigantic space and water cascaded down, she decided she wasn't going to ever leave this amazing shower. Though the scent of Kian's shampoo and body wash made her think of him in ways she didn't want to, she had no choice but to use it, knowing she was going to be thinking of him each time she inhaled today.

Maybe she'd pull herself together enough to stop being so selfish and would forget all about their night together and the fact that his smell was now coating her. She doubted it, but she could dream, she assured herself.

Taking a far shorter shower than she would have liked, she ignored the ache of her muscles and the soreness between her thighs. It had been a long time since she'd made love, more than four years, in fact, and, unfortunately, she was going to be reminded about it over the next few days whether she wanted to or not.

Right now, her only focus should be on her niece. Maybe her sister and she hadn't ever been close, but Roxie would have never wished her only relative to perish in the way she had. She was filled with regret that she hadn't tried harder to bring them back together. It wasn't her sister's fault she'd turned into the woman she had. They'd both been raised by their father, who'd been an abusive drunk. Pamela had turned to drugs and men, while Roxie had decided to freeze anyone and everyone out of her life. They both had demons to bear; they'd just chosen to deal with them in entirely different ways.

Grabbing a robe from the back of the door, she wrapped herself in it, ashamed as she stepped back into the bedroom. She really had no other choice but to put on the same clothes from the day before. Luckily, though, she'd spotted a hair dryer in the bathroom, so she grabbed her strewn clothes from the floor and slipped back inside before Kian could return to the bedroom.

She cleaned her panties and dried them off before dressing in her wrinkled clothes. Roxie had never before had to do a walk of shame from a man's house, but it appeared as if she was going to experience many firsts in her life with Kian. Why change things now?

Though she had no idea what his address was, she decided she'd figure it out and sneak from his place as quietly as possible and call a cab or Uber driver. She didn't think she could bear to be in a vehicle with him with his eyes raking over her. There was too much up in the air, and for now, she wanted to do what she did best—run away.

When she stepped from the bedroom and caught the scent of freshly brewed coffee, her mouth watered. But in order for her to get some, she'd certainly have to face Kian again. She was torn. As she began moving through his massive house, she decided escape was more important than caffeine.

Her cell phone was dead, and she needed to find a phone. She was sure there was one in the kitchen, but she couldn't remember where that was. He had to have an office somewhere with a phone. Hopefully, on the side of the house opposite from where he was. She didn't mind running right now. It seemed to be her best option.

As she turned another corner, the smells of coffee and bacon made her stomach rumble so loudly, it was as if thunder was crackling. Embarrassment made her cheeks flush as she came face-to-face with a tiny woman, who smiled at her.

"Good thing I've made a large breakfast," the older woman said with a laugh as she pointed to the table. "Grab a cup of coffee and sit down. I'll dish you up."

"I can't stay for food. I have to . . ." Roxie began before her words faded. She wasn't sure what she was going to do now.

The woman tsked at her while she began piling food on a plate. Roxie knew she could ignore the woman and run from the room, but she'd always had a difficult time hurting anyone's feelings. She assured herself her desire to stay had nothing to do with the fact that she was starving, and the woman's cooking smelled fantastic.

"I need to make a phone call and collect my niece," she said, attempting to leave the room again.

"Lily has already eaten, and she's lying in the living room watching a cartoon," the woman said.

"Oh." She was already failing as a parent. Someone else was taking care of Lily's basic needs. That wasn't a good thing.

"She's a beautiful little girl," the woman told her. "Get your coffee."

She decided to quit arguing. Lily was safe, and Roxie really didn't know what she was going to do next, anyway. She just really wanted to avoid Kian after her pathetic night of begging him to love her. Not exactly the homecoming she'd been expecting or wanting.

By the time she was done making her coffee, the woman had dished up enough food to feed three people. With the workout she'd gotten the night before, sadly, she could probably eat that amount.

"Thank you," Roxie told her quietly, wondering how many times this woman had fed Kian's mistresses. The thought was enough to ruin her appetite. The lady didn't seem at all surprised to find a woman in the house. Forcing herself to push that thought right out of her mind, Roxie ate, barely tasting the delicious meal.

The woman continued moving around the kitchen as she cleaned up the dishes she'd used to cook and keep the food warm on the stove. There was no sign of Kian anywhere, and Roxie assured herself that was a good thing. She finished her meal before realizing how rude she'd been.

"I should have introduced myself. I'm Roxie," she told the lady with a sheepish smile.

"I know about you," the woman said, and for some reason the way she said it made Roxie's cheeks heat again as she looked down at the table. She in no way wanted to ask the woman for an explanation of that statement. "I'm Tilly."

"It's great to meet you, Tilly. Can you tell me where the nearest telephone is?" Roxie asked.

Tilly picked up her plate before Roxie could grab it and began moving toward the sink. Roxie didn't try to stop her.

"Take the hallway to the left, and there's one in the third door on the right," Tilly said, already distracted with her cleanup.

"Thank you again," Roxie said. It was time for her to step back out of this fake world she'd been brought into the night before.

When Roxie stepped into the large room, she immediately spotted the phone on a desk. She began moving toward it when Kian's deep voice stopped her in her tracks.

"What do you need a phone for?" he asked.

She whipped around and found him sitting back in a comfortable chair, his laptop resting on his thighs, a cup of coffee in his hand.

"I need a cab," she told him, defiance dripping from her tongue. She turned away from him and grabbed the phone, hoping to make the call quickly and be on her way.

She'd barely begun dialing information when Kian's hand reached out, disconnecting the call and grabbing her arm. She was instantly angry with him.

"I need to figure out what Lily and I are going to do next," she snapped.

"That's for both of us to decide," he told her, his voice equally firm.

"I'm not ready for this discussion," she said. She backed away.

"Whether you're ready or not, it's something that has to happen."

He was right. She knew he was right, but that didn't make any of this any easier. All she was thinking of right now was escape.

He sighed after a few moments, and she waited to see what would come next.

"I called in some favors, and your sister's place is clean and ready for you to go there," he told her.

"With Lily," she said. It wasn't a question. If she kept her resolve firm, then maybe he would leave her alone.

He glared at her, but then his shoulders drooped. "For now," he told her.

She didn't want to ask for any further explanations. She felt as if he had way too much power as long as they were in his house. If she got away from him, then maybe he'd forget he was a father. Okay, that was a ridiculous thought, but still . . . she could hope for that, at least. She reached for the phone.

"What in the hell are you doing?" he snapped.

"I need a cab," she said as if he were stupid.

"Anywhere you're going, I'll take you," he insisted, his eyes narrowing in that way she remembered so well. When Kian made up his mind, the chances of changing it were slim to none. But she'd changed a lot as well since she'd last been with him, and he couldn't so easily run over her and get his way.

"No," she said, deciding she didn't need to explain herself.

He raised an eyebrow, the corner of his lip turning up just the slightest bit in a way that made his face entirely too appealing. She forced her warm feelings for him down as she glared even harder.

"You can stop pretending you didn't enjoy our time together last night and act like a mature adult, or you can continue to sulk and glare," he said with too much mockery in his tone. "But either way, I will be taking you *and* my daughter to the house."

The steel in his tone was something she didn't remember, but she could see how he'd changed with those words more than anything else she'd witnessed from him in the past ten hours or so. Her entire being wanted to submit to him. Because of that, her spine stiffened even more.

"Screw you," she told him, before swinging around and walking away from him. Hell with it, she'd collect Lily and walk to the house, even if she didn't know how far away it was or in what direction.

A low growl from behind her was her only warning before Kian grabbed her, spinning her around so quickly she almost lost her balance. There was no chance of her falling, though, because he tugged her against him, locking her in his tight embrace.

"Damn you," he said. He didn't give her a chance to reply before his head descended and his lips locked onto her, taking away her breath and her anger as she instantly was lost in the familiarity of his touch.

His body was hard, and she realized she couldn't fight him. He was too much for her, consumed her so easily, it made her lose all concept of reality. It was just as it had been before she'd run off. Only that thought made her able to pull away from him.

He allowed her to go. She had no doubt it wasn't her strength that had gotten her away. They were both breathing heavily as she took a few unsteady steps. She couldn't look him in the eyes now.

Finally, she heard him sigh as he moved over to his desk and pulled keys out.

"Let's get your things together," he said. There wasn't any emotion in his tone now to tell her what he was thinking or feeling. Suddenly she was incredibly sad. This wasn't what she wanted. The problem, though, was she didn't know what she did want.

She decided to quit fighting him. It just wasn't worth it. Some battles could be won, and others were lost before they'd even begun. She had a feeling this was the latter.

The next hour was emotional as she gathered Lily, trying to explain why they were leaving this luxurious place to go back to a house that held haunted memories for the child. Was she truly so selfish she'd risk Lily's happiness over her own? Roxie didn't know. She just knew that she had to think, and she couldn't do that as long as Kian was in a room with her.

By the time they left the house, Kian had stopped trying to speak to her, and they drove in silence. For this moment, Roxie couldn't even begin to think about the fact that Lily was Kian's daughter. It was too much of a reality she didn't want to explore.

That would be saved in her brain until later, until she could properly process what all of that meant. For now, she wanted nothing more than to figure out what she and Lily were going to do now that the immediate danger was over.

She could keep telling herself that tomorrow would be a new day, and important decisions could be made then. As long as she did that, she could choose her own reality. It was working for her . . . for now.

Chapter Eight

It was always a surreal moment when you found yourself standing beneath a hastily set-up tent with rain coming down on the other side of it and people beside you whispering words of comfort you aren't able to process in your fuzzy brain.

Roxie wasn't focusing on the closed box in front of her. No. That wasn't her sister inside there. It was just a body, an empty vessel that had once held the spirit of her sister, a woman Roxie had been too selfish to get to know.

The preacher spoke words of praise of Pamela as a strong woman who loved her daughter, who'd overcome great odds to be a person others were proud of. Roxie didn't look away from the drops of water falling on the other side of the preacher's head.

When she squinted just right, she could slow down the motion and watch individual drops drip from the canvas and hit the ground. If only the preacher would shut up, she might be able to hear the splash.

Why wouldn't people just be quiet? Enough had been said already.

"Are you okay?" Kian asked.

She heard his words, but even those wouldn't process in her brain. She held Lily in her arms, clutching her tightly as she continued staring at the drops of rain. She could feel Kian's presence, knew his hand was touching her, but she felt so disconnected. This was a dream, wasn't it? It had to be. There was no possibility that she was at a funeral for her sister—for her beautiful niece's mother. No. It wasn't even in the realm of possibility.

And she didn't even live in this town anymore. She lived in Portland. She'd left this place—left her sister, her friends, and her lover. So, Kian couldn't be standing beside her, couldn't be whispering words in her ear. She couldn't be holding her niece. This was nothing more than a bad dream.

"Do you need to take a walk?" Kian asked.

Roxie tried to make her lips move, tried to figure out what it was he was saying, but she still couldn't process it. In the back of her mind, she could hear voices. She even noticed that the preacher's voice was no longer interrupting her focus on the water droplets, but still she couldn't figure out what to do. It was so odd.

Her head turned the slightest bit to the side as the preacher moved, obstructing her view of the current raindrop she'd been tracking.

"Let me take Lily, sweetie," someone said.

Everything seemed to be happening in slow motion. The man with the soft voice standing in front of her had kind eyes, she decided. But she had no idea who he was. She must have seemed confused because he gave her a gentle smile.

"I'm Sherman Armstrong, and I've known your family for a long time," he told her. "I went to school with your grandpa. He was a good man."

Her grandpa? A flash of white hair and a beard flashed through her mind, the smell of tobacco instantly invading her senses, making her bottom lip quiver. Her arms tightened, and Lily made a sound that snapped Roxie back to the present.

She shook her head and looked at Sherman, whose expression hadn't changed. She turned and found Kian looking at her with worry. The rest of the people around them seemed nothing more than blurs. Tears finally stung her eyes as she felt her heart begin to thunder.

This wasn't a dream. It was real. Her body began shaking.

"Can I take Lily so you can say goodbye?" Sherman asked again.

Lily looked at him and gave a shy smile while he held out his arms. Her niece leaned toward him, shocking Roxie. The traumatized little girl didn't easily go to people, clinging instead to Roxie, which filled her heart with warmth.

Sherman pulled Lily close to him, and her niece snuggled against him as he rubbed her back in comforting strokes.

Her arms empty, Roxie turned to look at the oak box in front of her. Though she was aware this wasn't a dream, it still didn't feel real. She stepped forward, noting that Kian stayed by her side. His hand rested on her lower back, and though she knew she should push him away, she also realized he might be the only thing keeping her from collapsing into a heap on the wet ground.

He was lending her a quiet strength she desperately needed but was too prideful to admit she wanted. Warmth coated her cheeks before turning cold as tears descended. Kian reached up and wiped her face with a soft pressure of his fingers. That only made more tears fall.

"I'm sorry I didn't check on her, sorry I didn't take care of her," Kian whispered.

Roxie realized in that moment that Kian was the reason her sister had turned her life around. Yes, there was some bitterness there, and yes, she was allowed to be mad about what had happened, but she could also appreciate that her sister had found love when she'd delivered Lily.

"You gave her Lily. You gave her purpose," Roxie said. She meant the words.

She met Kian's surprised gaze for only a moment before turning away from him and the casket. That wasn't her sister, and there was no reason to stand there any longer. She cast her gaze over the small crowd of people who'd given her space to do what she needed to do.

That was when she found Sherman standing beneath a large oak tree, cradling Lily as the two of them spoke. Roxie knew for sure she'd fall over if it weren't for Kian at her side. Later, much later, she might regret leaning so heavily on him in this moment, but for now, he was keeping her grounded.

Her thoughts stopped altogether as she listened to Sherman and Lily.

"Where's Mommy?" Lily asked.

Sherman's smile was so kind and full of love, Roxie couldn't stop her tears or stop her heart from bursting. Lily was a lucky child indeed to have so many people care about her. Maybe the child hadn't believed Kian and Roxie when they'd explained her mother was gone; maybe she needed to keep hearing it. As painful as it was for Roxie to say it over and over again, she would do whatever it took to help ease her niece's pain. But for now, she was glad it was Sherman speaking with her.

"She wants to be here with you forever, but she's been called to help millions of people," Sherman told her.

"Was I bad?" Lily asked, tears falling down her sweet pink cheeks.

"Oh no, honey, you've never been bad," Sherman assured her. "There are just times in our life we don't get a choice on where we go or why."

"I didn't help, though, when she cried," Lily said.

Roxie was about to completely lose control. Kian pulled her into his arms and held her as she shook uncontrollably, and he whispered that everything would be okay.

"You did help your mommy," Sherman insisted. "You stayed safe, and you've been so strong. That's what she needs and wants most."

"I want a mommy snuggle," Lily insisted.

"Every time you close your eyes and sleep, your mommy is holding you tight and keeping you safe," Sherman told her.

"Why can't she hold me when I'm awake?" Lily asked.

Sherman was quiet for a moment as he searched for the right words. Roxie was grateful Lily was asking him, because she didn't have the answers and was afraid she'd traumatize Lily even more than she already was.

"If you are really missing your mommy, then all you have to do is close your eyes and picture her arms around you, and she will be right there with you," Sherman finally said.

"When I open them, will she still be there?" Lily asked with a hope that was tragic.

"She can't be there when your eyes are open," he said quietly as he wiped away her tears.

"But she was there in the hospital when I opened my eyes. Then she was gone again," Lily said.

A chill ran through Roxie at Lily's statement. She hadn't said anything about this in the two weeks she'd been in the hospital.

"Maybe she needed to give you love and tell you goodbye for a little while," Sherman said.

"Is that mean man going to come back?" Lily asked so quietly Roxie nearly missed the words. This time it was a cold chill that traveled down her spine. She felt Kian's body tense against hers.

"No, honey, we will all keep him away," Sherman said, his voice still calm, but Roxie could hear the fury running through him, as it was through all of them.

"Okay," Lily said as she snuggled trustingly closer to Sherman. "I don't want to be alone."

"And you won't be," he promised.

Both of them were silent as the tears slowly stopped dripping from Lily's eyes. She looked over Sherman's shoulder and spotted Roxie and gave her the sweetest smile; Roxie's knees grew weak again.

"Auntie," she said, almost on a sigh.

Kian released her so she could step up to Sherman and gratefully take Lily back into her arms. Lily smiled at her as she lifted her tiny hand up and cupped Roxie's cheek.

"I love you so much," Roxie told her.

"Love you," Lily said before leaning forward and kissing Roxie's cheek.

Roxie looked at Kian, whose face was full of pain as he gazed at Lily. Fear and protectiveness filled Roxie. She couldn't let Kian take Lily away. They needed each other too much.

"I want to go home," Roxie said.

"Okay," Kian said.

The four of them walked silently from the graveyard, and Roxie then thanked Sherman before climbing into Kian's truck and allowing him to take her and Lily home. It wasn't far, so she sat in the back and held on tightly to Lily, unable to let her go right now.

Kian walked her up to the door, and she knew he wanted to come in, but she couldn't take anything else on this day.

"I need you to go now because I can't discuss anything, Kian. Please give me more time?" she begged.

"How much more?" he asked. It wasn't easy for Kian to take a vague answer. That much hadn't changed in the years she'd been without him.

"I don't know," she admitted.

There was frustration in his eyes, but she had to give him a small amount of credit for the step he took backward, for the space he was allowing her.

"Goodbye for now, Roxie," he said. His eyes dipped down momentarily to look at her lips, but he jerked his gaze away and said nothing else as he turned and walked away.

Roxie was so confused, she wasn't sure if she was happy about that or not. It didn't matter what she felt; she knew she'd made the right decision. She needed space and time. She might never be able to find enough of either.

Chapter Nine

One Month Later

As Roxie stood in the small house her sister had so lovingly decorated, had made into a real home, she had a difficult time not expecting Pamela to walk through those doors, her signature smile lighting her beautiful face.

It was so much easier for Roxie to picture her sister when she was young, when neither of them had known how harsh the real world could truly be. Those days, they hadn't been worried, hadn't been burdened by the bad choices they'd one day make. That was how she wanted to remember her sister.

Pamela had grown up and led a difficult life, and things had just begun to go a little bit better for her, only to be so prematurely snatched away in a moment that still didn't have a resolution. Maybe that was why Roxie didn't feel as if her sister was truly gone; maybe it was because she hadn't been able to lay her memory to rest.

Returning home to the city of Edmonds, Washington, hadn't been easy for Roxie, especially with her past and all the memories flooding back, and she didn't even want to think about her first night back and her time with Kian. She shuddered as she thought about what she'd run away from four years earlier, and what she'd so easily fallen back into. But that had been one mistake out of many, and she refused to allow herself to dwell on the past, even if it had already bitten her once since her return.

She couldn't focus on all she'd done wrong. She had her niece to take care of, and though she wanted to fall apart every second of every day, she couldn't allow herself that luxury.

The trip home to move out of her apartment had been pathetically easy. Though she'd had to give up her job, it hadn't been difficult, and, sadly, she hadn't had anyone to say goodbye to. Even after living in the bustling city of Portland for four years, she'd never taken the time to make lasting friendships.

So, she was in Edmonds, in her sister's place, a small two-bedroom house in a quaint neighborhood, with her few possessions still in boxes. What she should do was place those boxes back into her car and drive away, start somewhere fresh, somewhere away from the memories, away from Kian Forbes.

As soon as she had the thought, she dismissed it. It was no longer just herself she had to take care of. Now she had the responsibility of raising Lily, who was beautiful and kind, and who had asked about her mother often in those first couple of weeks. Sadly, her niece was already forgetting her mother, was already attached to Roxie, even though, much to Roxie's shame, she hadn't spent time with her niece since her birth. They'd practically been strangers to each other before now.

Kian was most definitely putting pressure on Roxie to communicate more, but he wasn't being cruel. In reality, it was more likely that he was letting out the fishing line, and soon—much sooner than she was ready for—he'd begin reeling it back in. She was so afraid of what he was going to do next that she chose instead to live in denial and hide her head in the sand. She'd managed to avoid him *and* the attorney who'd been calling.

People said ignorance was bliss, and she believed them. If she pretended there wasn't a problem, then there wasn't, right? Well, obviously, that wasn't the case, as her time was running out already.

At least she had a few positives going for her. Thankfully, the house she was living in was paid off. It was the only possession her sister truly owned, and that was only because it had been passed down to her from their father. Technically, the place was in Roxie's name as well, but she hadn't hesitated to let her sister have it. Once Roxie had made the decision to move away from Edmonds, she hadn't looked back.

Now, she didn't want to leave the place and head to the attorney's office. This was it; this was where she'd find out if she had a battle ahead of her she had no chance of winning. She hung her head as she grabbed hold of Lily's hand and walked from the safety of their home.

She couldn't help but appreciate the town of Edmonds as she made her way through it. Though Edmonds was only about fifteen miles from the bustling chaos of Seattle, a person really wouldn't know that when they stepped back in time to the historic town.

This was a place where people still helped their neighbors and still smiled and waved at strangers. It was a place you had true relationships with people and where you called the family attorney *uncle* instead of *sir*. It was a place she'd run from quickly, and if she wasn't so guarded, she might admit she had regrets about doing that.

When Roxie arrived at the attorney's office, she stopped at the front door and wiped away the sweat springing up on her palm as she clutched Lily's hand with her other. Her young niece clung to her, as she often did these days, and she looked up at Roxie with a hesitant smile on her sweet pink lips.

Roxie had pored through her sister's photo albums, and there wasn't a single picture in them where Lily wasn't smiling with pure mischief in her eyes, even when she was an infant. To see her so much more subdued than what those images revealed was another heartbreaking realization for Roxie. She was determined to see that same light shine again in her niece's eyes, and to see it sooner rather than later.

As Roxie opened the door, Lily scooted a little closer to her. Soon only her short brown curls could be seen as she peeked out from behind the safety of Roxie's body. This made Roxie's eyes sting as she fought the need to cry again.

Lily's life would never be the same again, and even if it did make Roxie a bit uncomfortable being back home, her niece had been through enough, and Roxie could bite the bullet and make a sacrifice for the sake of this precious child.

"We're just fine, Lily Bear, I promise," Roxie said as she bent down. "We're just visiting with Uncle Sal."

Lily nodded bravely, but she didn't say anything as Roxie stood up and moved into the brightly lit hometown office. Before she managed to shut the door, a surprised gasp emerged from in front of the two of them, causing Lily to cling desperately to Roxie's legs as they both gazed ahead.

"Well, look what the cat dragged in," a woman cried, her lips turned up in a beaming smile, her eyes practically sparkling.

If Roxie thought she'd be able to do this meeting without any fanfare and then slip back to her small place and think some more about running away, that thought had just been brutally pushed from her mind.

Standing in front of her wearing a surprised-but-delighted smile was her former best friend, Eden Skultz. They'd been through thick and thin together all through their school years, and Eden had been one of the people Roxie had left behind. Guilt instantly filled her as she gazed at the woman who had been by her side for all the important events in her life.

"Hi, Eden," Roxie said with a fake smile in place. "It's great to see you. I'd forgotten you worked here," she added far too lamely.

"Well, you've been gone a long time, so I can see the memory lapse," Eden said with only the smallest hint of betrayal in her voice. She paused for only a moment before she rounded the desk she'd stood up from and came over to throw her arms around Roxie in a crushing embrace.

"Yeah, it's been a few years," Roxie said. She was perfectly aware of exactly how long it had been since she'd run away from this town, run away from Kian Forbes, but she didn't need to say that out loud.

Finally, Eden let her go, but took her arm and walked with her to the sitting area, where coffee and snacks were laid out.

"I'm here for a meeting, but I don't want to interrupt you," Roxie said with a slight smile. She really just didn't want the two of them to get into a discussion about the good old days, because she feared that would hurt too much.

"You know it's always been relaxed here, and the two of us can definitely visit before you see the old man," Eden countered as she took a seat and invited Roxie to do the same. Roxie didn't have much of a choice without seeming rude. It was odd to have such thoughts around someone she'd once been so comfortable with.

"You're looking great," Roxie said, noting that her friend hadn't changed at all in the years they'd been apart.

Eden laughed. "I'm a single woman. I have to at least try to maintain some semblance of my youth," she said as she picked up an orange and began to peel it. "But you're the one who's been gone. I want to hear all about you since you've left our small town to travel the world."

Roxie cringed. This was the type of question she'd expected from her small-town friends, but it wasn't something she'd been looking forward to. It wasn't as if she could tell them she'd gone out and conquered the world. For one thing, she'd been running away, not running toward something. For another, she'd accomplished a big fat zero. That wasn't something someone wanted to admit to.

Before Roxie was able to say anything, Eden zeroed in on Lily, who was clinging to her leg. The child was so quiet, she would be easy to overlook at this point.

"Well, looks like at least one thing has changed in your life," Eden said, making an assumption about Lily. This would be the hardest part that Roxie had to play in her new role in life, especially since she wasn't sure what she could say.

Lily looked bored, and though Roxie had been playing the parent role for only about a month, she already knew that look meant trouble. She quickly dug into her oversize purse for the small figurines and handed them to her niece, who gratefully took them, instantly absorbed. Roxie let out a relieved breath.

"I have to admit, I'm a little jealous of how amazing you look," Eden said with another warm smile, contradicting her words. "You haven't changed a bit."

"I . . . um . . ." Roxie trailed off.

"And now you're a mom," Eden said, sadness in her eyes, though the words should be spoken in joy.

"Not really. I'm just trying to not screw things up," Roxie admitted.

"You won't," Eden assured her. "I'm really sorry about the loss of your sister."

The words nearly ripped Roxie's heart from her chest. Of course, everyone would know about her sister, and know Roxie had Lily. Roxie wondered if they also knew about Kian's role as her father. To even think about that gave Roxie an instant headache.

"Thank you," Roxie finally said, not knowing what else she could add.

"We won't dwell on that," Eden assured her. "Tell me instead about your life. Are you married?"

So much had changed in the past few years that though it might appear on the outside that Roxie hadn't grown much, she knew very well that she was a new person. She wasn't as naive as she'd once been—that was for sure. Her looks might have matured the slightest bit since she was now a respectable twenty-six years old, but she had aged what felt like ten years on the inside.

She'd certainly matured in other ways—emotionally and physically. But maybe those were things that were so much more obvious to her than to an outsider. She cringed a little when thinking of Eden as an outsider. This was her best friend—or at least she'd once been her best friend, and now Roxie didn't know her at all. She didn't know anyone from her past anymore.

She really thought of her life in two parts. Her time in Edmonds, which was most of her life, and her time away, which was about four years. Though the time away was far shorter than her time growing up, the past four years were truly what had shaped her. She'd been little more than a girl when she'd left. She had no doubt she was now a woman, though she still didn't know exactly who she was.

Was it sad that she had come back around in a seemingly endless circle? She was back where she'd begun, but she'd made no true progress in life. And now she was jobless, low on money, and responsible for her niece, whose life could forever be changed by any decisions Roxie made. That was a responsibility she didn't want to take credit for.

Finally, Roxie thought about Eden's comment about a husband. Though Roxie wasn't wearing a ring, that didn't seem to matter nowadays. She could see how people would assume she was in a happy little unit—husband, check, child, check, white-picket-fence home, check. If only life could be wrapped up so neatly with a pretty red bow on top.

But Roxie hadn't managed to sustain a relationship, not since leaving Kian four years earlier. It truly wasn't fair to the opposite sex when a woman dated a man like him first. No one seemed to compare. She'd make it on first dates, but then never could go back for a second, even when she berated herself, trying to make herself go. She always found an excuse and got out of it. That was her life now, it seemed.

Lily shifted in her seat and looked up at Roxie as if she was drawing from her uncertainty and nervousness. The child was bound to grow up neurotic having Roxie as her main caregiver. Roxie had the sudden urge to beg for forgiveness as she clung tightly to her niece. She somehow managed not to do just that. Eden was waiting patiently as Roxie wrestled with all these thoughts. It felt like hours, but only seconds had passed.

"I'm not married," Roxie said with a fake smile.

"Looks like neither of us has changed much," Eden said with a somewhat false laugh.

"I don't know whether that's good or bad," Roxie said. She laughed, but even to herself, the sound came out hollow. "But I do know that Lily and I are now facing the world together, so that's one thing that's different."

Sympathy instantly flashed across Eden's face, and Roxie cringed. She didn't want sympathy. She just wanted to go back to some semblance of normalcy in her life, whether that was possible or not.

"You always were stronger than you thought," Eden said.

"I'm glad someone thinks that," Roxie said, this time with a real smile. "I did fail my sister, though, and that doesn't show any strength at all. I just have to live with the guilt of that knowledge, and I have to try to be a better aunt than I was a sister, for not being there for her while she was falling apart. Maybe if I had been there, this situation never would have happened."

She finished off with her smile fading away. She somehow felt bad when she did feel a moment of joy. Was it okay to feel good when her sister never could experience life again? She didn't think so.

"You can't blame yourself for someone else's actions," Eden quickly assured her. It wasn't taking Roxie long to remember why she had loved this person for so many years. "And it's certainly not selfish to strive for your own dreams. It wasn't as if you were doing it at someone else's expense." There was more passion in Eden's voice as she finished her words.

"You were always that friend that made me feel better about myself at the end of a conversation," Roxie said. "I can't believe I ever forgot that."

"Things got rough for you in your last months here. I understand," Eden said. The warmth in the woman's eyes made Roxie glad she was sitting. She didn't understand how forgiving Eden was acting toward her, considering how easily Roxie had walked away.

"I'm sorry I left the way I did," Roxie said.

"You had to do what you had to do. But you're home now. Is it permanent?" With those words, Roxie could see Eden had a little bit of her own guard up. She was still being more open than Roxie had the right to expect, though.

"I don't know yet," Roxie admitted.

"Well, you're here for now, and you have your beautiful niece with you, and you know the people of this town will embrace you both."

"Yeah, sometimes it's a little overwhelming to have so many people watching every action you make," Roxie said.

"Tell me about it," Eden said with a sigh that had Roxie wondering if there was a story there to be told.

"Is there any special man in your life?" Roxie asked.

"Ah, you didn't pay attention when I said I was a single woman," Eden pointed out as she held up an orange. "I would be eating chocolate if I were in a relationship," she added with a laugh.

"You've always looked amazing. I don't think you need to abstain from anything," Roxie said.

"We're getting old," Eden said with seriousness, her eyes wide as if this were a fate worse than death.

This did make Roxie laugh, a real laugh, something she'd needed to do for a while now and something she couldn't remember doing in so long, the sound was odd to hear.

"How sad for us that we think being in our midtwenties is old," Roxie said when the laughter faded away.

"When the average marriage age of our group is about twenty-two, I feel old," Eden told her.

"What about . . . ?" She trailed off. She probably shouldn't say that name and was glad she stopped herself when sadness entered Eden's eyes.

"We haven't been together in a while. He left," she said, a sparkle in her eyes. "And it was for the best."

"Then we won't speak of it," Roxie assured her. She could see questions in Eden's eyes, but she was grateful her friend hadn't brought up Kian. Since the two of them had dated brothers, they were very aware of each other's circumstances.

"I think that's enough talk about men or husbands or any of that," Eden said. "It's better to focus on the fact that you're a mother now."

"I'm not a mom; I'm an aunt," she said as she reached over and ran her fingers through Lily's hair. The amount of love she felt for this child was unbelievable. Lily was oblivious to the conversation they were having as she played make-believe with her small horse figures.

"You *are* a mom now," Eden insisted. "Your niece can't be more than three," she pointed out.

"Almost four," Roxie said. Her heart was racing.

"She's going to think of you as her mom. You will be, in every sense of the word," Eden said gently.

"I . . . I don't . . ." Roxie couldn't even form a thought to that statement, let alone say actual words.

"I'm not trying to stress you," Eden quickly said. "Maybe I should keep my opinions to myself. A few people have told me that."

Those words pulled Roxie from her panic attack as she focused on Eden. "Your advice always had a way of grounding me," she admitted. "But that's just something that hasn't crossed my mind. I don't know why not. I guess I've never really thought of myself as being capable of being a mother."

"Because this is all happening so quickly," Eden said. "But why don't we push it out of your mind for now and take a stroll? It's my lunch hour, and Sal isn't here right now. He got stuck over at Ms. Martha's house and probably won't be here for another hour."

This made Roxie grin again. "Is it an official meeting?" she asked with a sly smile.

"He thinks we all actually believe that," Eden said with a chuckle.

Martha and Sal had been secretly seeing each other for more than ten years under the pretense of client and attorney, but everyone knew the truth. Why the two of them wouldn't admit they were in love was a mystery. Maybe the clandestine meetings added excitement. Roxie wasn't even offended he was late to see her.

"I would love to take a walk," Roxie said.

"Perfect." Within a minute, Eden set the phones and had the place locked up. They stepped outside, and Roxie took in a breath of fresh air as Lily once again clung to her hand and looked around.

"We have this great new park that an anonymous donor contributed to, but we all know it was the Forbes family. They just don't like to be in the limelight for some reason. There's a great new volunteer program in town, too, that is helping higher-risk kids do things in the community and giving them a chance to earn scholarships for college and put résumé-building skills on their applications. I'll take you over to the park, where we will probably see some of the kids doing cleanup work and repairs," Eden said with excitement.

"Sounds like a lot of things have changed around here since I've been gone," Roxie said.

"I know. I remember we used to take part in community projects, but it was so difficult to get someone to head things, and now there are more than enough people willing to jump in and lead the kids. I give as much time as I can, and I love every minute of it," Eden said.

"Who heads the volunteer program?" Roxie asked.

"Martha's in charge of it, so she's coming into the office all the time and asking for me to do something or other. I think I get caught in the middle in her excuse to visit with Sal," she said with a wink.

"Martha is perfect for the task since it was always impossible to say no to that woman," Roxie said with a chuckle.

"Tell me about it. I've even done trash cleanup," Eden said. "But let me tell you, after doing that, if I see so much as someone throwing a gum wrapper on the ground, I won't hesitate to yell at them until they pick it up."

"I'm glad to be warned," Roxie said before turning to Lily. "Better be careful, little girl, or Eden will be putting you to work."

Lily clung a little tighter to Roxie's hand as she glanced at Eden with a shy smile.

"I wouldn't make you do anything that wasn't fun," Eden promised with a wink at Lily. "And sometimes, treasures can be found when you're going through garbage."

It was a warm day, and many people were milling about town, some sitting outside eating lunch, while others stood by buildings, visiting. It looked exactly the same, and yet subtle changes were showing throughout, such as planter boxes with bright flowers lining the streets, and new businesses that had customers walking in and out with bags. The town seemed to be thriving. It was a beautiful sight.

"Mr. Cortnick opened up a bakery over there," Eden pointed out. "It's absolutely sinful, and I know I'm going to gain ten pounds because I do good all day eating healthy and then get off work and swing by there. As soon as the door opens, I'm slammed in the face by mouthwatering smells and then buy half the case. I drop most of it off at the volunteer center, but not before consuming at least one pastry. I don't know what that man does, but I've never tasted such good food," Eden grumbled.

Roxie laughed. "We'll definitely have to stop in there on the tour," she said.

"Do you like chocolate doughnuts?" Eden asked Lily, who looked up and smiled.

"Yeah," she said.

"Then for your sake, we'll have to go there," Eden said with too much enthusiasm.

"I remember our old bake sales—he would come in with the best treats. I'm glad to see he's made a business of it now," Roxie told her.

"I'm not," Eden said. "He's making me fat."

"You know you haven't changed one little bit," Roxie said. She was amazed at how easy it was to slip back into her old routine with her friend. It was making her homecoming a lot better.

"Have you noticed my hips? I've gone up a pants size," Eden said.

"I'm sure half the men in town have noticed your hips. They're stunning," Roxie said.

Eden laughed. "You don't understand." She lowered her voice and looked around before she spoke more quietly. "I was feeding Scooter, and I bent down and heard a horrible ripping sound. I was afraid to reach back, but I felt the breeze, so I already knew what had happened. My favorite jeans split down the middle. My ass has gotten so huge that I ripped out my jeans." Her final words were spoken as a horrified gasp.

Roxie tried desperately to keep the laughter in, but between the horrified look on her friend's face and the urgently whispered words, Roxie couldn't keep it in. She bit her lip and still couldn't stop herself. Laugher rolled out of her in waves, and soon she found herself bending over as she clasped her stomach as more and more laughter escaped. The longer the laughter continued, the more her stomach hurt. It took several moments for her to gain control over herself.

When she was finally able to stand upright again, she looked at her friend, who was wearing a bemused expression as she tried to look offended. She wasn't pulling it off very well.

"I don't know what to tell you, because you look great," Roxie finally said.

"You can be horrified with me," Eden suggested.

"Are you working out?" Roxie asked.

"Every day!" Eden said, her voice rising.

"Then maybe you are building that booty in beautiful waves. Don't men like a good butt?" Roxie asked.

"Or maybe I just need to avoid the bakery," Eden pointed out. Then she looked at Lily. "But not today, 'cause I can't disappoint Lily."

"Of course you can't," Roxie assured her. Her friend truly was beautiful, with what didn't look to be an ounce of fat on her. She'd always been so thin in school, and now she looked like a woman with curves Roxie was almost envious about.

"Now that you're back, maybe you can come work out with me sometime. I'm almost obsessive about it. I had so much pent-up tension in my life after my breakup, and I discovered I'm a much happier person when I lift weights. If only I could stick to my diet, I'd probably be in the best shape of my life," Eden assured her.

"You *are* in the best shape of your life," Roxie said. "And if weight lifting can relieve tension, then maybe I'll have to take you up on that offer."

"Yeah. I always love to bring newbies with me," Eden said.

They made it to the park, where several people were enjoying the warm, sunny day. They continued chatting about different people in the community, and Roxie found herself smiling and laughing easily, as if she hadn't ever left. She'd needed this time with her friend more than she'd realized. For too long she'd been suppressing her feelings, and being with Eden for less than an hour had begun cracking the careful wall she'd built around herself.

Maybe she'd been protecting herself when she hadn't really needed to. Why had she let her feelings for one man influence her in so many ways? She'd kicked women like that in the past for being weak, and yet she'd turned into that. Maybe she'd now have the power to stop such negativity.

"There's a group of the kids from the volunteer place," Eden pointed out.

Five kids, two boys and three girls, were over at the restroom area with paint and brushes. They were laughing as three of them painted, and two were carting materials in and out and performing cleanup. She instantly recognized two of the boys from the hospital and felt panic stir in her. Would Kian be there? She'd avoided him since she and Lily had returned to Pam's house, but this was a small town, and she knew the more she got out of the house, the more likely she'd see him.

"Who's supervising them today?" Roxie asked, hoping her voice sounded casual. She didn't want to admit to Eden she was afraid Kian would be there.

"Not sure who's with them today, but most of the volunteer coordinators don't hover, wanting them to feel like they're capable and appreciated, not needing their hand held," Eden said.

"I'm definitely going to have to get involved if I stay here," Roxie said, but as soon as the words were out of her mouth, she realized that might make her run into Kian as well. This was all just too damn complicated.

"A lot of these kids come from troubled homes, or they have emotional or mental issues they're dealing with. But this center is really great about not putting any of them into a category. They want them to be just like their peers, and the more respect they are treated with, the more stable they feel," Eden said.

"Yeah, I know there's a really thin line some of these teens walk. They can go one direction or the other. I'm so glad to see a program like this in place," Roxie said. She was looking about her, but became more relaxed when she didn't spot Kian anywhere.

Eden filled her in on the different programs, and Roxie was impressed by how involved this group was. She was also impressed by the number of elite community members giving their time. The kids who got involved felt it was cool to do so since they were supervised by people they hero-worshiped.

Looking down at her watch, Roxie noticed that almost an hour had passed, and as much as she didn't want this visit to end, she knew she had to get on with her business. She didn't have time to play all day, as she still had to look for a job and make sure she would even have time to volunteer. Her number-one priority right now was providing for Lily. It wasn't all about herself anymore, which was an odd concept to delve into.

The word *mom* flashed through her mind again. She wasn't a mother, couldn't even fathom being a mom, but as she glanced down at her niece, she knew that was all changing. She was this child's sole caretaker for now, and Lily wasn't even four years old yet. Roxie might want to push Kian away, but he would be her father whether Roxie was willing to think about that reality or not. And Roxie also decided she would keep the memory of Pamela alive in Lily's mind and heart. She might be acting as Lily's mom, but Roxie would be certain the child knew who she came from.

What if she failed, though? She'd screwed up so many times in her life. Would this be the ultimate catastrophe for her? Would she fail this precious child in ways that would lead her to needing a place like the volunteer center to save her? A shudder rushed through Roxie's body at the thought.

Roxie had to push those types of thoughts from her mind, because if she dwelled on them for too long, she would sink deeper and deeper, and then she wouldn't be doing herself or her niece any good. Her eyes stung as she blinked away the tears that wanted to come and spill over. She hated that she allowed herself to dwell on things she couldn't control.

"We should probably get back," Roxie said, hating to break up their pleasant time together.

"I know, but I don't want to. I've missed you," Eden said with a sad smile.

"I'm sorry I left that way, I truly am," Roxie told her again.

"I don't want you to apologize anymore. Just don't leave now that you're back," Eden said. Her voice was serious. She didn't even try to cover up her words with a joke or a forgiving smile.

"I . . ." Roxie stopped speaking as she noticed the man walking up to them.

There went her wish to not see Kian. Damn! Eden looked at Kian, then at Roxie, then back at Kian. It was obvious there was massive tension between the two of them, more than there should have been if they were just seeing each other for the first time in four years.

"Hi, Kian," Eden said, breaking the silence.

"Eden," he said with a nod, his gaze never leaving Roxie's face. He addressed Roxie next. "You've been avoiding me."

What in the world was she supposed to say to that? Eden looked as if she were searching for the popcorn while getting comfy to enjoy the show. Roxie couldn't guarantee she wouldn't feel the same if she were on the other side of this situation.

"Yes, I have," Roxie admitted. What would be the point in lying?

His lips twitched the slightest bit, as if he were fighting back a smile. But then his gaze focused on Lily, and Roxie felt her stomach tense. There was such possession in his gaze that she wanted to grab Lily and run. She knew he had more rights to the child than she did, but for some reason she couldn't begin to fathom, she knew to the very roots of her soul, she couldn't let Lily go.

"Can we go somewhere and talk privately?" he asked.

"I'll just take a stroll and check in on the kids," Eden said, disappointment oozing from her voice.

Roxie didn't have to say anything as Eden disappeared. She felt betrayed because she didn't want to be alone with Kian right now.

"This isn't the time," she told him.

"Too bad," he said.

The determination in his voice made the color drain from Roxie's cheeks. Something had changed within him, and she knew the battle was very much on between them. Was she going to be strong enough to fight?

Chapter Ten

Kian wasn't normally a patient man on any given day. With Roxie back in his life, his patience and attitude were being tested on a daily basis. The woman needed time to grieve and accept this new reality the two of them had been thrust into together, but he was done with her avoidance, and he was done missing out on his daughter's life. Enough was enough. He'd driven by her small place several times, stopping often and pounding on her door. She was either very good at hiding, or she was making sure to be gone a lot. Being able to hide in the small community of Edmonds was pretty impressive.

But now, seeing her so casually strolling in the park with *his* daughter was truly pissing him off. She could run all she wanted, but she could no longer expect not to be chased, not when she had the one thing in his life he wouldn't give up.

He'd been giving her time to accept what had happened, but because of his damn feelings for Roxie, he'd lost another month in the life of his daughter. He was finished being the nice guy. That obviously hadn't gotten him anywhere in the past few years. However, he didn't want to have a public fight, especially in front of his little girl.

When he looked back at Lily, he noticed she seemed to be growing bored with just standing there. She was beginning to fidget in her aunt's arms, and it appeared as if Roxie was having a difficult time maintaining her hold on the child. His fingers twitched with the need to grab his child.

Though anger flooded him again, he refused to acknowledge it, pushing it deep down inside him. He wasn't going to get anywhere with Roxie if he was yelling at her, and that certainly wasn't going to make a good impression in front of his daughter as he tried to get to know her more, tried to work up the courage to tell her who he was and then find an explanation for why he hadn't been in her life so far, without saying anything bad about her mother.

But the urge to hold her wasn't going away. He didn't have to take her. He could be a lot more respectful than that, he decided. Resolve sat firm in his gut as he looked Roxie in the eyes.

"Can I hold her?" he asked. There was so much raw emotion in his voice, he wanted to be able to push it down, but he couldn't. His words came out practically baring his soul. She could do with that what she wanted. He couldn't care right now.

"Um . . . okay," she said after a slight moment of hesitation. She wasn't letting Lily go, though.

"I'm not going to run off with her," he told her. *At least not at this moment,* he added silently. He wasn't going to promise her he wasn't going to want custody of his child, but he didn't need to say that right now. If she remembered anything at all about him, then she should know he *was* going to raise his daughter.

Kian stepped closer to the two of them, Roxie's subtle peach scent drifting over him, taking him instantly back to their last night together. He'd never been able to resist her sweet scent. She'd giggled once when he'd told her just that and said that knowing that, she would always make sure to wear something good so she could get her way. As bitter as he was now, he'd think she was wearing the scent on purpose to get to him, but she'd been far too horrified to see him for her to have known they would run into each other today.

He reached out for Lily, and though she looked curious and gave him a little smile, she didn't let go of her aunt. He wasn't being too smooth at the moment, and he felt the sting of rejection filter through him.

"Lily, do you want to let Kian hold you?"

Another pang rushed through Kian. Roxie had called him Kian, not referred to him as Lily's father. He wanted to be Dad, or Daddy. He didn't want to be Doc, Kian, Mr. Forbes, or any other name.

But his rational mind knew you didn't just tell a child he was her father out of the blue. It would be easier on her if she knew him, trusted him. But the need to claim her was so strong, he was having a difficult time being rational. And though he *was* her father, in her eyes he was little more than a stranger. If he rushed this, it wouldn't go well for either of them, and he couldn't stand a lifetime of his daughter not trusting him. That thought helped keep him calm, helped him make positive choices.

Kian gave Lily what he hoped was a warm smile and reached for her again. This time she released her aunt and accepted his embrace. He gently pulled her in close and held on, being careful not to clutch her too tightly in his enthusiasm for holding his child.

She buried her sweet little face against his neck, her dark curls tickling his nose. The amount of love and joy he felt was so overwhelming, his eyes stung with the need to free what he was feeling. He closed his lids to keep his feelings to himself, unwilling to give Roxie a glimpse inside his soul. This was a moment between his daughter and him, and Roxie had severed her right to see the real him when she'd left so long ago.

Lily was an unusually delicate child, with small limbs and just the slightest bit of baby fat on her cheeks. He wondered if she was getting enough to eat, if she had warm clothes. He wondered if she had been taken care of. Now that he was holding her, he didn't know if he'd be capable of letting her go again, of giving her back to her aunt.

He looked over at Roxie, who was closer than appropriate, her fingers twitching. He knew the feeling. His own hands had been aching with the need to hold his child. He imagined Roxie wanted to take her back before he got too attached.

Too late.

He might not turn around and run with her, but the need to do just that was so overwhelming, he had to force himself to calm down. He didn't want his tension to radiate outward and stress Lily.

"Are you settling into the house?" he asked. He noted that she seemed reluctant to share anything, and she took too long a pause before replying.

"It's okay for now," she admitted. He tensed again, not knowing what the *for now* meant.

"It's a solid place, even if it's small," he said, trying to remember the layout of the place.

"I'm not sure how long we're going to be there," she said. He knew she wasn't trying to threaten him, but she apparently didn't want to lie any more than he did. At least they still had that much respect for each other.

"Where would you go?" he asked.

"I need to find work," she said, avoiding the question of where.

He had to force himself not to tense up again. He was holding his little girl, and that was what mattered.

"I hate to interrupt this, but Sal is back for a limited time, and we should go now," Eden said as she returned.

"Of course," Roxie said, before he could tell the woman to go away.

Roxie reached out for Lily at that moment and took her from Kian's arms. He wanted to refuse to let the child go, but he wasn't going to have a tug-of-war with Roxie over his daughter. The second Lily was out of his arms, though, he felt the horrific emptiness of not having her snuggled to him. He didn't like the sensation in the least.

The sooner the two of them got this custody situation resolved, the better it would be for him and for Lily. Roxie might end up hurt over losing Lily, but Kian wouldn't forbid her from being in the child's life. He wasn't cruel.

"I have to go," Roxie said. "We will have to talk about this later."

Without a conscious thought about it, Kian fell into step with Roxie and Eden as they made their way through the park and back to the office where Sal worked. Eden gave him a glance before looking back down, but he could see she had a million questions for Roxie and resented him being there.

Well, he had a million questions for the woman next to him as well, but he was sure as hell forced to wait, and he didn't feel in the least bit bad that Eden was going to have to stand in line for answers just as long as he did.

Besides that, he wasn't leaving until he and Roxie had a chat about where things were headed. He didn't need to tell her he was planning on obtaining full custody of his daughter, but he was going to put his foot down on visiting with her until that happened. He needed to make sure Lily trusted him. This transition was going to be difficult for all of them.

They got to the office, and Kian could see the surprise on Roxie's face when he followed them inside. She was looking more and more uncomfortable by the minute, the longer he stuck around. Too bad.

"Kian, my boy," Sal said in his cheerful voice as the three shut the front door behind them. "I'm glad you're here. I was going to have Eden give you a call."

"What do you need?" Kian asked.

"We're here to read Pamela Gilbert's will now that Roxie has quit avoiding it, and as you know, your name is there, too," he said.

Kian looked at Roxie and saw definite panic in her eyes.

"Then we should get under way," Kian said, trying to keep a positive note in his tone. Roxie wasn't saying a word. She also looked on the verge of tears as she gripped Lily tightly enough in her arms that Kian was getting a little worried about his daughter's ability to breathe.

"Why don't I keep Lily out here so you guys can talk without interruption?" Eden offered as she stood in front of Roxie and Kian, eyeing them warily as if they were both cobras about to strike.

"That would be great. Thank you," Roxie said. Kian felt a small buzz of irritation that Lily went to Eden without hesitation when he'd had to coax his daughter to come to him. He pushed that down, though. Soon she'd be running and jumping into his arms, he promised.

"Come on, Lily, I've got some great pictures of your aunt somewhere around here in full cowgirl gear at a barn-raising dance," Eden said with glee. A pang ran through Kian at this thought since he remembered those dances, remembered being there with Roxie in his arms.

"Oh, those should be dead and buried," Roxie said in horror.

"Nah, those are the good old days," Eden assured her. "Now you will get to teach Lily how to do it." Kian was more determined than ever to be a part of that dance.

Sal went ahead of them and gave Kian a moment alone in the hallway with Roxie. He grabbed her arm and halted her midstep. She eyed him warily as she waited for what he had to say.

Bending closer so he wouldn't be overheard, he whispered, "Our conversation is in no way finished. I don't want you running off when we're done in here. We're going to talk privately."

"I figured as much," she said, but there was fear in her bright eyes as she looked caught between anger and heartbreak. He wasn't going to soothe her. The two of them helping each other had come and gone. Now, they'd have to be civil for the sake of Lily, but they didn't need to go above and beyond anymore.

"Good. Just wanted to make sure you understood that," he said. His voice was firm and maybe just slightly husky at her close proximity. He wasn't thrilled at *that* particular thought. He was over her, dammit.

"I understand," she said, her eyes narrowing as she found some of the fight inside her she had seemed to have lost since coming back into his life in such a big way. It was enough to almost make him smile. He always had enjoyed her spirit.

Shaking his head, Kian pushed that sort of thinking out of his brain. He couldn't think about her in terms like that anymore. He was now a father, and he'd better behave like one. With a new resolve firmly in place, he let Roxie go and followed her inside the lawyer's simple office. She wasn't his friend or lover anymore. She was now the one trying to keep his daughter from him.

Sadly for Roxie, even though the battle might just be beginning, the reality was that Kian Forbes always came out the victor—no matter whom he was up against.

Chapter Eleven

Roxie was now very much aware of how someone escaping death must feel. Her heart was racing, her palms sweating, and her entire body shaking. She felt as if she'd just run twenty miles through a desert without water.

She should have known better than to think she could avoid Kian forever. But being in this attorney's office with him at her side was making the situation so much more real. He was Lily's biological father—at least that's what Pamela had told him in the hospital, and the fact that Sal said Kian was in her sister's will pretty much confirmed that fact.

Roxie didn't have a chance at all in a battle with Kian. He had money, prestige, and was a doctor in demand. He was a Forbes, dammit, and that meant something not only in this small town, but all over the United States. Hell, probably all over the world. She wouldn't be surprised if he went golfing on a regular basis with whatever judge was assigned to their case when he took her to court.

Now, not only did she have to deal with her unresolved feelings for Kian, which she had hoped would become more subdued through the years, but she also had to face the fact that her one true love had enjoyed a one-night stand with her sister, and a child she very much loved was the result of what she could only see as the ultimate betrayal.

He would take Lily away from her. He had the legal right to raise her, and he certainly had the money to beat her in court. So, though she might feel as if she'd just escaped death, the worst was yet to come. She had no doubt about it. What was she going to do? She could go on the run, but she had no money and no way to sustain a life of running. Besides that, she didn't think there was a place far enough for her to get away that she could hide from Kian. If he wanted to find his daughter, he was damn well going to.

She wasn't that person anyway, she reminded herself. She couldn't do that to him or Lily, now that she knew the truth. But she didn't want to give up her niece. She might not think she was the best possible care provider for her delicate Lily, but she knew no other woman would love her as much as she did.

That thought only led her into thinking about Kian finding a woman to be Lily's mom. He'd want to do everything he could for his daughter, including giving her a normal two-parent household. Tears stung her eyes to even begin to form that picture in her mind. She couldn't go there or she knew for sure she would fall to pieces. And this absolutely wasn't the time to do that.

Roxie felt as if she was completely out of options. She couldn't fight Kian. She didn't have the will for it, even if she had the money. He was too powerful in his own right, but to top that off, he had the Forbes name, and all the power associated with it. His family were basically celebrities in this community.

She wished they were monsters so she could hate them and justify running, but they weren't. They were truly good people with hearts bigger than the average family. They were tight-knit and incredibly intimidating, and there wasn't anything they wouldn't do for the ones they loved.

All of that led her right back to the place of not having a clue about what she was going to do. And while Kian had a huge network of people, she had not a single one. When she'd moved from Edmonds, she'd purposely burned every bridge leading away so she wouldn't turn around and run back with her tail tucked between her legs.

That might not have been her smartest choice ever, but she'd been thinking with emotion instead of her very smart brain. She had good insight when she chose to use it the way she was supposed to.

Growing up with an alcoholic father had been hell, and when her sister had begun following that same path, Roxie had pulled away from them. They wouldn't even have the house if it weren't for their grandparents being smart enough to leave it to them. It was their way of saying they were sorry for having such a horrible son.

Roxie's mother had left when Roxie was still a baby. Why she hadn't taken her girls with her, Roxie would never know. Her father had refused to talk about her, and their family had moved to Edmonds after her mother was gone, so no one knew who she was. Her bitter father hadn't so much as kept a picture.

By the time Roxie was old enough to try to find leads that might lead to who her mother was, she'd hated the woman. Any person who could leave her children with a man like her dad wasn't someone Roxie wanted to know.

So, the bottom line was that she had no one to turn to and nowhere to go. She wished she'd given her sister more of a chance and that she'd communicated with her. But it was so much easier to give up on her. Now, she wouldn't give up on her niece. Lily was all she had left.

It sent a pang through her heart knowing that her niece would be better off with Kian, though, with his loving family. Was she truly so selfish she would keep her niece from having that privileged life? She shook her head, pushing those thoughts away. Roxie also deserved happiness and love. Just because she didn't have money and power didn't make her less than Kian or his family. But in the end, if it was best for Lily to grow up without Roxie, then she would make that sacrifice. Though it would be tougher for her to give her niece a great life, she believed she could give her so much that money couldn't buy—loyalty, love, and affection—and she would always keep Pamela alive in Lily's heart by looking through picture albums and telling stories about her.

And Roxie was her blood. That mattered just as much as it did that Kian was Lily's blood, too. Besides, Roxie was a nurse and would get back on her feet, and maybe she'd even marry someday—marry an ordinary man who would love Lily as his own.

She took a moment to glance over at Kian, who was standing near the door of the office, probably to make sure she didn't rise up and make a run for the door. She quickly looked away again.

Even if she were to marry a nice guy, Kian wasn't going anywhere. The only doubt she faced was where she was going to fit in this picture. Maybe the reading of the will would help with that. Her sister had nothing monetary to give, so Roxie knew this could only have to do with custody. If her sister left custody of Lily to her, didn't that mean she would get to keep her? Roxie had done Google searches and still didn't know how the law worked. Who had more rights? She wasn't sure. But looking at Kian and the confident smirk on his face wasn't helping to ease her nerves.

"Go ahead and sit down," Sal said. Roxie needed to pay attention and not get lost in her own thoughts. She didn't want to sit and have Kian towering over her even more than he already was, but she feared her legs weren't going to keep holding her up, so she did as Sal suggested and sat. She pressed her still-shaking knees together to keep from showing her nervousness.

"You too good to sit?" Sal barked at Kian. Roxie didn't look in his direction, but she imagined he gave an eye roll. She did hear his steps as he moved in closer. Now that she was sitting, maybe he felt as if he could let his guard down enough to step away from the door.

He sat in a chair that was slightly behind her, giving him the advantage of being able to watch her without her seeing him. She was sure he'd positioned himself that way on purpose. Roxie was beginning to think every move he made was calculated.

"First off, darling, I have to tell you how sorry I am for the loss of your sister. I know you two haven't been close in a long time, but she was your sister, and she was trying to turn her life around," Sal said. His words instantly brought tears to her eyes, and she was too emotional to hold them back. They spilled over and soaked her cheeks. Sal handed her a hankie. An actual hankie. She hadn't known those still existed.

She gratefully dabbed the moisture on her cheeks as she tried pulling herself together. She could fall apart later that night, after she'd managed to get Lily to sleep and the day fully sank in. For now, she had to keep it together. It took massive strength, but she stopped the flow of tears and looked at Sal.

"I'm sorry. It's been a long day," she told him.

"It's okay to fall apart, Roxie. You don't have to be strong for me," he said before looking sternly at Kian. "And Kian won't judge you for it, either." That last part came out as a threat and nearly made Roxie smile.

"What I'm going to read might be a little hard for you, but your sister made me promise," Sal told her before he opened a folder on his desk.

"I can just read it myself," Roxie told him. She wasn't sure she wanted Kian to hear what her sister had to say. There was so much emotion filtering through Roxie. She almost wished she could hate Pamela for sleeping with Kian. Though Kian might not have known who Pamela was, Pamela certainly knew who he was. She'd been jealous of Roxie's relationship with him, once telling Roxie she'd managed to snag herself a rich one, and she'd better hold on tight. Roxie had been horrified at how cynical Pamela had become.

"No, that's the purpose of the reading of the will; it must be read aloud," Sal said. This time Roxie didn't try to argue; she just nodded as she waited for him to begin. "I want to start by saying your sister actually wrote this about a week before she died. She was truly frightened in the end. She came to see me with this typed out, and she signed papers to make it official; she was planning on speaking to you both but never got the chance," Sal said, his voice heavy.

Roxie wanted to ask a million questions, but she was hoping at least some of them would be answered with the letter. She said nothing as she waited for Sal to say what he needed to say.

"I did this pro bono for your sister because she didn't have much money, and she was scared. I didn't realize the seriousness of what was happening or I would have gotten more involved. I have to apologize to you both for that."

"None of us knew. We can't have 'what ifs' if we're going to move forward and protect my daughter," Kian said. Roxie's gut clenched, and she clutched her thighs tightly while trying not to shake.

"Thanks for that," Sal said, but there was pain in his eyes. "Let's get started." He looked down at the letter in his hand.

"Well, I have to say this sucks mighty badly, because if you're hearing these words, it means I'm dead," Sal read aloud. He gave Roxie a bit of a smile as he said this, and Roxie felt her own lips twitch the slightest bit.

"I never thought I'd be the type of person to write out a will, but then I had Lily, and my life was no longer as important as hers. I know, I know, hold the phone, that was actually me saying that. I'm admitting someone else just might be more important than me."

Sal paused, and it almost felt as if Pamela was in the room with them.

"At first, I didn't tell anyone who Lily's dad was because I loved holding the power over him, even if he didn't know I was doing it. I also loved the fact that I felt I had won some game I finally realized I was the only one playing. The truth is I was bitter and jealous and wrong. I was so wrong. I'm also scared right now. I'm having another baby, and I can barely take care of my sweet Lily as it is. How can I do this?"

"I would have taken care of them both," Kian said. Sal didn't acknowledge his words. He just continued to read.

"I got into a really bad relationship and tried to end it. He's not a good man. He's threatened me, and I'm scared something might happen. I have nowhere to run to. Well, that's not entirely true. I know Lily's father would help her, but I'm so scared of losing my little girl. That's how selfish I am. I'm willing to put both our lives in jeopardy just so I won't lose her."

Kian growled beside Roxie, and it took all her willpower not to turn and look at him, to comfort him. She was sure he was furious and hurting. Someone had attacked his little girl, and he would have protected her had he only known what was happening.

"Kian Forbes is Lily's dad. I'm so sorry, Roxie. I was so mad at you. I was jealous that you had everything I'd ever wanted, and then you left. You walked away. You left Kian, who worshiped the ground you walked on, and you left me. How could you leave me? I needed you so much."

Again, Sal paused as he gave a sympathetic look at Roxie. This time she didn't try to hide her tears. These were the last words she'd ever hear from her sister, and they were full of pain and anger. Roxie felt lower than a squished spider on the bottom of a shoe. She was too ashamed to look at Kian now.

"So, one night I found him at a bar. He was beyond drunk with some of his buddies. I made my move. I walked over and threw it all out there, promising Kian a night he'd never forget. I knew he had no clue who I was, but that only made me feel more smug. He took me to a hotel and, well, the end result was Lily. When I woke up in the morning, he wasn't there and, at first, I was furious. But when I sobered up, I knew I was nothing more than a free whore. Roxie, you were always going to be the one he loved."

Sal sighed, but he didn't look up this time to check on Roxie. She was grateful. This moment was too painful for her to say a single word. She really wished Kian wasn't in the room with her. This was too intimate a moment, and she was far too raw.

"When I found out I was pregnant, the first thing I wanted to do was stick it to Kian in every way I possibly could. I was so arrogant. I had him—I had a Forbes in the palm of my hand. Not only that, but

I had the man my sister loved. I was the winner, for once in my life. No one could take this from me. I didn't love the baby growing in my stomach. It was nothing more than a tool to be used to give me the life I always wanted. I didn't tell Kian. I wanted that baby in my arms to make a full impact on him when I walked into that hospital and smugly told him he now had to pay for me for the rest of my life."

Sal stopped again and cleared his throat. Roxie was mortified at these words being so casually spoken. She wanted to stop him, but it was like a runaway train, and nothing was going to put the brakes on it at this point.

"Then Lily was born. The moment the doctor placed her in my arms, my life changed. She was no longer an object to be used to get what I wanted. She was my darling little girl. She looked up at me with those perfect eyes, and she opened that tiny mouth and let out a squall like you wouldn't believe. I fell in love for the first time in my life. I was in shock at how much I loved this tiny, screaming human."

There was a smile in Sal's voice as he read these words, and there was a smidgeon of hope in Roxie's heart that her sister had truly felt love, maybe for the only time in her life.

"I knew then that I couldn't tell Kian about the baby. If I did, he wouldn't support me; he would take her away. Sure, he might throw some cash at me like a street bum, but he would take this precious girl away from me. He wouldn't want his daughter to be raised by trash like me. So, I decided in that moment I was going to change my life. I was going to get a great job and take care of my Lily on my own. I was planning on telling both you, Roxie, and Kian about Lily when she was older. But I was so ashamed of what I'd done and who I had become that I had to do something with my life to make you both proud of me before I could do that. I was beginning to get back on track, too."

Sal turned the page and continued.

"Then I met Greg. He was charismatic and said all the right things. I even thought I was actually falling in love with him. I hadn't ever been with a man before that I didn't want something from. But I got pregnant and things changed. He began hitting me, and I started to grow worried that he'd hurt Lily, so I broke it off. He's threatened to kill me, and I'm writing this because I think he might actually do it. You know I made a lot of mistakes in the past, and I was afraid to go to the cops. I was afraid they'd take Lily from me. I know that's stupid, and I'm trying to work up the courage to do just that, but my past has been so bad. I can do it for my baby girl, I know I can. I just need some time to figure it out. That is, if I have more time. I just don't know."

Sal had to pause as he cleared his throat.

"I know you will take care of our daughter, Kian. I know you will love her. Please don't tell her what a monster I was. Please tell her I loved her with all my heart, and she was wanted. I made Roxie's life a living hell for a lot of years, and Lily is the only family she has left in this world. I know as Lily's father, you have every right to take her, but you need to know that Lily and Roxie need each other. I'm leaving full custody of my precious Lily to Roxie Gilbert and Kian Forbes. Take care of her together. And though Kian isn't the father of this precious baby inside me, I also leave her to Roxie Gilbert and Kian Forbes. I wish I had money to give you, Roxie. I wish I had anything at all worth keeping, but, sadly, I haven't gotten my life on track enough to do that."

Sal again cleared his throat before he finished.

"I truly am sorry for what I did, Roxie. I thought I hated you, thought I'd sought the perfect revenge, but now I'm devastated at what I did. Don't blame Lily for my mistakes, and don't let her go. You two need each other. We're the end of the line, and our family needs to continue to show the world that our destiny isn't decided by where we're born, but by what we make of ourselves. I love you more than I can ever express. I hope I'm the one to read this letter to remind myself of who I can be instead of who I've always been, but if you're the one hearing it, then go home to Kian and be a mama to my babies. And, also, it's okay to cry about this situation, and to mourn me, but don't do it too long because I want you to be happy that I grew up and didn't turn into the same kind of parent as our father. I woke up, Roxie, and I loved big, and my Lily loves me. That's so much more than many people in this world can ever say. So, continue the love with Lily, and you and she will save each other."

Sal turned and gazed at Kian directly.

"And for Kian Forbes, wake the hell up and stop your destructive behavior. You have a daughter to set an example for now. And everyone in this damn town knows you are head over heels for my sister, so suck up some pride and tell her. She will forgive you for your transgressions, if you ask. It was a great night, baby, and I don't regret it for a second because you gave me Lily, which gave me my life back. Carry on, people, and live. I believe in ghosts, and I will be haunting your asses if you don't do what I say."

Sal stopped, and Roxie waited for him to go on, but he was silent as he shut the folder. Roxie didn't know what to think or say as she sat there a little stunned. Her sister certainly had enjoyed writing *that* letter.

"Do they know who this Greg is?" Kian asked, murder in his voice.

Roxie turned to look at him, and he was now standing, his body tense, his hands clenched into fists. He looked capable of murder at that moment, and though Roxie knew he was mad at her, she was certainly glad she'd never put that light into his eyes.

"No, there are no pictures, no real name, and no evidence," Sal said.

"But the police are investigating," Kian demanded. It wasn't a question.

"Yes, but Pamela didn't have a lot of clout, and it's not high profile," Sal said. That's when Roxie noted the bit of smugness in his eyes. She almost smiled. She now knew that the power of the Forbes name would go into this investigation. The mother of Kian Forbes's daughter had been brutally murdered. The killer *would* be found. That gave Roxie the slightest sense of peace.

"It hasn't seemed real until now," Roxie said quietly. "Can I have a copy of her letter? I want to read it again . . . privately," she said, the last word coming out a whisper.

"I want a copy as well," Kian said, his voice not quiet at all.

Sal pulled two copies out of his desk, obviously anticipating their requests. "She told me to read this out loud with both of you in the room. She wanted to make sure you heard her final words. I'm sorry for your loss, and again sorry I didn't do anything to help her," he said.

"She made a lot of mistakes in life, but at least she was trying to make up for that," Roxie said, quick to defend her sister now that she was gone. "And she's reached out to me a lot in the past few years, and I was only barely interested. I have a lot to make up for with Lily."

"She's not your redemption," Kian snapped. His words made the hair on the back of Roxie's neck stand up, and she jumped from her seat as she turned to face him.

"I know that," she yelled. It felt good to feel anger instead of fear, anguish, or guilt. "I might have abandoned my sister, but Lily is my blood, too, Kian, and you can't take her from me no matter how much power you wield. Pamela kept her from you out of fear. Are you going to prove her right and take away my only living relative?" she challenged.

His eyes glowed hot embers as they glared at one another. She didn't back down, and neither did he. This might just get nuclear before one of them put up the white flag.

"Yelling certainly won't get us anywhere," Sal said, trying to get in between them.

"But it sure as hell feels good," Kian snapped.

"Yeah, that's about *all* we agree on," Roxie said.

"You two have to put aside your differences for the sake of that precious girl out there," Sal told them.

Neither of them was anywhere near ready for compromise.

"She's my daughter and should be raised by me," Kian thundered.

"You didn't know about her, or want to know. At any time, you could have checked in on my sister and been aware she had a child. You'd rather live in the dark. For that matter, you better go down the long list of women you've screwed to see how many miniature Forbeses are running around out there."

At those words, Kian flinched, finally breaking the glare between them. Instead of her words feeling like a victory, they cut the inside of her heart. She might have been yelling them in anger, but the frightening reality was that he could have more kids. This man she had loved so much had turned into nothing more than a slut who didn't care to even remember the names of his conquests. She was feeling more and more shattered by the second.

Without warning, the office temperature felt like it had climbed about fifty degrees and all the oxygen in the room had been sucked out. Her head grew fuzzy, and Roxie clutched her throat as she fought to draw in a breath. She began to tilt on her feet as the edges of her vision dimmed.

She heard her name called out as if through a long, dark tunnel. She tried to breathe, tried to stop the wobbliness, but she was no longer in control of her own movement. She was sinking into an abyss.

"Breathe, just breathe," came the concerned words of Kian. She felt the pressure of his hand on her back, gently rubbing as he spoke in her ear. His chest was against her cheek as he held her in the safety of his arms. The buzzing began to fade, and the darkness receded.

"Breathe," he repeated, his tone calm, his hand gentle. The last of the dizziness evaporated, and Roxie sucked in a much-needed breath of air. Tears fell down her cheeks, but the panic attack went away.

She stood there in the safety of his arms for a few more much-needed seconds, and only when she was sure she wasn't going to slip down in a puddle at his feet did she take a step back. She was mortified she'd shown such weakness. She might as well hand over Lily now, because he'd never think her suitable enough to raise the child. She couldn't even take care of herself.

When Roxie was able to gain the courage to look up at Kian, she thought she'd see smug awareness in his gaze, but she only saw worry in the tense lines of his forehead. He seemed ready to dart quickly back to her in case he needed to catch her again. She forced more breaths in and out. She couldn't afford to lose control like that again.

"I'm fine. I'm sorry," she said, tearing her gaze away from Kian and looking over at Sal, who looked frozen in place as if unsure what had just happened.

"Let me get you some water," Sal said, and before she could stop him, he darted from the room. She didn't want anyone to know what had just happened and hoped he wouldn't say a word to Eden.

It was odd, but there was comfort in knowing time hadn't changed Kian. He was still the man who'd be there to rescue a person, even if he didn't like the person he was saving. He'd be the person in battle to patch up the wound he'd just been forced to inflict. She had to love him for that, even if she was mad at him, or even if she feared he was going to take her niece away.

After what she and her sister had both put him through, it would have been well within his rights to let her fall to the ground and writhe in pain and agony. No one would judge him for it. Well, she might judge him a little if she were being honest, and Sal would most certainly judge him, but they wouldn't really have the right to.

Roxie just needed this meeting to be over so she could collect her niece and hightail it out of there. She didn't think she was capable of going through anything more—not on this day. After she was alone, she could read the letter again and maybe get some focus on what was happening in her life.

As long as her head continued to spin, she wasn't helping in any situation. She had to get away. Sal came back in and gave her water, and she gulped it down.

"The house is all yours now," Sal said. "I know that's the last piece of business, but I wanted to give you that reassurance."

"Thank you," she told him.

"Do you want to keep it or sell it?" he asked.

He didn't turn and look at Kian as he asked this, and she was grateful. This had nothing to do with him. She felt him tense behind her, though. His reaction was great enough that it seemed to almost send out an electrical pulse through the air.

Roxie wanted to say she was going to sell it and take her niece and run far away, but she knew that would only start a war. There truly was no use in fighting Kian at this point. The only thing she could do was try to work with him. Then at least she'd have a shot of getting to keep her niece. It was a small shot, but at this point she'd take it.

"I'm keeping it . . . at least for now," she said.

There was an audible sigh behind her. She wasn't sure if it was stress release or what, but for now there was a semitruce in the room. She couldn't offer more or ask for more. The battle between Kian and her had only just begun.

Chapter Twelve

Relief. Sweet, blessed relief was what Kian felt at Roxie's words. He hadn't even realized he'd been holding his breath, but it escaped from him in a beautiful rush as she told Sal she was keeping the house, not putting it on the market. She and Lily were staying. He couldn't miss any more of the firsts in Lily's life, and he wanted her to know who he was and how much he loved her. He'd just met this beautiful girl and already she owned his heart.

If he didn't bring her into his life soon, then she'd never realize how much she meant to him or how much he wanted her. Yes, Roxie would be able to see Lily anytime she wanted—within reason—but Kian was well aware that wasn't the same as waking up with the child every morning, or tucking her into bed at night, or having access to her company each afternoon. No, this was going to be very difficult for Roxie.

On the other hand, he reasoned, she seemed perfectly capable of walking away from those she said she loved. Maybe he just thought it was going to be hard on her, but maybe she was planning on the freedom this was going to afford her. Who was Kian to decide what was and wasn't difficult for the woman he'd never stopped loving?

When Kian did have Lily with him, he was going to have to harden his heart more firmly against Roxie, if she decided to stick around. Their time had come and gone, and to think of them in a relationship again was impractical and just wasn't going to happen, so he'd have to get used to seeing her, and he'd have to deal with it.

The out-of-sight, out-of-mind philosophy hadn't worked out too well for him, anyway. He might have been able to push her from his thoughts when she'd been rude enough to enter them, but he'd been able to do nothing about his dreams of her—and she'd come to him often in that manner, causing him to wake up in a cold sweat with an incredibly hard body.

Kian in no way had time to dwell on those thoughts. Not if he didn't want to be judged for the reaction that was sure to follow. There had never been another woman who affected him the way Roxie had. Sure, he could work up enough enthusiasm to scratch the itch, but with Roxie, it had been otherworldly. Kian shook his head as he turned away from the woman in question.

He was pissed at her, he reminded himself. He in no way wanted to have erotic fantasies about her. He also didn't want to focus on the ways in which she'd pissed him off. Because he was either going to be turned on, or thinking of strangling her, and neither was an acceptable action at the moment.

The two of them had been given a lot of new information in the last month. Their initial meeting after four years hadn't gone too well, until they'd ended up in the bedroom, but he couldn't think about that. And just because they had a lot of baggage didn't mean they couldn't have a civil relationship for Lily's sake.

They were adults, after all, and they could be civil to one another. Hell, he'd been civil to people he hated, so he knew it was possible. Because as much as he'd wanted to hate this woman over the past four years, he hadn't been able to accomplish that.

He was glad he hadn't. They were now bound to each other for the rest of their lives. Lily needed them both in some form or other. Lily's shy smile flashed through his mind, and he felt his fear and anxiety begin to fade. They were bound together through this beautiful little girl. How could he be angry when he was thinking of Lily? He couldn't. Kian would simply choose to think about his daughter now, not about the past couple of years he'd missed. He was going to look forward to what was to come.

Heck, there were a lot of firsts to come, he realized. He was going to teach his daughter how to ride a bike, a horse, and a sheep. He would take her to the swimming hole and teach her how to do a cannonball and how to dive. They'd have lazy afternoons of fishing, and exciting nights of rodeos. She could be anything she wanted to be—whether it was a ballerina or a NASCAR driver, or possibly she'd follow in her father's footsteps and be a doctor. That filled him with unbelievable pride. The sky was the limit with his daughter, and he'd show her love and kindness and support for whatever it was she wanted to do in life.

So, he might not be happy he'd lost a couple of years, but when he realized how much more was in store for the two of them, he couldn't help but feel optimistic. Kian looked at Roxie, who was gazing at him with a furrowed brow, worry clearly dominant in her expression.

His gains were her losses. He knew this, and it pained him, but he couldn't think that way. He might have made a mistake in whom he'd shared a bed with, but he wouldn't ever be able to think of Lily as a burden. She was his, and he was glad he had her. No one would keep them apart. He just wished Roxie didn't have to be hurt for him to have what he wanted. He'd once loved her too much to cause her this type of suffering.

Kian knew he'd made many mistakes in his lifetime, but he'd been raised by incredible parents who had shown him love and support in all he'd done. He'd been scolded when he was wrong, but he'd been held as well. Kian knew he'd have a million questions for both his mom and dad, and he knew they'd answer him honestly. He'd been loved his entire life, and now he'd give that same love to his daughter.

And maybe someday . . . he didn't even want to think the thought, but maybe Lily would have siblings. Kian's face turned as he looked at

Roxie again. But he forced his eyes away. That ship had come and gone. There was a time he'd wanted children with her, but she'd walked away from him—and Kian Forbes begged no one for a single thing.

All these thoughts passed through Kian's mind in a matter of seconds. It might feel as if he were alone on an island, but he was still in the room with Roxie and Sal, and no one seemed to be saying anything. What could be said after the revelations that had been exposed today? Not a hell of a lot.

"We're finished here," Sal told them, and Kian was glad there weren't any further revelations. He didn't think his system could take anything else—at least not today.

"Good," Kian said. He stepped forward and shook Sal's hand. "I'll have my attorney get ahold of you if he has any questions."

"We can talk without another attorney," Sal said, instantly scowling.

"I'm not jeopardizing anything when it comes to my daughter," Kian said, his normal humor gone from his tone.

Sal stared at him a moment, but then relented, nodding. Kian then faced Roxie, who had lost all color in her cheeks. He couldn't think about that right now. He was doing what had to be done.

"Why don't we walk out together?" he said, holding out his arm in a sort of peace offering. She looked at the arm as if it were a snake about to strike. Then she shook her head and turned to Sal, skipping the handshake and giving him a hug.

"Thank you for this gift of my sister's last words," she said, her voice much more under control now. She'd pulled herself together and was maintaining her hold on her emotions. He wondered if she was having difficulty doing that, or if she was truly that calm. He wasn't sure.

"I'm glad I could be here for you both," Sal said.

Roxie nodded and then turned and walked from the room. Kian was right on her heels. He didn't need her pulling another disappearing act. Not right now.

They reached the front entrance and found Lily playing on the floor with Eden, her giggles music to Kian's ears. She looked up as they approached and gave Roxie a big smile as she climbed to her feet and ran over to her aunt, holding up her arms. Roxie pulled her up and gave her a loud smacking kiss on the cheek, making Lily giggle more.

"Thanks for watching her," Roxie told Eden.

"It was my pleasure. You have a beautiful niece, and I hope to watch her again anytime you need," Eden assured her. She climbed to her feet and came over and gave Roxie a half hug before she moved back. "See ya, Kian," she added flippantly as she turned and walked back to her desk.

"See ya," he replied with a big smile. He'd been dismissed, and he found it incredibly entertaining. He followed Roxie from the building and down the street to her car, which he glared at.

"That's what you're driving?" he said in disgust.

Roxie glared at him. "There's nothing wrong with me driving this. It gets excellent gas mileage," she pointed out.

"Were you on the freeway in that thing?" he gasped, remembering she'd driven from Portland.

"Of course I was," she said, opening the back door and setting Lily in her car seat.

"Don't take my daughter on the freeway in this," he demanded. It was interesting, because he practically saw the hackles sprout on her back as she stiffened.

Somehow, she managed to keep it together long enough to buckle Lily into the seat before she handed his daughter some toys and calmly shut the door. Then she turned around and fire leaped to life in her eyes.

"I've been caring for Lily for a month now, since her time in the hospital, and I wouldn't do anything to hurt her. Don't you dare imply I would," she hissed.

"She's my daughter, Roxie, and it's taking all I have not to snatch her from that seat in that pathetically small death trap of a car you're driving and march her over to my giant-ass truck," he said, getting equally worked up.

"It's a newer Ford," she snapped.

"It's tiny and will be crushed faster than a can in a flattener," he pointed out.

"I don't plan on getting in a wreck," she said, throwing her hands in the air.

"No one *plans* on a wreck, but if they happen, you should at least be in something you have a chance of surviving in," he yelled.

Some people across the street turned and openly stared at them. It wasn't often people got into yelling matches on the sidewalk in Edmonds. Kian tried to calm his voice as he spoke next.

"We'll find another vehicle right away," he said.

Roxie gaped at him. "Not everyone has the luxury of buying a new car just because they feel like it," she thundered.

"I do, and I say we're doing it."

He knew the second her eyes narrowed he'd said the wrong thing. Shutters flew over her eyes, and she took a step closer to him and stabbed him in the chest with her surprisingly sharp finger.

"You might think you have all the power in the world right now, but you haven't ever seen me truly angry, Kian Forbes. Right now, you're getting a small taste. You aren't my boyfriend, my lover, my anything. You don't get to tell me what to do or how to live. I'm an excellent guardian to Lily and haven't done anything to put her in danger. Don't you dare try to imply I have simply because I can't afford to go out and buy a damn Hummer. This Ford is perfectly equipped with all the latest safety features. Now, I'm tired and emotionally drained, so we will continue this conversation later," she growled.

Then she stepped away, and it took him a second or two to realize she was planning on leaving just like that. Hell no, she wasn't!

Kian grabbed her arm just before she managed to jump into her car and speed away. They glared at each other, and Kian didn't even care at the moment if anyone was watching them. He had a daughter, and the world could know about it. Heck, he wanted to shout it out from the rooftops.

"I'm going to allow you to go home tonight and rest. But I want to know a time and place for tomorrow for us to finish this. Do you want it to be in private or public?" He was very pleased with how quiet he was able to keep his voice when he wanted to roar.

She glared at him. "Allow?" she challenged.

"Yeah, allow. Got a problem with that?" he asked.

Oh, she certainly had a problem with it, and he didn't care.

"Fine," she snapped, obviously figuring out she wasn't leaving until she made plans with him. "Meet me at the café on Main tomorrow at two," she said.

He nodded and then allowed her to leave. It took all that was in him not to follow them to her place, just to assure himself they'd arrived. It also took everything not to sit in front of her place to make sure she didn't leave.

He had a daughter now, and he didn't want to let her go for even a single night longer. He knew he wasn't going to get much sleep that night. Not much at all.

But, soon his daughter would be sleeping in his house with him. He certainly had some shopping to do. He wished he could ask Roxie to help him, but he knew how that would go. And it wouldn't be a happy conversation.

It was okay, though. It would all be okay. Why? Because he was a daddy.

Chapter Thirteen

Kian almost felt the need to duck and cover as he entered the high school his brother chose to work at. What was wrong with Arden that he'd put himself through all this torture? His brother was a wealthy man; hell, they all had more money than anyone could ever spend in ten lifetimes, but they still found a love for life and for their individual passions.

Arden just happened to think being a history teacher and football coach was about as great as it got. Kian normally didn't seek his brother out at school, but he had to speak to him. Kian loved all his family members equally, but Arden might just edge out his other siblings as his favorite, even if he wouldn't admit that anywhere but in his own head.

The office staff knew Kian and had smiled with glee when they told Kian his brother was in the school cafeteria. They knew Kian would rather poke himself in the eye than enter that place.

As Kian walked in, the noise level alone was enough to make his head spin. His muscles were taut as he fought his way through the crowded room to where he spotted his brother at a table with a bunch of nerdy-looking kids. Arden was laughing so loudly, the sound echoed off the walls. It actually made Kian smile. Arden did have an infectious laugh. Kian quickly made his way to his brother's table.

"I see you're making an entrance," Arden said, laughter in his voice as Kian looked around at all the kids staring at him, the noise levels so high he was getting a headache.

"Can't you get these kids under control?" Kian grumbled.

"You can sit here, Dr. Forbes," one of the boys said as he tripped while getting up quickly to give up his seat.

"You don't have to move for me, Matt," Kian insisted, but the boy was grinning.

"It's no problem at all," he insisted as he held out his hand.

Kian wasn't going to be rude, so he sat down across from his brother, who looked like he was enjoying Kian's discomfort at being in the cafeteria.

"What brings you to the zoo?" Arden asked him.

"It's hard as hell to see you these days," Kian grumbled.

"I know. I've been busy with school and practice. But you know you can join us on the field anytime you want. The kids love having the star running back from Stanford at our practices," Arden said.

"Yeah, come to practice," Matt said.

Matt was a smaller boy and not the most coordinated, but he'd joined the football team the year before because all the kids loved Arden so damn much. Kian had to admit his brother had a gift for teaching these kids, and he'd done a hell of a job of breaking the typical stereotype of what an athlete should look like. Sure, Arden looked as if he could be a linebacker for the San Francisco 49ers, but that didn't matter. He respected talent, but he respected drive more than anything else. If the kids were trying their hardest, he'd give them a place on the team.

"How's your running time?" Kian asked.

Matt beamed. "I'm the fastest guy on the team," he said. The boy barely stopped himself from pounding his chest.

"Way to go," Kian said, holding up his fist so the kid could bump it.

"I gotta run. I have a science test today, and I have more studying to do. The coach is harsh on grades," Matt said. He might have been complaining, but there was a proud light in his eyes that made Kian smile.

"Go kill it, kid," he told him.

Matt took off. Kian looked at the tray of crap Arden was eating and felt his stomach turn just a bit.

"I don't know how you survive on this food," he said.

Arden laughed. "Hey, food is food, and you know I have to show the kids I'm not too good to follow the same routine as them."

"Yeah, well, I think I'd have to put my foot down at what I was putting into my stomach," Kian told him. He did reach over and snatch a carrot from Arden's plate, though. He'd missed lunch, and he was hungry.

"I c-could g-go and g-get you a t-tray," Jenny said. Her stutter was getting much better, but right now she was nervous. She was so willing to please both Kian and Arden that Kian knew he couldn't turn her down. It looked as if he was going to have to eat the crap they called food.

"That would be great, Jenny. I'm starving," he said.

The girl bounced to her feet and ran off to the front to get him food.

"Good boy," Arden said with a grin.

"Yeah, yeah," Kian muttered.

Jenny was back far too quickly and set a tray down. Kian looked at the food, and since he couldn't identify what was on his tray, he knew it was going to take some effort to force it down his throat. At least he'd be back at the hospital soon in case he had to have his stomach pumped.

"Thanks, Jenny," he said.

The bell rang and the kids jumped up from the table. "See you in class, Mr. Forbes," a couple of the kids said, and then the cafeteria quieted as kids rushed off to their next period.

"Do you have to run?" Kian asked. He was picking at the food on his tray. He took a bite and was surprised it wasn't too bad.

"No. This is my free period," Arden said. "What's brought you down here?"

Kian was quiet for a minute. He wanted desperately to share what was happening in his life, but he wasn't sure what he should or shouldn't say. He squirmed in his seat as he tried to hash it all out in his mind.

"Come on and spit it out. I don't have that much time," Arden insisted. His brother finished off his food, then snatched Kian's tray and began to eat *his* food. Kian reached for the banana and peeled it as he tried to get as comfortable as he could on the hard bench.

"I'm having a hell of a time with my daughter not living with me, and I'm alternating between wanting to get in a knockout yelling match with Roxie and wanting to pull her into my arms and kiss her into submission," he spat out.

He looked up in time to see Arden spit his drink of juice down the front of him before he began coughing. Arden glared at him.

"Wow, a little warning next time would be nice." Arden pulled himself together quickly. "Why don't you tell me how you really feel," he added with a chuckle.

Kian sighed, then he relayed his frustrations to his brother, who didn't interrupt once. He had to respect the man for that. Kian wasn't sure he'd have been able to keep quiet for so long.

"What does Roxie plan on doing about all of this?" Arden asked quietly.

"I can't read her anymore. I'm beginning to think I never was able to, and maybe our entire relationship was all in my head," Kian admitted.

"I don't think that at all," Arden disagreed.

"The entire family liked Roxie," Kian said. "I loved that at the time, but now, with these new developments, I'm thinking you all are gonna side with her and turn against me," he said, only half kidding.

"No matter what you do or don't do, we'll always have your back," Arden assured him.

"You should have gone into counseling instead of teaching. You're good at it," Kian said.

"Yeah, I've been told that before. But teaching is a lot like counseling. I love these kids, and I believe in them," Arden insisted.

"They know it, too," Kian assured him.

"There are days I don't think I can get through to some of them, and then there are other days I feel I'm making progress. Sometimes I want to give up, but then I'm around a kid like Matt, who has an atrocious home life, and I see him glowing now, feeling a real part of the team and doing great with his grades, and I know I'm where I belong," Arden said.

"Plus, you get to be a bum all summer," Kian pointed out.

"Hey, we have football practice for half the summer. I'm not slacking," Arden said.

"Football isn't work," Kian insisted.

"It is when it's ninety degrees out," Arden argued.

"I think you just like to get all sweaty and shirtless for the cheerleading coach," Kian said with a wink.

"The cheerleading coach is sixty and happily married." Arden laughed.

"Well, maybe it's for one of the hot teachers. I hear some kinky stuff goes on in schools when the lights go out," Kian said, finding himself quite amusing.

"I've had a few desk fantasies with one or two of the staff members." Arden winked again.

Right then the seventy-year-old librarian walked by and winked at Arden, and Kian busted up laughing as his brother's face turned a nice shade of red.

"I think Ms. Myrtle's interested in helping you out."

"Shut up," Arden grumbled.

Kian was serious for a moment as he looked at his brother. "Thanks. I've been sufficiently distracted." He flashed a crooked smile.

It had only taken a few minutes, and Kian was feeling much better. He'd made the right decision in coming to visit his brother. They might rib each other like crazy, but at the end of the day, there wasn't anything they wouldn't do for each other.

"Mom and Dad haven't called me for a few days, so I'm assuming they're consumed with being grandparents," Arden said with a chuckle.

"They didn't last long with keeping their distance, but I think it's good for Roxie to have them in her face. They have respected her, but now that they know for certain that Lily is my daughter, they don't want to miss any more time with her," Kian grumbled.

"You're upset about this?" Arden said, obviously confused.

"No, not at all. I just want to be with Lily as well. I knew Mom and Dad would be incredible, and I love that Lily has this family with open arms. She's my daughter, and that's all any of our family needs to know in order to love her. I just want her to have the full benefit of grandparents and aunts and uncles. I want Roxie to have that, too."

"She has that," Arden told him.

"But we're broken right now. It's wrong. Mom has told me how beautifully Roxie is doing as Lily's mother." Kian sighed because Roxie was allowing his mother in and not him. "Maybe I'm failing as a father. Maybe I'll never get it right."

Arden laughed before slapping Kian on the back. Kian wasn't too thrilled about that. He waited to see what his brother had to say.

"I love seeing this humble side of you," Arden said. "But don't let it last too long. It sort of freaks me out."

"I'm being a little bitch, aren't I?" Kian chuckled.

"Yeah, but I'll forgive you," Arden said. "Now quit whining, and you can walk me to class."

"I've got nothing better to do at the moment," Kian said.

It took both men a few seconds to get out of the table. For just a moment, Kian felt trapped and wanted to break the damn thing, but he might get his brother in trouble if he started smashing school property.

"Did you get a call from Dakota?" Arden asked as they made their way down the hall.

Their little sister had married Ace Armstrong last year. And though all the brothers had wanted to smash Ace's face in at one point for not only putting Dakota's life in jeopardy, but also for knocking her up without being married to her, they all really liked the man now, and his entire family. The Armstrongs were good people.

"Not in a few days—why?" Kian asked. He was instantly worried. Their little sister might be married now, but that didn't mean they didn't worry about her. If Ace ever hurt her, they'd have to kill the man.

"She's about to pop at any time," Arden said.

"It's unreal how much is changing in such a short period," Kian remarked. "Now there will be two grandkids for our parents to lavish attention on. You know they'll be hungry for more."

A shudder went through Arden as a light of panic entered his eyes. He laughed, as if pushing it aside.

"They have four other children to give them all the kiddos they want. I will focus on the overgrown toddlers in this high school," Arden finally said.

"I don't think they will see it that way," Kian argued.

They reached Arden's classroom, and Kian propped himself up on one of the kids' desks as he faced his brother.

"My students aren't going to like your ass print on their desk," Arden pointed out.

"I have a great ass. They won't mind." Kian winked.

Arden laughed as he sat in his chair and pulled out some papers to be graded.

"Want some help?" Kian asked.

"You'd just give them all *As* and call it good," Arden told him.

"Yeah, I wouldn't actually read that crap. I've been through enough schooling to last a lifetime."

"You're the one who wanted to go to medical school," Arden pointed out.

"And every single day, I'm still happy about the decision." He flashed through the night he'd lost Pamela in his ER and thought he might not be so grateful every day. But he didn't need to say that out loud.

He chatted with his brother a few more minutes before making a hasty retreat. He definitely wanted to be out of that school before the next bell rang and the halls filled with obnoxious kids. He'd leave the teaching and counseling to his brother.

Right now Kian had one thing on his mind, and only one thing. He had to figure out a way to make things right with Roxie, and he had to do it before he lost too much more time with his beautiful daughter. Just knowing he had a little girl had brought a new optimism to his life he hadn't felt in a long time.

Kian smiled as he jogged out to his car. Arden really had helped improve his mood.

Chapter Fourteen

There was a mixture of relief and apprehension filling Roxie as she walked from the interview with the emergency department at the same hospital Kian worked at. She'd applied at three other places, and none were hiring, telling her to come back in six weeks. She didn't have six weeks to find work. She had to do it yesterday. She had a little girl to take care of, and no matter what her sister's will had said, she wasn't planning on sharing her with Kian.

He was a doctor, for goodness' sake, and busy all the time. She would calmly talk to him about Lily being raised by an aunt who adored her, or a nanny who didn't have anything invested in her at all. Roxie would find a new job where she'd take as many night shifts as possible so she could be with Lily during the day.

Kian, on the other hand, worked a massive number of hours. If the man wouldn't be reasonable, then maybe a judge would see it in Lily's best interest to be with family versus nannies. If Roxie truly thought about it, she knew she had no rights, but she couldn't think that way. It scared her too much.

Luckily, Roxie had gotten Eden to babysit for her while she'd done this job interview, so she hadn't had to try to juggle her cranky niece while doing it. She wanted to seem more than capable of getting the job. She knew not working would look really bad for her if this did end up going to court. She was desperately hoping to avoid that.

Her entire life, Roxie had always been that girl to look on the positive side of things. She'd correct people when they only saw the bad in any situation, and now here she was fighting to find the positive. She vowed she wasn't going to do that anymore. She would have a job and a bright future ahead of her. She wasn't even going to think about the road bump in the way named Kian Forbes. Nope. He was just a blip on her radar. That was all. Nothing more and nothing less.

Roxie was on her way down the hallway when she stopped. Ahead of her, in his white coat that showed his shoulders to perfection, was Kian, walking quickly before he slipped into a room. Though she'd only seen him from the back, she would know that confident gait of his anywhere. He walked how he talked and how he faced life—with determination, as if there was nothing at all in his way. To be honest, it was slightly intimidating.

The two of them were scheduled to meet at the café in two hours, and what Roxie should do was quietly slip from the hospital and prepare herself for that meeting. She'd stayed up half the night making a case to present to him on why Lily was better off with her full-time and him part-time. She was quite proud of it.

But almost as if her legs were working outside of her control, she found herself moving down the hallway in the direction of the room Kian had just slipped into. It was so wrong for her to be following him, but even knowing this, she couldn't quite get herself to stop her forward motion.

If he caught her, he'd think she was spying. What would that say to him about her? Certainly not that she could be a responsible parent to his daughter. That thought made her feet pause. It wasn't something she was allowing herself to think of right now. She didn't like thinking of Kian as a father, especially to Lily. But Lily was indeed Kian and Pamela's child. They had shared a one-night stand, and Lily was the result. Those thoughts hurt her in so many ways, she wasn't sure she would ever be able to heal from it. The pain it caused was devastating.

But she had no other choice but to move forward. She couldn't hate him for having sex with another woman when they were broken up, and she couldn't hate her sister for sleeping with him, because her sister had hated herself enough as it was. She certainly couldn't hate her niece, who was the only light out of all this. That left her with no one to hate but herself, and she wasn't going to do that, either.

Roxie knew she should turn around and leave the way she'd come into the hospital, but even as she had that thought, she found herself moving forward again as she heard the sound of Kian's rich laughter travel down the hallway. Her steps quickened, as she wanted to see what was amusing him.

It truly was none of her business, but she couldn't seem to convince herself of that. She was now too curious to turn away. She'd just take a quick peek and then be on her way, and he would never even know she was there. Mission accomplished.

The closer she got to the door he'd gone in, the more Roxie felt like some damn teenage stalker about to be busted by the mall police. She glanced guiltily around her as she looked to see if anyone was paying her the least bit of attention. Would the doctor who'd just interviewed her take away the potential job offer if he could see her now? Probably. She certainly would hesitate to hire a nurse who was prone to stalking doctors. Even with these chastisements running through her head, she still moved forward until she was right at the door Kian had walked through.

His rich voice sounded sweet as he spoke to the obviously elderly woman on the other side. The woman's replies came out childishly in her sweet, high voice. Kian laughed as she told him not to suck all her blood like a vampire. Roxie felt her lips turning up as she decided to just peek inside. She wanted to see what the woman looked like now that she had an image in her head.

Roxie was a nurse, and she'd seen it all in her years of medical service. She liked to try to imagine what her patients would look like just from their charts or the sound of their voices. She rarely ever got it right. Once in a while, though, she was 100 percent correct.

She imagined this woman as a sweet, petite, white-haired granny with glasses. Her voice was just too sweet to be anything other than that. She probably had a dozen grandbabies and two dozen great-grandkids. Roxie didn't even want to think about the fact that she'd be lucky to have her own child, let alone grandchildren. That was a thought to ponder on another day.

Finally, she peeked into the room and then had to cover her mouth before she let out a surprised gasp. The woman was absolutely nothing like she'd imagined. She was pretty petite, that much was clear, but she wore shoulder-length purple hair and had bright-pink lipstick on her lips, and blue eyelids she was batting flirtatiously at Kian.

He was sitting next to her as he held her hand and laughed at another joke. He seemed besotted with the woman, who was old enough to be his grandmother, and the woman was eating up every single moment of it.

"I've told you I used to dance over at the corner of Pearl and Seventieth Street, right?" the woman said in an attempt at a raspy voice, but she went too low and caused herself to cough. Kian turned her slightly and patted her back.

"Yes, Millie, you have, and I wish I would have seen you," he said. "But you have to slow down a little bit," he warned.

"Are you trying to tell me I'm old?" she asked, her lips forming into a pout.

"Not at all," he insisted as he let go of her hand and held her chart, glancing at the numbers. "But you had a close call. It's okay to listen to our bodies and slow down. I don't want to see you in my ER again unless it's to stop and say hello." His voice was warm and firm at the same time. He commanded respect because he gave it. Roxie hated that she felt her guard slipping as she stood there gawking at the two of them.

"I will most definitely stop in for a visit. If you do a good job and get me out of here quick enough, I might even bring you a coffee," she said, her practiced pout back in place.

Kian chuckled. "I wouldn't turn down coffee at any hour of the day. I swear the stuff they serve here is truly just car wax with a little bit of flavor," he told her.

She had a perfect little melodic laugh that had Roxie smiling again. She had a difficult time not joining the two of them in merriment. This patient right here was why Roxie loved being a nurse so much. Patients who were full of spirit and life and who didn't allow age to be anything more than a number.

"When my knee isn't acting up so much, I might have to show you one of my dances," Millie told him.

Roxie knew not to be jealous of a patient even if she and Kian were in a relationship, which they weren't, but even with that knowledge, she felt just the slightest stirring of that green-eyed monster light up inside her. It was so much better for her peace of mind to not see Kian at all, and certainly to not think about him at any club looking at dancers who were far younger than Millie and who liked to go home with men like Kian. It didn't matter if he did that. He was his own man, and she was her own woman. That was the beauty of a breakup, she assured herself.

"I would love to see you dance," Kian said, his voice still warm. "You were in a line, right?" A line? Roxie was confused.

"That's right. We could dance all night. I did partner dance, too. I once danced a mean tango," Millie assured him.

Roxie felt like even more of a fool now. The woman hadn't been offering to strip for him. She really needed some coffee or something. She definitely needed to sneak away before she did something foolish and got caught gawking at Kian and Millie.

Roxie was getting ready to slip away when Millie's surprisingly bright eyes looked over and caught her. Roxie grinned and tried to slip away quietly before Kian could turn around, but Millie wasn't having any of that.

"Who are you, darling?" she asked, her voice just as childlike when she raised it. Roxie wondered if that was truly her voice or if the woman had perfected it over the years.

Kian turned, and now Roxie was certainly caught. If only she'd been able to tear herself away thirty seconds earlier, she could have been in and out without anyone being the wiser. But the old woman had mesmerized her and, unbelievably, caused the slightest bit of jealousy, and now she had to try to explain why she was standing in the doorway like some loony stalker.

She couldn't figure out what to say, let alone come up with a reasonable excuse while they both looked at her waiting expectantly for a reasonable explanation. Kian's gaze narrowed as he refused to look away, and that only made it worse. Roxie's cheeks heated, and she looked guilty as she shifted on her feet, searching for an explanation she didn't have ready.

"Um, I was just walking from the hospital and thought it might be your voice I heard, so I just glanced in for a moment and then heard Millie tell a story about dancing, and I . . . um . . . love dancing, and I paused too long," she said in a hesitant voice. Roxie never had been a good liar, especially on the spot like this.

One time she'd been busted cheating and had actually said she'd seen a squirrel run across her classmate's table and was looking at the desk to see if there were any scratches. The teacher had been so impressed with the creativity of her excuse, she hadn't gotten busted that time, but she'd gotten a stern lecture to never cheat again. She hadn't so much as turned her head a quarter of an inch during test time after that, afraid her teacher would be looking, and she'd end up blurting something out like *The sky is falling*.

"Dancing, huh?" Kian said, sounding utterly disbelieving.

"Yeah, dancing. I used to dance a lot," she said defensively. In reality, she had two left feet and zero rhythm, but they'd never gone dancing together, so it wasn't something he would know.

"Oh, you like to dance, huh? Show me your favorite one," Millie said. She looked so excited, Roxie hated to disappoint the woman, but there was no way she was going to do a dance in front of them and show how very bad she was, proving herself a liar. Why couldn't she have come up with a better lie?

"Yes, please show us," Kian said, amusement now dripping from his voice. Millie didn't seem aware at all.

"There's no music. I have absolutely no rhythm without it. Maybe next time," Roxie offered, thrilled with her excuse. That was until Kian pulled out his iPhone and smiled.

"Name the song and I can pull it up in three seconds," he said, his voice utterly helpful. He was calling her bluff.

"Maybe the two of you can do the waltz for me. I know this room is small, but if you're careful, it can be done," Millie suggested.

That was the moment Roxie realized Millie hadn't really been flirting with Kian at all, because the woman was certainly in matchmaker mode at the moment.

"This room is far too small, and I wouldn't want to accidentally unplug something," Roxie said. She moved into the room and came to stand beside Millie, hoping to distract the woman from her request. "Why don't I fluff these pillows for you? They look quite lumpy."

"That would be lovely, but then you dance," Millie said firmly, her eyes surprisingly bright and alert. Roxie had a feeling she wasn't getting out of this. She glanced from the corner of her eye to see Kian smugly sitting there.

"I'll move my chair back to give you more room," he offered. She gritted her teeth.

Roxie remembered she'd once taken a line-dance lesson just to get some socialization. Line dancing didn't take a lot of rhythm for those beginning songs, if she remembered correctly. Some of the damn people there looked amazing, their hips and shoulders moving in sync to their feet, but there had been others like her who could barely manage to move their feet, let alone clap hands and swing hips.

"I don't think it would be proper to play music in the hospital," Roxie said.

"I'm the doctor in charge this afternoon. I'll okay it," Kian said. He was now leaning back as if he planned on getting real comfortable.

"Don't you have patients who need you? I can do the dance for Millie. You don't need to stay," she said, almost begging him.

"Nope. I always make sure Millie is my last patient so I don't have to rush away. She always tells me the best stories," he said before looking down at Millie and winking. "I don't know, Millie. Maybe she can't dance, and she fibbed to us," he said in a loud, conspiratorial voice. "What do you think?"

"Oh no, she definitely has the hips to dance. I think she's just being shy," Millie said.

Self-consciously, Roxie moved her hands across her hips as she thought about the conversation she'd had with Eden the other day. She wanted a mirror right now.

"Yes, she definitely has the hips," Kian said. The hunger Roxie witnessed in Kian's eyes as he said those words while his gaze moved steadily up and down her body sent any thoughts of being fat right out of her mind and made heat pool in her core. That wasn't a good idea. She couldn't even begin to have thoughts like that when it came to Kian.

And now, as Kian's gaze took its time appraising her, she felt hunger that she'd managed to push down for years spring to life in a roaring manner that had no business consuming her.

Clenching her thighs together in fear that any movement might make things happen she really didn't want happening in public, Roxie focused on Millie instead of Kian as she tried to calm her now-erratic breathing and rapidly beating heart.

"I haven't danced in a while," she said, pleading with the woman to let her off the hook.

"That's okay; once a dancer, always a dancer," Millie assured her. She pushed a button on her bed and sat up.

Again, Roxie wondered why she hadn't run away when she'd had the chance. She either had to admit defeat or she had to dance. Roxie never had been one to give up, even if she knew she was going to be humiliated.

"Play 'Watermelon Crawl,'" Roxie said through clenched teeth. She was flashing through her thankfully near-photographic memory as she tried to remember the dance. She could do this. It was just a few steps, a little side to side and front and back. She could do this, she assured herself. It had been two years, but she could do this. And she would do this without hurting the nice old woman.

Kian didn't say a word as he pulled up the music and hit "Play." His lips were turned up in a smug smile, and Roxie wasn't going to allow that look to stay plastered on his face. So, she was about to humiliate herself. Wouldn't it just be better to walk away? *Nope, it wouldn't,* she assured herself.

She lined up as centered as she could in the room, then counted to eight and began the dance. Her eyes were closed as she tried to focus on the images in her head, and she felt as if she were actually doing it. She followed along with the images that felt like a television screen and danced away, and "Watermelon Crawl" played softly on Kian's phone. She turned, did it again, turned, and did it once more.

Millie was clapping, calling out that Roxie was doing beautifully, and that gave Roxie the confidence to finish off with a little turn as the song drew to a close. Maybe she should have opened her eyes, because she did her turn and tripped on Kian's foot, tumbling down straight into his lap.

Her eyes shot open, and her gaze was captured by his, his lips only inches from her own, her butt cushioned on his lap. Her breath caught in her throat as her eyes got trapped by his, and if she wasn't mistaken, which she very well could be, there was a throbbing thickness beneath her butt that was making her core pulse with need, and making heat flood her body. Her nipples peaked, painfully rubbing against her bra, and for a moment, just a single moment, Roxie forgot she was in a hospital room with a patient watching them, forgot she'd left Kian with nothing more than an aloof note, forgot he wanted to take her niece away from her, forgot they'd been apart for four years.

Roxie began reaching for his lips, desperately hungry to close the small gap between them. She felt his fingers tighten on her hips where he held her and watched fire leap into his eyes. She thought of nothing but his touch . . .

That was until Millie clapped and called out, "Bravo." Both she and Kian froze at the reminder that they weren't alone. Roxie ripped her gaze away from Kian and gazed at Millie with a shocked expression.

"That was wonderful, darling. Please come back and do it again," Millie said.

The old woman had to be blind, because Roxie knew she might have gotten the steps right, but even with getting them right, she had no rhythm and certainly had slaughtered the dance.

"Wonderful, just wonderful," Millie repeated again.

"You need to take her to a proper place where she can really dance," Millie told Kian.

"And you've had too much excitement for one afternoon. It's time for rest," Kian told her.

Roxie knew this was her only chance to escape. If she and Kian left that room together, she wasn't sure what would happen. And right now, she was hormonal, and her head was fuzzy. She might make a wrong decision.

She didn't even say goodbye to Millie, deciding she'd slip back in there later when she knew Kian wouldn't be around. She liked the old woman and didn't want to hurt her feelings. But more than that, at the moment she was fighting for her own survival, and that meant she had to get away from Kian, and she had to do it right now.

So, she rushed from the room, then speed-walked down the hallway. She was just passing the on-call rooms when a hand snagged her around the waist, and she was pulled inside the darkness.

Kian's lips smashed against hers before she could even think of objecting. And protesting went out the window at the first touch of his familiar mouth.

Chapter Fifteen

Kian's mind went blank as he pushed Roxie against the wall in the private on-call room. It was dark as midnight, and the only sounds were the rapid breaths escaping them. He was so hard and thick, he feared he'd explode from just the feeling of his clothed erection against her backside.

"Are you playing games, Roxie?" he asked, his voice low and guttural. "I know how to play, too," he insisted. He had the front of her body pressed against the wall, his own body acting as a cage behind her. Reaching up, he stroked a finger along the curve of her jaw and felt her tense beneath his touch.

She wasn't in any way repulsed by him. She was just as turned on as he was, and she was running. It was exactly what he should do. He had no business dragging her into this room. There was too much between them, too much lost. And their one night together already hadn't fixed things.

Even knowing he should let her go, he wrapped his fingers in her hair and pulled her head to the side as he descended, his lips soothing her skin before his teeth sank into her flesh, his tongue wiping away the sting.

Moving his mouth up the sweet curve of her neck, he traced the outline of her ear and whispered, "Do you want me, Roxie? Do you want this ache soothed?"

A shudder racked through her body as she tensed beneath his hold. He could feel the erratic beat of her heart as it pulsed against his lips while he sucked on her neck, growing harder by the second with the need to claim her.

Never could he have forgotten how it felt when he was buried deep within her, but even after four years, his hunger had been woken up a month ago, and now he wanted more and more. He'd once taken her in every position, in every fantasy come to life, but never at the hospital. He wanted her here, where he worked, where he could walk past this room and grow hard just thinking about it. This should be the opposite of what he wanted, but he had to have her. If she denied him now, he might not be able to walk from this building, he'd be in so much pain.

"Our passion could break us. It was always so consuming, so hot," he said, enjoying the shudder that passed through her responsive body. She couldn't hide how she felt, no matter what she said, but Kian wouldn't take her without her permission. She had to ask for it, had to admit she wanted him, too. Her silence wasn't enough consent.

"Do you want to break with me, Roxie? Tell me," he demanded as he pressed his thickness against her. "Don't deny us this." His voice was urgent, his need overwhelming. He didn't care about anything else in the world at this moment; he just had to have her.

He sucked on her neck again, his hands rubbing down her sides. She squirmed against him, but he stopped waiting to hear her consent before he gave them what they wanted. He didn't move, but his grip was loose enough for her to get away. It was hell while he waited for her decision. She pushed her backside against him and caused him even more pain, but he didn't respond. It felt like an eternity as he waited, his hot breath caressing the smoothness of her throat.

"Yes," she whispered so quietly he could barely hear her. Joy filled him, but he wanted more. He wanted her pleading with him.

She would beg, he decided. His hands roamed her body, sweeping across her covered skin with precise movements to make her whimper in pleasure and desire. His touch was sure, filled with purpose, and everywhere he touched responded. He peeled her clothes away, needing her naked and panting.

She lifted her arms as he tugged off her shirt and bra. He wanted the light on, wanted to see her flesh, but he wasn't going to do anything that might break this moment, that might wake them both up to the reality of what they were doing. He touched every beautiful inch of her as he stripped away the barriers keeping him away from her hot flesh.

Soon she was naked, her body ripe and ready for him. He wanted to touch her all over. "What do you want?" he asked, his voice guttural, barely recognizable. His pants were still on, though he wrenched his shirt off. If he stripped that final barrier, he might take her too fast, end this too quickly.

She shook before him and answered. "Everywhere. Just touch me," she begged, her words barely a whisper.

"Hmm," he said, his lips rumbling against her skin as he sucked on her neck before turning her so her back was now against the wall. He filled his palms with the sweet weight of her breasts, her nipples hard against his palms. "Perfect," he said in utter reverence.

He'd once memorized her perfect body, and touching her again brought those memories to the surface. She was just how he remembered her, sweet and lush and full of fire, her skin so hot to the touch he was surely getting burned.

Once again, Kian turned her and pressed his hardness against her sweet backside while he cupped her breasts, rubbing the nipples between his fingers, causing her to cry out.

"Yes, let me know how you're feeling," he said, the sound of her desire almost more than he could take.

She bit her lip and groaned, trying to suppress the sound.

"Don't hold back. I want to hear you," he demanded. He was losing more control by the second. The longer he had her in his arms, the more fried his brain became. He desperately wanted to see the look in her eyes while he squeezed her chest and she whimpered beneath his touch. But the lights were too bright in here, and he had no doubt it would kill the mood. He wasn't taking the risk.

He squeezed her nipples again, and she cried out, this time louder. *Yes!* He wanted to own her total loss of control. He didn't care if they were at the hospital; he didn't care if someone passed by the door. He was out of his mind with lust, and he wanted her right there with him.

"Your body is amazing," he told her. "So soft in all the right places, so firm in others. Perfection. You are utter perfection," he said with a reverence he'd never felt with another soul. "Only you, Roxie, only you are this perfect." Maybe he was giving this woman too much power, but at this moment, he didn't care.

"Only you, Kian," she said, her voice breaking, her body his— *only* his.

Roxie panted as he pressed his fingers more tightly over her nipples, squeezing them hard before he tugged; a whimper escaped her. It was just enough pressure to give the slightest pull of pain, with mind-boggling amounts of pleasure to follow.

She squirmed beneath him, and he could practically taste her orgasm in the air. Only he knew how to touch her, knew every nuance of how she responded to him, knew the moment her pleasure neared. He'd brought her to the brink of pleasure too many times not to know how to do it before backing off, building her explosions to molten levels.

"Please, Kian, please," she begged. She was losing control more and more. He wouldn't please her until she let go all the way. He wanted to own her, at least for this moment, and nothing less would be acceptable.

Needing to see her, Kian remembered the yellow corner light, and he turned her around, giving her body a shove that made her fall to the bed. She gasped as her hot body came into contact with the cold, sterile blanket. Kian stepped to the lamp and hit the switch, then turned to find her sprawled out on the bed, her legs wide, her eyes huge, her mouth panting.

"Damn," he said, his voice choked, his body pulsing. His erection hurt as it pressed against the silk of his underwear and tented out against his scrubs. He reached for himself and squeezed, trying to relieve some of the pressure. It didn't help.

"Spread wider," he demanded. He wanted to look at her beauty. "Wider," he told her, his tone harsh in his excitement. "I want to look at where I'm about to bury myself."

He glanced at her eyes, at the utter pleasure in them, and nearly ripped off his pants and sank into her right then and there. Playtime was just about over. But Roxie always had enjoyed him making her hot and bothered before they connected. He didn't want to displease her now.

Roxie planted her feet on the bed and spread her legs wide open, her stomach quivering as she gripped the cool blanket beneath her. Her confidence in her smoldering body nearly made him come in his pants. He was afraid to take a step closer, afraid he was about to lose control.

With a strength he hadn't known possible, Kian crawled onto the bed and braced himself above her, leaning down and rubbing his tongue across one sweet nipple before kissing a path across her luscious mound and swiping his tongue over the other one. He moved from nipple to nipple, licking and sucking until she buried her fingers in his hair and pulled hard.

"Do you want my mouth all over you?" he asked.

"Yes, yes, yes," she begged, her fingers tightening in his hair.

He wanted the same. He trailed his lips down the soft curve of her stomach, his tongue dipping into her navel before he moved lower. The bed was too small, so he slid from it as he grabbed her hips and tugged her along with him, positioning her beautiful opening in front of his mouth.

The first taste of her heat had him nearly crying. She was so hot and wet, he was quickly losing his mind. He pushed her quivering thighs farther apart as he leaned in and sucked her hot flesh.

Kian gazed up Roxie's quivering body, and their eyes met. Hers were nearly delirious in her pleasure, and he felt his tongue slip from his mouth and coat her taste over his lips, which she seemed to like as her entire body jerked from the bed. Slowly, keeping his eyes connected with hers, he leaned forward and ran his tongue along her hot slit, sliding it in a circle across her most sensitive bundle.

She twisted her head, breaking the hold he had on her eyes as she called out her pleasure and demanded more. She was on fire, and he felt the heat scorching him. Electricity sizzled through his own flesh, all stopping and pulsing in one place that demanded he finish this.

Slipping his fingers inside her tight heat, he sucked on her flesh again, feeling her begin to tighten beneath his expert touch. He knew what she needed, what she wanted, and what she didn't even know she desired. He knew all of this about her, and she'd still left him. That thought made him clamp his mouth around her bundle and suck hard, causing her to scream as she neared completion.

Anger and pleasure rode side by side inside him, making him have something to prove. She was his, had always been his, and he was more than determined to prove why. He'd been the first to take her, and something primal was overriding his normal senses.

He added two fingers and pumped them inside her body as she said his name over and over again. She screamed as he lapped up her release, but he didn't relent. He wanted it all; he wanted her too sated to ever fight him again. She was his, and he owned her pleasure.

"I . . . I can't," she cried out as he sucked her flesh, pumping in and out of her.

"Give me your pleasure," he demanded when he let go of her flesh long enough to speak. She cried out again when his lips clamped over her quivering mound again and his tongue lapped at the sensitive spot.

She writhed on the bed beneath him and then cried out as her core clamped hard and fast over his fingers, making it difficult for him to move them within her. She whimpered as he kept going, kept giving and giving until she couldn't possibly take another second.

Roxie whimpered and tried to pull from him, her body too sensitive. Kian wouldn't let her go, holding on to her thigh as he tasted her over and over again. He'd never get enough of her taste, never be done with her. This was far from over.

He took his time tormenting her, building her pleasure again until he was nearly out of his mind. And then he couldn't take it another second. He had to be buried inside her.

At this moment, he was grateful there were condoms in the room. A lot of people used this space, which was why they had fresh linens you had to change the beds with when you were done. He'd never before used it, but he was grateful now.

Reaching into a small drawer, he pulled out protection and quickly slid it on, never taking his eyes from Roxie as she twisted on the bed, seeking out his touch, her legs still wide open, her body knowing it needed the ultimate fulfillment of him buried deep inside her.

Kian wouldn't disappoint her. He pushed her back on the bed and climbed over the top of her, lining their bodies up perfectly. Her face was damp and flushed, her hair wet with her hot pleasure. He buried one hand in her hair, and the other gripped her hip as he positioned her perfectly.

He was too out of his mind to make this slow and sweet. "Look at me," he demanded, and her eyes slowly lifted open.

Kian pushed forward, burying himself deep within her heat, making her eyes flash the rest of the way open as she gaped at him in awe and wonder. It was the same look she'd given him the first time he'd buried himself deep within her. Then, there'd also been a flash of pain, but she'd slowly adjusted to his girth, and then it had all been about pleasure. So much pleasure.

The next day when he'd seen her walking funny, he'd been concerned. She'd turned shades of red he hadn't known were possible, and he hadn't left her alone until she'd explained what was wrong. She'd told him she was sore from the sex. Pride had filtered through him as he realized he'd pleasured her so deeply, she'd been marked. He wanted to mark her again, make sure when she walked away, her body screamed his name.

Kian was nearly delirious as he moved faster, his body pounding into hers as he said her name, as he looked at her flushed face, as he leaned down and ran his tongue over her swollen bottom lip she'd been biting.

Then, with a gentleness he didn't think possible, he closed his lips over hers. He moved them, firm and demanding and then gentle and soothing. He told her without words what she had meant to him, and the hold she'd always had over him. He was hers in this moment as much as she was his, and this one woman had the power to destroy him. He hated her a little for that, and he loved her, too, but it wasn't something he'd admit.

He could have her body anytime he wanted. That knowledge was heady in its intensity, and it made him lose the last grip of control he had. His lips clamped over hers as he possessed her mouth and her core.

He drove inside her over and over again until she shattered, until her body gripped him without yield. And then he let go with her, each of their cries consumed by the other as they shook in each other's arms. The orgasm went on for an endless time, and Kian felt close to passing out when the last of his pleasure faded.

He sank against her scorching flesh, his face buried against her neck. Their breathing was erratic and harsh in the quiet room. It was a perfect moment in time before the storm of reality could hit them.

Both of them dozed in and out of consciousness for the next few moments, and then Kian felt her squirm beneath him. He knew his weight was too much for her to take for long. He shifted over to his side, his hand drifting against her hot flesh.

She squirmed beside him, then placed her hand against his. He felt more than heard her intake of breath, as if she was trying to come up with the right words to say. He was silent, deciding he wasn't going to help her worm her way out of this. She'd wanted it as much as he had.

"Kian?" she said, his name coming out a question.

"I would hope you know the name of the man you just got done having sex with," he said with humor.

"Of course I know it's you." She sounded slightly irritated. "I was just trying to find the right words, and you've helped me," she added.

"Oh, really. What are the right words?" he asked. He was too sated to care about whatever complaint she planned on making.

"I'm not going to pretend I didn't want that," she began, and he chuckled, feeling her tense beside him as she sat up and jumped from the bed as she searched for her clothes. He didn't move much, just enough to watch as she struggled with untangling her clothes so she could put them on. Her hands were shaking, so she was having trouble.

"I wouldn't think you'd deny it. You were pretty involved," he said, chuckling more when her eyes flashed fire at him. "Need some help with the clothes?" She didn't seem pleased with his offer, but he thought he was being quite the gentleman.

"I've got it," she said. She finally got her pants fixed and slipped them on—minus underwear. That had him all hot and bothered again, his body firming back up. She didn't miss that, and he enjoyed her sharp intake of breath.

"You're an animal," she muttered, but she ripped her gaze away from him. He lay there on his back as he eyed her lazily.

"If I were truly an animal, I'd jump up and mount you," he threatened. That thought had him all the way hard again. He'd have no problem bringing them both to satisfaction again.

"As I was saying, I'm not going to deny I wanted that, but it won't happen again," she said through clenched teeth, but he noticed her looking at his erection from the corner of her eye, so he reached down and grabbed himself, slowly stroking his fingers up and down his thickness as he gazed at her chest. She was beginning to breathe heavily again, but much to his disappointment, she threw on her bra and shirt. He continued stroking his thickness from base to tip as he stared at her.

She opened her mouth as if she wanted to say something, then closed it again and went silent. Then she moved to the door.

"Can you go ahead and lock the door? I'm not quite finished with the room," he said when she reached for the knob.

Her body stiffened, but then she opened the door and slammed it shut, not locking it. Kian knew he could get ticked, knew he could choose how to react. He chose to chuckle. The two of them were nowhere near finished with each other. He just wasn't exactly sure what that meant.

Now that she was gone, he had zero desire to keep touching himself. He let go and cursed a little when his swollen flesh stayed hard. He'd just had a mind-numbing orgasm. He should be good for at least a few hours. Damn woman. He always had been insatiable when it came to her. He'd have to figure out a way to seduce her again or live with a constant arousal. That wouldn't do him or his patients any good.

He got up and saw a flash of red just under the bed. Stooping down, he found her delicate panties, and his grin couldn't have gotten any bigger as he reached down and picked them up. He quickly dressed and threw them in his pocket, glad he was off shift now. It certainly wouldn't be sanitary for him to carry dirty underwear around to his patients' rooms. And he wasn't willing to toss them.

Kian left the on-call room in a hell of a good mood. He didn't even notice when he passed by the nurses' station and stopped the young girl at the desk from what she'd been doing. His happiness was contagious, and it was enough radiation to affect the entire floor as he continued walking.

If only every moment in life could be this perfect. He didn't need to think like that, though. He decided to just enjoy each piece of time as it happened. Kian left, a little disappointed when he didn't run into Roxie in the parking lot. He somehow doubted she was going to show up for their lunch meeting.

That was perfectly okay. He'd had a much more enjoyable meeting with her in the on-call room than he would've had in a crowded café. Kian figured he'd be smiling for a long time to come.

Chapter Sixteen

Lucian was on his feet as he paced back and forth in his office. Joseph and Sherman were sitting back, sipping on fine glasses of bourbon as they waited for him to gather his thoughts. He paced a few more times, and they knew they needed to give him space.

"Why hasn't that boy given an official marriage proposal yet? Too much time is wasting!" Lucian grumbled.

Joseph smiled. He knew well how this worked. They were strong men, and they had equally strong-willed children. Joseph wouldn't have it any other way. He loved his children and grandchildren. He was now itching to have great-grandchildren. Yeah, he knew he was greedy, but he could admit to that and even smile about it.

"I think it's amusing when he comes around, because you can clearly see his frustration. He wouldn't be happy with a weak woman. Roxie is certainly his match made in heaven," Sherman said.

"It's easy for you both to be calm; *you* get to be with *your* grandkids every single day," Lucian pointed out. "I'm trying to be patient to wait for Kian to get to know his child and convince Roxie he isn't a rogue so she'll marry him before I'm insisting on seeing Lily on a daily basis."

"That's true," Joseph admitted. "But you do want the boy to do this right. We're pushing all the buttons we can and throwing them together. Roxie is a stubborn girl, and that's a positive thing."

"That's why I've always loved her," Lucian admitted.

"Anyone with less backbone would never be able to handle Kian," Sherman said.

"That's true. My boys and my girl aren't easy to handle. We raised them to be strong and independent," Lucian said with a hell of a lot of pride.

"That's why it's worth it to be patient," Sherman told them.

Lucian glared at the two men. "Again, I tell you it's easy for you to say. I think we're going to have to either push Kian into moving quicker, or we're going to just have to talk directly to Roxie. She's in love with him, and when she can admit it to herself, we can all be one big happy family. My wife needs to hold her granddaughter."

"Ha!" Joseph said on a bout of laughter. "We all know you're just as anxious."

"Yeah, I really am," Lucian said with a beaming smile. "Lily looks just how my precious Dakota did at that age."

"I love all of my grandchildren equally," Joseph said before he looked around to make sure no one was sneaking up on them. Then his cheeks flushed a little bit. "But I have to admit there's something special about the first. Jasmine stole my heart from the moment I held that girl in my arms. There's no other that will ever take her place."

"She's going off to college, isn't she?" Lucian asked.

"Yep, she got accepted into Yale, of course," Joseph said, beaming so big it was a wonder his cheeks didn't split.

"That's a long way away," Sherman pointed out. Joseph's lips turned down.

"I know. I was excited she got into her first choice, but bummed she was going so far, but she promised I can visit anytime I want, and I will hold her to that. Don't tell Katherine, but I already bought a house close to the campus," he said. Sherman and Lucian laughed. "It's an investment," Joseph said in defense.

"Sure, the billionaire needs an investment in a small house," Lucian said sarcastically.

"It's not exactly small," Joseph said, puffing out his chest.

Both Sherman and Lucian laughed again.

"Thanks for that, my friend. I needed it," Lucian told him.

Joseph sat back and grumbled. He didn't like being the butt of the joke with his friends. He liked being the one dishing it out. So, he was a little overprotective of his favorite granddaughter. There was nothing wrong with that. Oops, he'd thought of her as his favorite again. He had to be careful about that.

"Well, let's talk about Kian, Roxie, and Lily," Joseph said, deciding it was time to change the topic.

"What should we do next?" Sherman asked.

Lucian smiled. "I have an idea or two."

The men grew quiet as they put their heads together and once again got up to no good. Their wives would kill them if they knew what they were planning. A little jealousy always seemed to help a romance move right along, though. And the guys knew just what to do next.

Chapter Seventeen

Lily's scream woke Roxie from a dead sleep, and she was on her feet and running before she was fully conscious. Rushing through her niece's bedroom door, she found Lily sitting up in bed, tears streaming down her face.

"What's wrong?" Roxie asked as she moved forward and sat on the bed. Lily scrambled into her lap, practically crawling up her neck as she buried her face against Roxie's neck and sobbed.

Looking around, Roxie didn't see anything indicating danger. Her skin was tingling, with the fight-or-flight mode fully in place. She rubbed Lily's back as the child shook uncontrollably and mumbled nonsensical words.

"It's just a nightmare, little one," Roxie assured her.

Roxie rose from the bed and carried Lily with her to her bedroom. She propped a pillow up and leaned back against the headboard as she continued mumbling comforting words to the terrified child.

After what had to be a half hour of sobs and muttered words, Lily gave a few hiccups and finally began to settle down.

"Do you want to tell me what scared you so much?" Roxie asked. She was almost afraid to do so. She didn't want Lily to fall back into a panic.

"Someone was knocking on my window. He's trying to get me," Lily said in between hiccups.

Roxie's entire body froze at her niece's words. She tried telling herself it was just a bad dream, that Lily hadn't truly heard anything. But what if . . .

"I'm sure it was just a dream, sweetie. Some dreams feel very real," Roxie assured her.

"No!" Lily cried. "He called my name," she said, leaning back, terror still clearly in her eyes.

Roxie's body froze in fear. Though she didn't want to think the man who'd killed her sister was still out there, was still wanting to finish the job he hadn't completed, she would rather err on the side of caution.

Without really thinking about it, Roxie found herself lifting her phone and dialing Kian. He answered before the first ring was even finished.

"What's wrong?" he asked, no trace of sleep in his voice.

"Lily thinks someone was knocking on her window," Roxie said, her words barely audible.

"I'll be there in five minutes," he said.

The call disconnected.

Roxie was sure not even five minutes had passed when Kian rushed into her house, finding her and Lily in the same spot they'd been in for the past thirty minutes. There was a wild flare to his eyes as he looked in all directions before his gaze landed on the two of them.

He nodded, then rushed from the room, and she heard each door open before closing again less than a minute later. She was sure he was checking all the locks on the doors and windows. Then she heard the front door open, and she felt her stomach tighten. Within five minutes he was back, his eyes still alert, but a bit calmer now.

"My brother and the sheriff will be here soon," he told her.

"What? Why?" she asked.

Lily had fallen asleep in the last few minutes, and Roxie truly felt comforted by having her in her arms.

"Someone could be here," he told her.

"It also could have been nothing but a bad dream," she insisted.

"I want you to move in with me." His voice was firm, as if that was going to get her to do what he was so foolishly commanding.

"We're fine. I shouldn't have called you," she told him.

Though she was reluctant to let Lily out of her arms, she had to use the bathroom, and she could really use a drink. Being careful not to stir her too much, Roxie laid Lily down in her bed, tucked her in tight, then stood over her for a few moments to make sure she wasn't going to wake up. Once she was sure, she moved to the bathroom and shut the door without bothering to tell Kian.

By the time she came back out, his brothers Declan and Owen were in her living room along with the sheriff. The four men were standing close, whispering. She approached cautiously.

"I'm sorry to have spooked you all. I'm sure it was nothing more than a dream," Roxie said.

"There are footprints outside Lily's window," Declan said. A new shiver of fear ran down her spine.

"That could have been Kian when he did a perimeter sweep," Roxie said hopefully.

"I don't think so," Declan said. The way he spoke was all business and was spooking her even more than she needed to be.

"It's okay, Roxie. We're going to keep you both safe," Owen assured her, the first of them to approach and pull her in for a hug she hadn't even realized she needed. She wrapped her arms tightly around him and took comfort from someone who had always been a great friend.

"She'd be safe if she just came to my place," Kian told her, his eyes narrowing as Owen's hand rested low on her back. She rolled her eyes at him as she let go of Owen and took a step back so Kian wouldn't think he could grab her next.

"I'll just add an extra lock or two," Roxie said, satisfied with her solution.

Kian stared at her for several moments, not wanting to back down. She looked right back at him, letting him know without words she wasn't a damsel in distress who needed rescuing.

He lifted his phone, punched in a number, and waited. Roxie could hear the irritated voice from six feet away as it snapped out a greeting to him. Kian didn't even blink as he interrupted the man.

"How soon can you get a security system installed?" he said. The command in his tone would make most people jump to do his bidding.

"Not good enough," Kian said. He waited a moment longer. "I'll triple it if you get someone here by morning." Again, there was a pause, and the person was no longer yelling. "Done." Kian hung up the phone.

"What did you do?" she asked.

"I'm not leaving tonight. A system will be put in tomorrow," Kian said.

Exhaustion was quickly pulling Roxie under, and she had no desire to keep fighting with him, especially in front of his brothers and the town sheriff, who appeared to be amused. Yeah, Kian was just a barrel of laughs.

"Blankets are in the closet. Good night," she told him without a smile. She did give the others a thank-you and a smile before turning around and going into her bedroom, firmly shutting the door behind her.

Even with the excitement in the middle of the night, Roxie didn't have any trouble drifting off to sleep again. She wouldn't admit, even under torture, that maybe, just maybe, it was because Kian was out there ensuring her safety.

Chapter Eighteen

After putting in a security system for Roxie, Kian was able to leave town for two days for an emergency in California. But he was back now, and he'd insisted on seeing Lily. He was trying to give Roxie some space and respect, and trying to be patient, but that certainly wasn't a virtue for him.

Kian wouldn't say life had been easy for him, but he'd been born with natural talent and the drive to succeed. It always seemed odd to him when others had to work so hard to make it in life. Didn't everyone want to have all they could? Apparently not. Some just wanted to skate by. Kian wasn't one of those people.

Now he found himself more nervous than he'd been the first time he'd held a scalpel in one hand and the life of a patient in the other. He paced around the children's park as he waited for Roxie to show up with Lily. He wanted to tell the child she was his; he wanted the world to know he was a father. But at least he was getting to visit with her. That was a step in the right direction.

He never should have had sex with Roxie again—twice. That had opened up a whole chain of emotions he hadn't been ready to open, and now he was even more reluctant to do what needed to be done in order for his daughter to be raised how she deserved to be. She was his daughter, and every single day she wasn't in his home was another day he lost.

But his feelings were clouded and getting more and more mixed up in Roxie. He couldn't stop thinking about the woman. He should be focused solely on Lily, but now he couldn't imagine Lily without Roxie. He wanted them both.

He watched as small children climbed up ladders and slid down slides, laughing and chasing one another. Never had Kian imagined himself smiling as he sat at a park and enjoyed the warm laughter of children. His life had changed in the blink of an eye, and he wasn't sure what to think about that.

Kian wasn't the type of man who could easily change his type of thinking, and he was obsessing about whether or not he'd make a good parent. At one time in his life, he hadn't hesitated to think about having kids of his own. He'd imagined Roxie and him sharing a home, her belly rounding with their child growing inside, a little girl with her eyes and hair running toward him. It had been a dream he'd been more than happy to have every single night. Until she'd left. Then that dream had turned into a nightmare.

Too restless to sit, Kian paced as he gazed from the playground to the parking lot. He was early, but he was still frustrated Roxie wasn't there yet. A girl called out, and Kian watched as a father pushed his daughter on the swing, her legs sticking out as she called for him to go higher. The man smiled, looking happy as he bonded with his child. That should be Kian every single day.

Finally, Kian recognized the unsuitable vehicle as Roxie pulled up. He wasn't sure if he should go over and help her or stand by and wait like he hadn't been crawling out of his skin in anticipation of their arrival. He took too long to decide, and then he saw Roxie pulling Lily from the back seat. His little girl struggled to get down, and then Roxie was clutching her hand as she tried to wiggle away to get to the playground.

The second they came through the gate, Lily shot off like a torpedo, running with her limbs twisting in every direction as she headed straight for the ladder and began climbing. Kian wasn't sure what to do. Panic slammed into him as he found himself holding his breath.

But Lily climbed up effortlessly, and then was shooting down the slide. She rushed back to the ladder as she instantly made friends with another girl about the same size, and they decided to race side by side down the slides again.

Roxie seemed hesitant to approach him, so Kian didn't say anything as he kept an eye on her out of the corner of his eye while she slowly approached. His main focus was on his daughter. He couldn't help but smile as she laughed with joy, instantly able to make friends with other kids at the park. He wanted to get her attention, but he knew this wasn't a sprint. He didn't want to smother her and have her be afraid of him.

Kian was anxious as he stood next to Roxie without speaking and continued watching Lily. How did parents do this? How did they not wrap their children in their arms and protect them? Lily ran fast over to the monkey bars and tripped, and he about jumped out of his skin. He moved to go to her, and Roxie placed a hand on his arm. It wasn't enough pressure to stop him, but it did.

"She's fine," Roxie said in a soothing voice. And she was. Lily jumped to her feet and was off again.

"How do I do this?" he asked. It was odd, but that moment of her touch against his skin and his heart slowed; his breathing evened out.

"I was just like this the first week, afraid of everything, but I've learned that she's smart and vivacious and independent. If we smother her, she gets frustrated. It will be fine," she promised.

There was so much Kian wanted to speak to Roxie about, but this wasn't the time or place. They would talk, but it would be when Lily wasn't around. Lily flew down the slide again and then came in a full-blown sprint toward them.

"Swing," she demanded, her head turning from Roxie to him. She didn't care which of them pushed her.

Kian grinned. "Let's go," he said.

She took off running to the swings, and he followed her, a smile engulfing his lips. He helped Lily up on the swing and pushed her gently. Her head swiveled around as she glared at him.

"Higher," she demanded.

His heart pounded again, and he added a little more pressure to his push. Lily squealed with delight, and each time she launched into the air, he felt as if he could have a heart attack, but the sound of her laughter more than made up for the fear he was facing.

This was what he'd been wanting, to have a carefree afternoon with his daughter, to do this normal type of activity, to feel as if the world wasn't continually spinning off its axis. He'd be happy to stay right where he was for the rest of his life.

Emotions he hadn't known it was possible to feel flooded through him. His heart felt twice its normal size, and his cheeks hurt, he was grinning so much. He needed his daughter. He loved her without question, just like that.

Looking up, Kian's gaze met Roxie's, and for a moment, just a brief moment, she let down her guard, and the two of them shared a smile, a carefree smile as they shared their time with this amazing child. But, too quickly, Lily demanded their attention, and the connection was broken.

Could Kian have it all? Could he have the life he'd once taken for granted? And have his daughter as well? He wasn't sure, but all of a sudden, it seemed like a real possibility. And for this small moment in time, everything in the world was right where it was supposed to be.

He felt a connection with both Roxie and Lily, but the uncertainty would be a constant. As long as he was aware of that, he'd be fine. Maybe he would finally learn to have patience. His mother always had said it was a virtue. He'd always thought that was a piece-of-crap line that those who had no goals used.

For people like him, who had to close the deal, patience was a weakness, but if he truly wanted to embrace his new role as a father, then he had to learn some new skills. The good news was that he was always up for a challenge.

"Done," Lily yelled.

Kian stopped pushing his daughter, then tensed when she launched herself from the swing while it was too high up in the air. He took a step toward her when she rolled on the ground, but she giggled and then was up like a shot again, running over to the monkey bars.

"I don't know how these parents seem so relaxed. I remember playing on this same type of equipment, but it didn't seem so dangerous back then. There's potential for bone breakage in every direction I look," Kian complained.

"Did you ever break a bone?" Roxie asked.

"Well, yeah, but not at the playground," he said.

"How, then?" she asked.

"I was sliding into home plate my freshman year of high school and twisted wrong, snapping my ankle," he said. "Hurt like hell, but I was safe, so it was worth it," he said smugly.

"Well, as long as you were safe," Roxie told him with a chuckle.

"Of course. If I'd gotten out, I'd have been pissed," he said. It was pretty logical to him.

Roxie laughed, and he decided right then and there, he wanted to make her laugh as often as possible. It was not only a beautiful sound, but it went straight to his gut and made his heart pound.

He'd thought he was over this woman, but he now knew he'd been living in denial. As much as he wanted to have his daughter living with him right this moment, he was having to go back to that *patient* word again, because now his goals were bigger. Now he found that he wanted them both.

Roxie loved Lily, and she would be an excellent mom for her. He could have his daughter *and* a wife. The past would always be there, but now they had more than themselves to think about. Now they had Lily, and she needed a mother and a father. They could do that together. Kian wasn't sure how he was going to go about reaching his goals; he just knew this was too important to screw up.

Roxie would have to watch out, though, because once he set his mind on something, he wouldn't quit until he got what he desired. And right now, he wanted Lily *and* Roxie.

Game on.

Chapter Nineteen

Roxie had no idea what to think or feel anymore. She wasn't sure she even trusted herself, let alone anyone else in her life. Confusion seemed to be the one emotion she could be sure of. Why, oh, why had she allowed herself to get pulled back into the orbit of Kian Forbes? Was she a glutton for punishment?

She'd told herself that chapter of her life was over, and then bam! On-call room. The sad thing was, she couldn't even regret it. The sex had been that good. The self-recriminations weren't the best after, but during, oh, during, had been well worth the fifty lashes she should give herself.

Of course, she couldn't allow her train of thought to go down that route. Nope. That got her kinky mind to thinking in bad, bad ways, and since Lily was in her car seat, napping, Roxie certainly didn't want to have sex and ropes and mouths and . . . Nope! Had to turn off those thoughts again. What in the world was wrong with her?

Maybe it was because, until that first night at Kian's after Lily was released from the hospital, she hadn't had sex since so brilliantly deciding to leave Kian four years ago. She'd almost forgotten how amazingly wonderful it actually was. But he'd awakened her in a big way.

She wondered if it would be wrong to do it just once more. No. She couldn't think like that. One more time would never be enough when it came to a man like Kian. He certainly knew his way around a woman's body, and though she hadn't been with anyone since she'd left him, she knew for sure *he* had.

Looking in her rearview mirror confirmed that for her. He'd not only been with other women, but one of them had been her sister. That made her cringe. Sure, he might not have known it was her sister, but still, it was disgusting. She felt a deep betrayal she couldn't figure out how to push away.

Besides the fact that he'd slept with her sister, what was happening between them was going at warp speed. From the moment she'd come back to town, the man had been everywhere, in person and in her thoughts and dreams. She didn't know how to handle that.

For now, Roxie was trapped in her car. Lily had fallen asleep, and as soon as her vehicle pulled up to home, her niece would wake up, and then she'd be grumpy because she hadn't slept long enough. Roxie didn't mind peaceful Sunday drives, though. There never tended to be much traffic out, and it gave her a chance to clear her head. She liked to explore new areas. But now that she had Lily with her, she was a lot more careful. She didn't need to get lost in some back-roads area where a creeper killer found her and she was never seen again. The things a person thought about with a child in the car were much different from what they imagined when they were responsible for only themselves.

As she continued down the road, her thoughts turned to Kian again. At one time, she'd been so in love with him, she hadn't known where he ended and she began. That had frightened her. She hadn't wanted to lose herself in another's identity. That hadn't been his fault, though. It was all on her shoulders. But even knowing that, she was scared to open that door again. Kian had changed in the past four years.

He'd always been a confident man—it was why she'd been so drawn to him. But now he was harder around the edges, not quite so trusting. She was tense around him, just waiting for the shoe to drop regarding when he'd serve her with papers to take Lily away. He seemed to be playing by her rules for the moment, but she knew that wasn't likely to last. He would give up on her eventually. Didn't everybody?

Unlike Kian, who had a beautiful family, Roxie had no one. The one thing she'd always been able to count on was disappointment. People came and went in life, but the truth was that they always did go. It wasn't a matter of *if*, it was a matter of *when*. Maybe that's why she'd left Kian. Maybe she knew she wouldn't have been able to handle it if he left her.

Ugh. She didn't want to go there. Her fingers tightened around the steering wheel, to the point that her knuckles turned white. She took in some calming breaths, knowing she couldn't get upset and start making mistakes while driving. She reduced her speed since no one else was around. It might even be safer for her to just pull over. Her mind was focused on just about everything except for driving.

But there wasn't any other traffic on the road. She'd only passed a couple of vehicles in the last hour. She'd turned around a while back and would be in town soon enough. Lily had gotten plenty of sleep. Maybe the two of them would make a trip to the bakery. With all the stress of the last week, Roxie was burning plenty of calories and could totally afford to eat some sugary delights.

Roxie saw movement out of the corner of her eye and realized too late that a yearling was bounding right into the road, straight in her path. Slamming on her brakes, Roxie swerved to the left, the rear of her car fishtailing as the front tires caught the gravel on the side of the road.

The deer was on the road, staring at her in horror. Their eyes met, and Roxie silently pleaded with the animal to move, but it didn't listen, and her front corner bumper slammed into the poor animal, sending it forward. Her car came to a screeching halt on the side of the road, and Roxie's heart was now lodged in her throat.

Her entire body trembling, Roxie pulled all the way off the road and killed her engine. Turning to check on Lily, she let out a relieved breath when she saw her niece shift in her seat, then rest her head comfortably again and start snoring. The impact had been minimal and had shaken Roxie up far more than the damage it had caused.

She still had to make sure everything was fine, though. She needed to stop trembling before she left the safety of her car. All she could think about was Kian telling her how unsafe her car was if she were to get into a wreck. Well, she'd proven him wrong. Both she and Lily were just fine, and they'd just had a minor accident.

Of course, she'd barely clipped the deer and had been going only forty-five, but still, the car seemed to be holding up well. Adrenaline was flowing through Roxie's veins as she gazed at her niece a few more moments while concentrating on her breathing.

Finally, Roxie emerged from her car and felt tears sting her eyes when she saw the yearling lying on its side, its legs moving in a running motion as it tried to right itself. Blood oozed from its shoulder, but she couldn't tell if anything was broken. The sound it was making was enough to make her sob, but she tried desperately to hold it together.

It was just a baby, and it was hurt. She couldn't possibly just leave the young animal there to suffer, but there was no way she'd be able to put it out of its misery. She didn't have it in her. She paced in front of the deer that appeared to be terrified, and she felt a tear slip free.

She had to call the game department or roadkill services. But it wasn't dead yet. Could someone help it? She felt terrible she hadn't managed to avoid the beautiful creature. Looking back, she saw that Lily was still sleeping in her car seat. Roxie didn't have to rush off. She needed to call someone.

Without giving it much more thought than that, Roxie lifted her phone and dialed Kian. He was going to think she was crazy, but she didn't care. If he could help the animal, then she'd take a little taunting. She didn't want to be responsible for the kill. It was a senseless death.

Kian didn't say hello when he answered. He never had been the greeting type of person. It was something she remembered from the many times she'd called him while they were dating. He always answered the phone as if they'd been having a conversation and he was simply continuing it. Surprisingly enough, his greeting helped to calm her.

"I was just going to dial you and see if you and Lily wanted to get lunch," he said.

"I'm out on the county road about fourteen miles in, and I hit a deer. It's still alive and needs help," she replied. The panic rose as she said this.

Kian was quiet on the other end of the line, and she wondered if he'd heard her. He had to act fast if they were going to save the deer. They didn't have time to ask and answer questions. She really wasn't sure what he could do about it, but this was reminding her of how she had always turned to him whenever she had a problem. It had been like that for years, and when she didn't have him anymore, she'd been lost for a while.

Heck, maybe, for that matter, she never had truly found herself again. Roxie wasn't sure. And thankfully, her mind was occupied, and she didn't really have time to think about it right now.

"Are you and Lily okay?" he asked, and that was when she noticed the panic in his voice. He'd been taking his time to control it.

She heard movement and then his vehicle start up. "Yes, we're fine," she said, her voice growing more urgent. "But the deer isn't."

"I'm calling the ambulance, and then I will call you right back," he told her.

"No!" she yelled, not wanting him to hang up.

"What?" He sounded confused. "I'm on my way, but we need to get the ambulance out there."

"No, I swear Lily and I are fine. It was only the corner of the car that clipped the deer. We didn't even feel the impact. Lily is in her over-the-top-safe car seat, and my seat belt held me tight. I might have a bruise or two on my chest, but other than that, I'm fine. I need help with the deer," she repeated.

"The deer?" He sounded confused.

"Yes, the deer. It's hurt." At least now he was listening to her.

"You want me to fix a deer?"

"What is so hard to understand about that? You're a doctor," she reminded him in frustration.

"I'm a *people* doctor," he told her slowly, as if she were dumb.

"So you can't help an animal?" she snapped. The deer looked at her with such sad eyes, Roxie felt like sobbing. "It's innocent."

"I'm on my way," he said, his voice placating. She didn't care. She knew he had a big heart, and he wouldn't let the animal die if he could help it.

"Good. I'm going to check on Lily again. Hurry."

She hung up the phone and missed whatever he'd been saying. But she had no doubt he'd be there quickly. He was probably driving at warp speed. Lily was still sleeping, so Roxie stood there at her car, keeping her eye on both the injured deer and on Lily, who was oblivious in the back of the car.

Now that she had a moment to think, she realized it had been Kian she'd thought of first in her emergency, and he hadn't hesitated to come to her aid. What that meant, she really didn't know. She only knew she could count on him when it mattered most.

Could she count on herself in the same way? Honestly, she couldn't answer that.

Chapter Twenty

It was unreal, the urgency and panic Kian felt as he raced down the road to find Roxie and Lily. She had told him they were both fine, but he wouldn't believe it until he was there, until he saw them, felt them, knew they didn't have life-threatening injuries. He'd warned Roxie that vehicle she was driving was a death trap, and less than a week later, she gets into a wreck.

One way or another, she was getting a safer vehicle. He didn't care if it ended in them in a knockdown brawl. It was going to happen. He was a doctor, so he knew there were some things that simply were beyond his control. That didn't mean he had to like it, and it didn't mean he was simply going to sit idly by while those he cared about died of injuries he could have prevented.

His heart pounded, and he couldn't get control of his breathing as he nearly broke the speed limit by double. It was okay with him if a cop started chasing him. Then he'd have emergency vehicles on the way to the scene of the accident. It had taken all that was inside him not to call that ambulance he said he was going to call.

Roxie had always been a stubborn woman. She could be injured and not wanting to make a big deal out of it because she was so focused on a damn animal. Not that Kian was against animals. He loved the furry creatures. It was just that he was more concerned about people.

Kian's first true breath didn't come into his lungs until he located Roxie's car on the side of the road. She was standing in front of it, and he couldn't yet see the deer. His eyes were focused fully on her. But as he came to a stop in front of her, he looked down, and sure enough, it was a yearling, the horns barely sticking from its small head. And the poor thing was twitching. Most likely, there was nothing he could do for the animal.

Roxie didn't look up as he climbed from his truck and approached her slowly. Her face was washed of color, and she was gazing despondently at the creature on the ground. Shrugging out of his coat, he wrapped it around her shoulders, and finally, she looked up.

"I'm fine, I promise. I need you to check on the deer," she insisted.

"I promise you I will, but I'm going to check you first," he said, his voice commanding. He was in his element now, with a patient who didn't think she wanted or needed help. He knew how to handle this situation.

"I told you I don't have injuries," she said, her eyes flashing to the deer again.

"Good, then this won't take long at all," he informed her.

She let out a frustrated breath but then allowed him to lead her to the side of the car. "I'd rather you were lying down," he said as he looked around.

"I'm fine standing," she said with a huff. "Get this over with."

Kian did as thorough an exam as possible on the side of the road. He pushed and prodded, took her heart rate, and listened to her lungs. She sounded fine, and though she had some soreness where her seat belt had dug in when she came to a sudden stop, she didn't appear to have any injuries. He'd feel a hell of a lot better if he could have her scanned as well, but those were expensive tests, and he knew she'd balk at them when there was no physical evidence indicating she needed them. Maybe he'd wait to begin that battle.

"You seem okay," he said.

"I know I am. Will you check the deer now?" she huffed.

"No, I need to check Lily first," he insisted. He opened the back door, and Lily was just waking up, her sweet little eyes shining up at him as she opened her eyes. She gave him a little smile before sticking her thumb in her mouth.

His heart melted right there in his chest as he reached for her and slid his fingers down her flushed cheeks. She didn't appear to be injured at all, but he'd still feel better doing a basic exam on her.

Having no idea how to undo the straps securely holding her in, he had to move aside for Roxie to get her out of the seat. He watched, though, so he'd be able to do it next time. This was important stuff to know, and he wanted to be an active parent. He didn't want his child raised by nannies or, if he took that route, solely by his wife. His own parents had been wealthy, and yes, they'd had staff in the house whom Kian and all his siblings had loved, but they hadn't let the staff raise the kids. His parents had come to their sporting events and school plays. They'd been an active part of their lives. That was exactly how Kian planned on parenting.

"Come here, sweet girl," he said after Roxie pulled her from the seat.

Kian's heart melted again when the sleepy girl willingly held out her arms to him and snuggled against his chest as she continued sucking her thumb. Her small body was languid and warm, and he ran his hands gently up and down all her limbs before he listened to the soothing sound of her heart and lungs.

"She's perfect," he said, not ever wanting to let her go.

"Yeah, she is," Roxie said, her own voice soft. She shook her head, and the somewhat glazed expression on her face cleared as she held out her arms to Lily, who grumbled when she was taken away from Kian. He wanted to grumble, too. "You need to check on the deer now," she insisted.

Kian sighed with frustration. He hadn't wanted to give up his daughter—not when she was being so dang snuggly. But he knew Roxie was going to be a wreck until he made a completely inappropriate medical decision regarding the damn deer.

"We need a vet here," he said. "If vets even treat wild game." Hell, he didn't know.

"It can't be much different from a person to an animal," she pointed out. "We both have organs and stuff."

"True," he said, unbelievably seeing her point. That wasn't something he would have ever thought could happen. But he did know that in some small places, people have brought their animals to medical doctors when a vet wasn't around. He had nothing to lose by trying.

Kian inched closer to the deer, which looked panicked as he neared. "Don't you worry there. I'm a doctor and only trying to help you," Kian said, feeling incredibly foolish for talking to the animal, which didn't appear reassured.

It kicked its legs weakly, as if it wanted to get away but didn't have the strength. He didn't think the poor thing was going to make it, but he sure as hell didn't want to tell that to Roxie, who had put her faith in him. If he messed this up, she might think he'd mess up everything.

Dammit. He was going to make sure the damn deer lived. Then, he'd have to make sure it went to a hunt-free zone, because he wasn't putting all this hard work into an animal just to have it be dinner. Not that he minded a good venison steak, but he certainly couldn't eat an animal he'd saved, or one that he put a face on. Crap, now he was getting all philosophical. He needed more sleep, he assured himself. Then he'd be back to normal.

As he knelt by the animal's side, he continued to talk softly, and surprisingly enough, it began to calm. He ran his hands along its body and tried to feel for anything out of the ordinary. Nothing seemed out of place. He didn't know deer anatomy, but it didn't seem to have a swollen stomach and didn't appear to have any broken bones. The thing might just be in shock and needing the cuts sewn up and disinfected. He might actually be able to save this thing.

"Is he going to make it?" Roxie asked, standing right behind him.

"I don't know," he said, not wanting to raise her hopes only to dash them. "But I think I'll call Doc Evan and get him taken in. We might be able to."

Doc Evan was a local vet with magical hands. Kian had seen more animals saved by his hands than by any other vet. He was in high demand, and it was a good thing the guy owed Kian a favor or two, because this was going to cost him.

Kian placed the call and explained the situation to the doc, and then had to grit his teeth as the guy laughed so hard, he couldn't speak for several moments. Kian turned away so Roxie couldn't see his scowl as he waited for the doctor to calm down.

"Man, Kian, I am loving this. You're out there performing CPR on a deer to impress a girl. I gotta see it in person," Evan said between bouts of laughter.

"You're a damn vet. Aren't you supposed to want to save animals?" Kian pointed out.

"I don't typically make it a habit of saving roadkill," Evan told him after a few more chuckles.

"Well, obviously, the damn thing isn't roadkill yet," Kian snapped.

"Okay, okay, I'm on my way," Evan said before hanging up.

There wasn't much the two of them could do as they waited for Evan to show up. Kian had no idea why Roxie was so invested in this animal. Maybe it was because she'd been the one who had hit it, or maybe she just needed a miracle, but because she was invested, that meant he was, too.

"Why don't we let Evan take the deer to his place and we can swing by the hospital and have a scan or two?" Kian asked.

Roxie rolled her eyes at him. "I'm not going to tell you again that I'm fine. I'm staying with the deer," she said, her voice firm. Both she and Lily appeared perfectly okay, and he wouldn't insist any of his patients undergo unnecessary tests, but Roxie wasn't just any patient. She was special, and Lily was his daughter.

Still, he'd been watching them for thirty minutes straight, and there were zero signs of injury. He might have to let this one go. Taking a loss wasn't easy for him to swallow.

Doc Evan showed up and cracked a few more jokes at Kian's expense, then the two of them sedated the frightened deer before loading it in the doc's trailer. Roxie insisted on following him back to his farm, where he had secure places for animals to recover.

Kian was at the back of the parade, not wanting her to drive the damn car, but since she insisted on not leaving it, he had no choice. He was tense the entire thirty-mile drive. He was buying her a new car and then dropping hers off a damn bridge. That thought cheered him up immensely.

They got to the farm, and a couple of the local kids were doing volunteer work, including Jeff, who ran up to see what was happening. He insisted on helping Doc take the deer into the barn, and there really wasn't much for Kian to do.

"Want to get your hands dirty?" Evan asked.

"Nah, do you know what these hands are worth?" Kian said with a smug smile.

"Not much, in my opinion," Evan told him with a wink.

Kian wasn't at all offended. Evan had grown up with money himself but had never taken advantage of it. Evan hadn't been as lucky as Kian and his siblings, though. His family had been super assholes who had treated Evan like shit. If it hadn't been for his grandmother, he wouldn't have received a dime to even go to school after his dad ran away with the nanny and his mom married some rich foreign guy and fled the country.

His parents were both pissed when his grandmother left her entire estate to Evan, and instead of giving either parent a dime, he invested in the community and continued his work as a vet. He was a good guy and somebody Kian easily called a friend.

"Can I take Lily to see the pigs? Mama just had a litter last week, and they're pretty cute," Jeff said.

Roxie looked to Kian for confirmation that their daughter was safe with Jeff, and he nodded, his chest puffing out that she was turning to him to ask.

"That would be wonderful, Jeff. Thank you," she said, and the boy glowed at being trusted. It warmed Kian's heart. It also went right over his head that he'd thought of Lily as their daughter. That might freak him out if he took the time to think about it.

"Can you grab that antiseptic, Roxie?" Evan asked.

"Of course," she said, and for the next hour, she was Evan's assistant, and Kian found himself on edge as the doc flirted shamelessly with Roxie, making Kian grind his teeth. He knew his friend was doing it on purpose to get a reaction from him. He also knew Evan wouldn't make a move on her since everyone in the town knew she was his, but that didn't mean Evan wasn't going to torture the hell out of him. Kian looked forward to payback. He wouldn't forget, not even if it took a few years.

"I think this guy might actually make it. He sure as hell is lucky you're the one that hit him," Evan said as he sat back on his heels, surprise in his eyes, his clothes bloody and hairy.

"Really? You aren't just saying that to make me feel better?" Roxie said, wringing her hands.

"I really think he'll make it," he said again.

Kian found himself clenching his jaw so tightly, he was surprised his teeth didn't snap when Roxie launched herself across the small space between her and Evan and held on tightly as she gave him a big hug.

She pulled back and gripped his cheeks, and for a moment, Kian saw the doc completely mesmerized by her. Yeah, she had that effect on people.

"Thank you so much, Evan, thank you," she told him before hugging him one more time and giving him a smacking loud kiss on the cheek. "You're the best."

"Well, hell, if I'd have known I'd get that reaction, I would have been trying to hit deer just to save them," he said with a chuckle.

"Yeah, you're a true hero," Kian grumbled.

"Damn straight," Evan said as he winked at Kian. "I saved the day this time, and you had to stand by and watch me work."

Kian grumbled at the doc, trying to decide if it was okay to punch him now that the animal was out of danger. He decided that might not earn him too many brownie points with Roxie, and right now he needed all the merit badges he could get.

Jeff and Lily came running back into the barn right then, both of their cheeks flushed as Lily talked a million miles a minute about how cute the pigs were.

"Can I have a pig, please, can I?" Lily asked, her eyes wide in her excitement.

"We don't have anywhere to keep one," Roxie said, and Kian felt his own heart breaking when tears sprang to Lily's eyes and spilled over.

"I'll bring the pigs to my house," Kian said. The girl could have asked for anything, and he would have granted it, just to make that heartbroken expression disappear.

She turned to Kian and gave him a watery smile. "Can we live there?" she asked.

Hell yes! He was about to yell just that when Roxie cleared her throat, and he looked up, finding her intense look on him. He would be toast if he said that. Of course Lily was going to live with him, but he had to do it in the right way.

"Why don't you come and visit first," he said. He wasn't going to tell her she wasn't going to live there because they all knew she was. But, for the sake of his relationship with Roxie, he could slow down his normally wicked-fast pace.

"Can we visit the pigs, Mama?" Lily asked.

Everyone went silent as Lily spoke those words. It seemed like time stopped altogether, but Kian knew only a second or two had passed. He looked at Roxie's radiant face, and his heart broke a little. She truly did love his little girl, and the slip of her calling Roxie *Mama* had sealed her fate. Lily needed Roxie. Kian needed Lily. It was pretty simple, in his own mind. The three of them would become a family. He just wasn't sure how he was going to make that happen.

"Of course we can, sweetie, but they won't be leaving their mama for a while, so we'll just have to come here," she said. Kian could hear the relief in her voice. She was afraid to come to his place. She was afraid of what she would feel. He had no doubt about it.

"I also have a cat that's going to have kittens at any time," Kian said, wanting to draw Lily back into insisting on coming to his house.

"Really?" Lily said, her eyes going wide again.

"Yep, so you and your . . ." He paused. Was he supposed to say aunt or mama? He didn't know. "Um, you and Roxie can come and see them, maybe even be there when they are born."

"Can we, please?" Lily asked Roxie.

Roxie was refusing to look at him. She was irritated he'd put her on the spot. Well, too bad. He knew what he wanted, and he wasn't afraid to go after it. He'd told a white lie, though. He didn't actually have a mama cat, but his brother had been complaining about a big pregnant cat that wouldn't leave his back porch. It appeared as if Kian was officially adopting the stray now. He'd pick it up on his way home and hope the damn thing hadn't popped already. He'd have to call his cleaning lady and see if she could pick up whatever the hell he needed to take care of a cat.

"I guess we'll have to do that," Roxie finally said, and Kian wanted to jump in the air and pound his fists. He wanted them to come to his place. Victory was his.

"Why don't you all come out here this coming Saturday?" Evan asked, making Kian turn. He'd forgotten other people were even around. Roxie consumed him so much, he felt sucked into his own world whenever they were in a space together.

"What's happening Saturday?" Kian asked. He wasn't sure how much he wanted Roxie around his very eligible friend.

"I'm having a barbecue to thank community members who volunteer," Evan said. Of course, at this, Roxie gave him a beaming smile.

"Oh, that's so thoughtful," she told him.

Never in his life had Kian had reasons to be jealous of another person, but he was feeling the green-eyed emotion pretty damn bad at the moment as the damn vet tipped his hat at Roxie and winked.

"I'm a thoughtful guy," he said.

"Humility looks fake on you," Kian said with a slight growl. Roxie turned and glared at him.

"You're being rude, Kian," she snapped. Then she turned back to Evan and smiled even more brightly. "And I think it's amazing for you to do that. Lily and I would love to come."

"I'll pick you both up," Kian said. There was no way he wasn't going to bring her. He was certainly keeping his eye on her around the damn vet.

"We can get here ourselves," she said. But he knew Roxie enough to know she wouldn't be willing to get into a fight with him in front of people.

"There will be a lot of cars here, and we don't want to take up too much room. I'll bring you both, and then you can feel free to have a drink without worrying about driving," he pointed out.

"Oh, I didn't think about that. It might be kind of nice," she said.

"Then it's all settled." Kian wouldn't give her a chance to change her mind. "You can also check on the deer and pigs."

"Piggies," Lily said, her face brightening.

Right then, Evan's old yellow Lab came lopping around the corner, and Lily was distracted by yet another animal. She went over, and the old boy rolled over on his back so she could scratch his tummy.

Kian couldn't help but laugh when the dog's head rolled side to side with his tongue out as Lily curled up into him and scratched his belly.

"She needs a dog," Kian said.

"I know," Roxie said. He looked up and saw guilt in her eyes. "I just can't afford it right now."

"I can," he insisted.

She gave him a stern look. "She's not deprived. I'm taking good care of her."

"We can both take care of her. She doesn't have to go without," he said. This argument was getting old.

"Sometimes, when children get too much, they turn into spoiled little brats. I don't want that to happen to her. I want her to work for the things she truly wants. She will appreciate it so much more then."

Kian was about to argue, but he saw her point. His parents hadn't handed him and his siblings anything. They easily could have, and there had been definite advantages in having money, but they'd all worked hard, and because of that, they had good ethics.

"You're absolutely right. Let's figure out ways for her to have the things she desires by earning them," he said.

Roxie seemed shocked by his compromise, and he wondered if he'd always been that much of a dictator that people didn't expect him to meet them halfway. He didn't think so, but maybe he'd have to ask his siblings their advice on the matter.

"I can agree to that," she said, and Kian felt as if he'd just won a gold medal. Damn, he enjoyed making this woman happy.

Roxie's phone rang, and she stepped out the door of the barn so she could take the call. Kian found himself wanting to know who was on the other end of the line, but he realized it was truly none of his business.

Lily rose to her feet and looked to the door, her sweet face worried for a moment, but then she zeroed in on Kian. She walked over to him and held up her arms. He gratefully lifted her into the air and held her tightly to his chest. She snuggled against him, and within what seemed seconds, she was still, her breathing even.

He felt pressure in his eyes at the love and trust his daughter was showing him. It was the best gift he'd ever been given. When he looked across the way, he saw Evan looking from him to Lily and back, his eyes rounding in surprise. Kian didn't even want to hide it.

"She's my daughter," he said, pride filling his voice.

Evan seemed speechless for the first time in his life. He opened his mouth, shut it, then opened it again. He knew there were a million questions, but Kian wasn't sure how to answer them.

"Okay, then," Evan said, and Kian's respect for the man grew even greater. Just like that, his friend accepted Lily as his daughter. He didn't try to pry, didn't need to ask questions. Maybe it truly would be that simple with everyone. Kian hoped so. He just knew he loved Lily, and because he loved her, anyone who knew him would love his little girl as well.

Roxie walked back in, looking tired and slightly stressed.

"What's wrong?" Kian asked.

She moved close to him and brushed back some hair from Lily's forehead. "She's had an exciting day," she said softly. Her stress seemed to dissipate as she laid her hands on Lily. The little girl certainly was good for taking away any ill feeling.

"What's the matter? Do you need to talk about anything?" Kian asked.

She looked at him, and he saw the conflict in her eyes. She was deciding if she wanted to share with him or not. He wanted to drag it out of her, but instead he softly rubbed his daughter's back and tried to keep his face neutral. He was just a friend there to listen if she needed it. She didn't have to see how much his heart was racing.

Finally, she sighed. "It was the detective. They have nothing new on the case with my sister. I would just really like some answers so I'm not constantly looking over my shoulder," she admitted.

"I know it might be difficult for you to talk about your sister with me, and I can't say enough how sorry I am about what happened, but just know you can share anything with me," he told her.

Moisture sprang to life in her eyes, and she looked away for a moment as she sniffed, then gave him a slight smile. "Thanks, Kian. I appreciate it. There's really nothing to tell right now," she said.

"Okay," he said. Though he wanted to know the entire conversation she'd had with the detective, he decided not to push her right then. The more she learned to trust him, the more she would open up. He reminded himself it was a marathon, and he wasn't in a hurry. It might feel like he needed to be, but they were building this relationship slowly so there'd be a solid foundation.

"I should get Lily home so I can get her settled for the night. This day has been pretty exciting, and she's going to have a difficult time sleeping," she told him.

The thought of letting Lily go caused an ache unlike anything he'd ever felt before, and Kian wanted to cling more tightly to his daughter than ever before, but he knew that would only cause Roxie to close up. If he wanted this to go smoothly, he couldn't just think of himself. He had to think of Lily, and of Roxie, too.

"Want some help?" he asked. He might not push her, but he'd keep offering his services.

She looked at him for an unguarded moment, and he held his breath, hoping she would accept his offer. He'd love to be there for their nighttime routine. Hell, for that matter, he wouldn't mind tucking his daughter in to bed, and then tucking Roxie in as well. He could certainly help her have an excellent night's rest.

She shook her head, though, and he felt utter disappointment. He hadn't really thought she'd let him come by, but he'd been hopeful all the same. This patience stuff truly was a load of crap.

"I'm pretty worn out. I think I just want to make a cup of hot tea and read until I go to sleep," she said.

"What are you reading?" he asked as he walked with her back to her car.

Her cheeks flushed, and he was incredibly curious now. He couldn't remember ever reading something that would embarrass him. Okay, maybe the copies of *Hustler* he'd read, solely for the articles, of course. If his mom had ever walked in while he'd been immersed in one of those magazines, he'd have been truly mortified.

"Oh, you wouldn't recognize it," she said, looking away. Now he had to know!

"Come on, you tell me what you're reading, and I'll tell you what's on my Kindle," he said in his persuasive doctor's voice. It always got his patients to open up to him.

Her blush wasn't going away. "It's just mindless entertainment," she grumbled.

Kian placed Lily in her seat, and she didn't stir at all, but her tiny fingers gripped his shirt and tugged a little bit more on his heart. He brushed Roxie's hands away and buckled his daughter in. He'd watched Roxie, and now he had it down. He only fumbled a little bit.

"It's called, um, *In the Heir* by Ruth Cardello," she murmured.

He carefully pried Lily's fingers from his shirt, and she grumbled before shifting her hand to her mouth and sucking her thumb. He had a hard time turning away from his daughter, but he was incredibly curious about Roxie's reaction to a book.

"What has you blushing?" he asked. He shut Lily's door and trapped Roxie against the side of the car, not allowing her to escape. He wasn't touching her yet, but now that it was just the two of them with no one else around and Lily asleep in her seat, Kian was getting a lot of ideas that had nothing to do with kids—well, maybe *making* kids, but that was for later.

"I'm not blushing," she insisted, but the color rose in her cheeks, completely contradicting her words.

"Oh, you're definitely blushing," he said. He stepped closer, his body fully coming to life. That flush in her cheeks made him think of how many other ways he could bring color to her body. She blushed all over when she was turned on, and that had him ready to explode in seconds.

"What is this book about?" he asked. She refused to look him in the eyes.

"I have a thing for romance books, okay," she told him in a huff.

"What's so embarrassing about a romance book?" He really was confused. He wasn't letting her leave until she explained.

"It's not embarrassing. It's just a romance book, and there might be a little bit of steam to it." She finished her sentence very quietly. At those words, Kian's imagination came to life.

"What do you mean by steam?" he asked. Now, only inches stood between them, and his lower region was throbbing painfully.

"Well, I don't read romance for the sex, but she . . . um . . . well, this author definitely writes some sexy scenes," she said. The heat coming off her cheeks could burn him now.

"What's this book called again?" he asked.

"*In the Heir*," she said.

"Hmm." There was no way he was admitting his curiosity.

"So, you like reading about sex?" Damn, he was turned on right now. He didn't know women read about sex. It wasn't like he'd ever seen a girl's porn magazine in the stores. Not that he'd looked for one, though. He couldn't imagine a bunch of naked men in a magazine would sell.

"No!" she insisted before calming her voice. "I like reading about *romance*," she told him.

"With sex?" he pushed.

"The sex just happens to be in there," she insisted.

"I can teach you all about sex," he said, leaning in closer, his body now brushing hers.

"You did teach me all about sex," she reminded him.

"And we had fun, didn't we?" he pushed.

He found his fingers tracing the curve of her cheek and jaw and was encouraged when she didn't push him away. Her eyes dilated, and he ran his fingers down her neck, finding the place her pulse was beating out of control.

"Yeah, but that was a different time. We were so young," she said.

"Just because we get older doesn't mean we have to grow up," he advised.

"That's exactly what it means. We can't act like kids forever," she told him.

"Why not? What's so wrong with being youthful? Take Millie, for example. She wears her hair in any color she feels like, and she still dances like she doesn't care. She will live her life until the day she dies and have no regrets as she releases her last breath."

"Your positive outlook on life was one of the things that drew me to you," she said, her guard down, her body relaxing against his as he continued pressing into her.

"It's been a long time since I felt positive," he admitted. "You make me feel like anything's possible."

It was true. When he was with Roxie, the world was at his fingertips. He loved it. She brought something out in him no one else could, and he didn't want to let go of the feeling, not ever.

"Maybe you just buried it," she said, but she was no longer looking in his eyes. Her gaze was on his lips, and he didn't even want to control the hunger drifting through him.

Bending down, he gently kissed the corner of her lips. She sighed as her mouth opened. He wanted to take her fiercely, but he didn't allow himself to. He had to remind her of their languid days of lying on a picnic blanket, worshipping each other's bodies.

He kissed the other corner of her mouth, and she wiggled against him. He pulled her bottom lip into his mouth and gently bit down before sucking on it. Her hips rocked against his. His hand drifted to the back of her head, and he held on tightly as he angled her just where he wanted her and closed his lips over hers, giving her a lazy kiss as his tongue traced her mouth before drifting inside and retreating again.

Her moan rumbled against his mouth, and he had to fight not to lose control, but this was about seduction, not satisfaction. He continued slowly kissing her as one hand drifted down her side, a shudder racking through her frame. He ran his hand down the back of her leg, then gripped her beneath the knee and pulled her thigh up so he could cradle himself against her heat.

She squirmed in his arms as she wrapped her hands behind his shoulders and gripped him tightly, trying to intensify the kiss. He released her lips, and she whimpered until he kissed along her jawline and sucked the skin at the base of her throat. She was melting in his arms, and he was losing the battle of keeping control of himself.

"Invite me over," he begged. He was more than happy to beg now. He'd started this as seduction, and now he just wanted to sink inside her and stay there all night long.

She sighed as her fingers tugged his hair. He kept licking her throat as he waited for her decision. But then she reached around the front of him and applied pressure to his chest. She wanted him to let her go.

Though he knew he could seduce her into submission, he wanted her trust even more than he wanted her body. He allowed her to push him back. Her cheeks were bright-red, and her eyes dilated as she looked at him.

"I need to go," she said, her voice husky.

He wanted to argue, but he didn't. He just caressed her cheek for a moment before taking another step back, then another. She didn't move. He was five feet away from her before he smiled. Damn, she was a sight to behold.

"Sweet dreams, Roxie," he said with a confident grin. Then he forced himself to turn around and leave. He whistled as he made his way back to his truck. Kian had plans tonight. He had a book to download, because he sure as hell wanted to know what it was that had gotten her all worked up.

The night was still young. Maybe, just maybe, he could talk her into a nightcap. He never had been one to give up hope, and with his pants scratching his very prominent arousal, hope was all that was allowing him to walk away.

Roxie was going to be his again. He'd make damn sure of it. They wanted each other and, even more than that, needed each other. He was going to prove it to her in any possible way he could.

Chapter Twenty-One

Throwing his keys down on the entryway table, Kian moved through the large foyer of his house, bypassing the double staircase and walking down the seemingly endless hallway. For some reason, the house seemed extra empty tonight. His footsteps echoed off the walls as he walked past pictures of his family, not bothering to look at them.

He didn't want to admit to what he was feeling, but loneliness came to mind before he pushed it away. He was a successful doctor, a brother, a son, and now a father. That last title got to him, though, because his daughter should be there with him. This place was meant to have children in it, was meant to absorb the sound of laughter. How much longer was he going to be able to stand not having Lily with him?

He knew he wouldn't last a long time. But he didn't want just Lily, he wanted Roxie as well. Of course, he would love and want his daughter just on her own, but he wanted it all now. He'd bought this place a few months before Roxie had left. He'd planned on sharing it with her. It had been getting a complete remodel in those months before she'd walked away, and she'd never even seen the inside of it.

Kian went to his den, normally a haven to him, and wasn't looking at anything as he usually did. Instead of enjoying the beautiful fireplace and hardwood floors, he only saw empty spaces where his child or, for that matter, children, should be crawling around. He wanted to sit in this room, cuddle up on the couch while a fire roared, with Roxie in his arms and Lily playing with action figures. Hey, a girl could be a superhero, too.

But instead, he moved to the liquor cabinet and poured himself a scotch. He couldn't stand being in the room, so he left, crystal glass in hand as he made his way to the back staircase. He moved up them two at a time and went down the hallway, stopping in front of a door. His hand caressed the wood, and he told himself not to open it. But Kian didn't seem to be listening to himself very well at the moment.

He pushed open the door and felt so much loneliness in that moment, he didn't know what to think. Stepping inside, he glanced around the room. A large princess bed sat in the center of the room, purple drapes hanging down from the tall posts. It truly was a bed fit for a queen, which his little girl was.

He'd had the room done the moment he'd known she was his. He wanted her to step into his house and feel at home instantly. He'd wanted her to never want to leave. Maybe the room would help accomplish this. He'd given his assistant carte blanche to do whatever she thought a nearly four-year-old would want. His sister had been impressed, so he thought it had been a pretty good job.

Not able to stand being in the empty room any longer, he quickly left and moved to his own room. It was almost as difficult to be in there as it was to be in Lily's quiet bedroom. But he couldn't kick himself out of the room he slept in. Not that he wanted to sleep there. He wanted to be with Roxie. Why couldn't the woman just admit she wanted him? He knew she wasn't fighting him so much as she was fighting herself. He just wasn't sure what to do about it.

He refilled his glass with a bottle he had in his bedroom, then took a quick shower and settled down on his bed. He had a book to download. A smile flittered across his lips. He had to see what had gotten

Roxie so embarrassed as she'd admitted to reading romance. He couldn't believe there were porn books for women. There was no way it could be any good, he thought. Maybe it would bore him enough to make him have a great night's sleep for the first time in ages.

Sitting in his nice warm bed, he laughed when he found the cover to the book. He double-checked it was the right title, then shrugged and hit the "Buy" button. He'd have to skim the thing because there was no way he was going to get into the story line. When Kian read for pleasure, he wanted action and murder, and always entertainment. He mostly read nonfiction, so his limited fiction time had better absorb him pretty damn quickly.

Kian was a fast reader, and an hour into the book, he was shocked. What the hell? He found himself laughing out loud at some of the scenes, and though he wouldn't admit to this, not even with a gun pointed at his head, he was entertained, for sure. This wasn't anything like he'd expected.

Was it real world? Hell, no. This sort of thing didn't happen in real life. But even as he thought that, he began to think of his own story with Roxie. Heck, he thought a book could be written about them, if someone wanted to take the time. They'd had their ups and downs, hell, were still going through a down time. It might make a decent story. He chuckled. Nah. His life wasn't entertaining enough to read about.

He continued reading as he got absorbed back into the story. If his brothers knew what he was reading right now, he'd never hear the end of it. Never! He wondered, though, if his sister had read the book. He wanted to ask her, but then she'd want to know how he even knew about it, and that was a question he wasn't at all willing to answer.

He found himself laughing again as the hero of the story, Brett, tried to give dating advice to the woman who was making him harder than a rock. Yeah, Kian definitely knew how that felt. He seemed to be solid 99 percent of the time he was around Roxie, even after having a perfectly good orgasm. He'd always been insatiable when it came to her.

No other woman had made him want to stay naked twenty-four-seven. Kian wouldn't lie, not even in his own head. He loved sex. He loved everything about sex. He could do it on a moment's notice. Hell, the species would die out if not for sex. It was his duty to perform the act. Yeah, he liked that; it was his duty, his obligation. But with Roxie, oh, with Roxie, it was so much more. He could run his hands along her smooth flesh morning, noon, and night.

Dammit! Now he was throbbing again. Maybe he should stop reading now. Nope. He was too into this damn story and wanted to see what else the hero could do to screw things up. People were so stupid sometimes. Why wouldn't they just be honest with each other? Maybe because playing a few games made life that much more interesting.

Hell if he knew all the answers. He didn't even know how his own mind worked, let alone what the answers to life were all about. Kian got to the next chapter of the book and found himself swallowing hard. Ah shit, this wasn't going to be good for his anatomy. He could tell right from the next line.

Alisha walked over to the door that connected her room to Brett's and laid a hand on it.

Stop now! He was already throbbing, and this book had proved to him he no longer needed to pick up a copy of *Playboy* to read something sexy. Not that he'd done that in a while, he defended himself. Instead of stopping, though, he continued reading. The heroine was thinking about all the nice things Brett had done for her. Smart lady. See! He wanted to call up Roxie right this instant. Look, in your book you're so enamored with, the heroine understands what a great guy the hero is. She's lamenting about the wonderful things he's done for her.

Kian grinned. Yeah, she's thinking about those nice things, and she's gonna get naked. He laughed out loud. Maybe it was good he was only having these thoughts instead of speaking them. He might come across as a pig. Hell, all men were pigs. Women had to know that by now. They were controlled by sex, food, and power. Love, too, he added. He did a lot out of love. Love for his family, for his career, for sex, *and* for food. He chuckled again, then continued to read.

I'm a survivor. If he breaks my heart, I'll pick myself up and go on.

Kian stopped. Those words hit him hard. Was that how Roxie felt? She had every right to feel that way. She'd survived so much. Was she broken in more ways than he could have imagined? Was there something more he could do for her to help her heal?

Shaking his head, Kian continued reading, then cringed. What the hell? He could do without male body parts being described.

Her gaze slid lower, across his flat stomach to his dark-blue briefs that did nothing to conceal his enormous erection.

Yeah, Kian would bet the guy had a giant sock in his pants. Not many men were as blessed as he was when it came to a satisfying cock. He knew what he had, and he was more than happy to please his woman with it. But in a book, he supposed an author couldn't exactly say something like, *His three-inch penis was gonna pound her so hard.* Kian laughed again. Maybe he should stick to doctoring and not try to write a romance book.

Her thighs quivered as warmth spread through her.

Now we're getting somewhere! Kian was picturing Roxie reading this, her thighs quivering, her hot core getting wet. He should stop. He really should stop. But there was no way he was going to now.

Thoughts evaporated from Kian's mind as he got absorbed in the love scene. His mind flashed with images of Roxie and him tangled up on his giant bed. He read the scene and imagined doing all the hero was doing with her. He wanted her so badly, he was about to explode without a single touch to his body.

. . . flicked his tongue back and forth over her nipple . . .

. . . tongue darted across her lower lips . . .

His tongue plunged in and out of her . . .

. . . dipped the tip of his cock into her . . .

That's it! He had to admit he was officially a romance-book fan. Kian threw down his Kindle, his breathing heavy. He needed Roxie, and he needed her now. He picked up his phone. How persuasive he could be?

Chapter Twenty-Two

Lily had been asleep for an hour, and Roxie was lying in bed reading. She'd forgone the tea, going straight for her bottle of wine. Her body was still on fire, and the worst possible thing she could do right at this moment was drink a couple of glasses of wine while reading a romance book.

But she'd been so busy with taking care of Lily and then moving and finding a job that she hadn't been able to finish her book, and it was a good one. She was a little bit in love with the hero of the story, Brett Westerly. He actually reminded her a little of Kian. Though Brett was a businessman and all, and Kian was a doctor, their attitudes certainly lined up.

And Roxie was very aware that the last thing she should be doing was reading about sex when her body was so hot as it was, but she couldn't seem to stop herself. She guzzled down her glass of wine and decided one more glass wouldn't hurt anyone.

She went and refilled, then climbed back into bed and grabbed her Kindle. Before she could get back into the story, her phone buzzed, showing she had a message. It was almost ten, and she couldn't imagine who'd be texting.

When she opened the message and saw it was from Kian, she felt a stirring of excitement low in her stomach. She could pretend she was asleep and dive back into her book, but she found herself putting down the Kindle and picking up her phone. Maybe it was the wine, and maybe it was the book, and maybe it was the hot make-out session from a few hours before. Whatever it was, she didn't think too hard about opening a door that should remain closed.

He groaned in approval and thrust his tongue deeply inside her.

Roxie was in shock as she read the message. She reread it again and felt moisture pool in her core. She squeezed her thighs together as an unbearable ache took over her body. He'd downloaded the book she was reading. He was texting her a line from one of the sex scenes, and she was as hot as hell. She'd never had a phone-sexting conversation before. Should she play along? It was a bad idea.

Squeezing her thighs tightly together, she decided to respond.

She put a leg over one of his shoulders and pulled him closer with it, urging him to continue.

It was too late to go back now. She'd responded, and she could see where he was typing. Rubbing her legs up and down, the friction on her thighs was driving her mad, but she couldn't help it. She grabbed her glass of wine and took another deep swallow, then licked her lips, imagining it was him doing it for her.

His tongue plunged in and out of her, deeper with each stroke.

Hot damn! She felt as if she were in the book, as if she were being stroked and teased, built up slowly. Though it wasn't exactly happening slow, not at all. She was hot and aching, and her fingers caressed the screen of her phone as she decided what she wanted to do next. Her room was dark and her head slightly fuzzy. She replied.

I'm hot, so damn hot right now . . .

Letting go of her inhibitions, Roxie's hand slid down her pajama pants, and she ran her fingers across her aching slit. Her body jumped from the bed at that gentle touch. She'd eased her own ache before but never while this turned on. It had been out of necessity before she'd thought she'd explode from the buildup, but it was always such a letdown, and she'd hungered to be filled; she hungered for one person to do it. She'd close her eyes and picture Kian on top of her, his sweaty chest brushing against her nipples, his solid erection penetrating her in the most filling way.

Slowly, Roxie's thighs opened as she slid her hand lower and slipped two fingers inside her heat. She bit her lip to keep from groaning as the next message popped up on her phone. It was difficult to see through the blurriness of her vision.

I want to make you hotter. I'm dying here. Let me come over and finish this. Please.

Roxie felt as if she were going out of her mind. She wanted fulfillment. She shouldn't do it, shouldn't allow this to happen, but she wanted him so badly, and she didn't think she was going to get the same release without him.

My hand doesn't come close to the tight hold of your wet heat. Let me come to you. I'm hard and aching. I want you. I'm lying here picturing your fingers deep inside that hot core, and I want to replace them with my own. I want to run my tongue along your tightness and push it inside before I bury myself deep within you. I want to take you deep, and I want to bury myself in your mouth and hot core. Just say one word and I'll be there in five minutes.

Kian definitely lived more than five minutes away, but she had a feeling he'd be here that fast. She could get the satisfaction she so desperately needed. Before she could change her mind, she found herself typing.

Yes. Key is under the pink flowerpot.

She hit "Send" and waited to see if there was a response. Nothing. Roxie pushed her pajama pants away and lay back, her eyes closed as she ran her fingers across her slick heat. She rubbed her swollen flesh and dipped her fingers inside, seeking relief that just wouldn't come. She needed Kian—only Kian.

There was a noise at her front door, and she was so delirious in pleasure, she couldn't even begin to focus on it. Then her bedroom door opened, and though it was dark, she could see the outline of Kian standing there. He began stripping off his clothes as she continued to rub herself, trying to see his face, but unable. A moan escaped her, and she wondered if all of this was a dream.

That was okay if it was, as long as she was able to come to completion at the end. She wouldn't mind coming again and again.

"You are so fucking hot," he said, his voice low and gravelly, nearly out of control—just the way she liked it.

"I need . . ." she panted.

"What do you need?" he asked. He crawled up on the bed, his flesh hot and hard.

"You, I need you," she panted. She was still touching herself when he grabbed her hand and pressed it into the bed.

She had to grab her pillow and push it over her face when his mouth replaced her fingers and he did exactly what he said he was going to do; he dived his tongue deep inside her, making her hips arch off the bed.

She exploded instantly, her heat clenching over and over as an orgasm nearly ripped her in two with the intensity of the waves. One touch from him had been all she needed. He stroked her slowly as she fell back down to earth, but Roxie wasn't even close to being fully satisfied. He'd woken up a hunger in her she wasn't sure she'd ever be able to sate.

She sat up, and with her eyes adjusted to the dark, she could see his outline. She needed to taste him. She missed the feeling of his fullness inside her mouth. Pushing him onto his back, she started at his neck. He reached his fingers into her hair and pulled. The sting grounded her and excited her all at once.

Kissing her way down his chest, she circled her tongue across his hard nipples and bit down on them, making him moan low in his throat as he pushed his hips up against her side. She felt his thickness against her and grew even wetter, her body dripping in pleasure.

She ran her tongue down the solid plane of his stomach, circled his belly button, and then went lower. His fingers were still holding her hair, tugging on her. She smiled as she kissed his lower stomach, her fingers lightly rubbing along his happy trail. That small arrow of hair had always turned her on so much when he'd go shirtless. She'd grow wet as she followed the line, knowing exactly what it led to.

She pressed her lips against his hip, wetting his skin with her tongue before she moved down his thigh. His groan encouraged her to keep going. She kissed across his pelvic bone, kissing the base of his thickness. He was solid, his erection pressed against his stomach, his pleasure moistening the head.

She ran her tongue up his beautiful length and circled the bulging head, her core clenching as she thought about the moment it would be fully inside her. Oh, how she ached to be satisfied. She wanted to do everything at once. But first, she had to taste him. She had to fill her mouth with him.

Gripping the base of his hardness in her hand, she sucked him into her mouth and swirled her tongue across the tip of him. His body arched off the bed as he let go of her hair and threw his hands above him. He pushed upward, encouraging her to take him deeper. She opened her throat and sucked him in, then swallowed, clenching her throat around his tip.

It was his turn to grab the pillow and cry out against it as he thrashed on the bed beneath her. Moving expertly up and down his thickness, she tasted him, squeezed him, and soaked him as she took her time, making him pulse in her mouth.

"Roxie, I need inside you," he commanded, reaching for her again. She pulled away from him, letting his slick steel pop from her mouth.

"Be good or you won't get to finish," she taunted before sucking him into her mouth again.

She knew how to tease him to the breaking point. He'd taught her well. He might be regretting that right now. But she'd enthusiastically learned how to suck him years earlier. She'd even looked up ways online to satisfy him. She'd loved pleasing him, loved making him lose control. Only Kian. He was her only lover, and in her abstinence, she'd grown hornier, it seemed.

She deep-throated him again and again; all the while her core pulsed with a need for fulfillment. He was losing control as he gripped a pillow to his face and cried out into it. She wanted to continue torturing him, but she couldn't handle it any longer. So, she let him pop from her mouth, then rubbed her fingers up and down his wet length a couple of times before she climbed up his body and sat over him.

His thickness rested on his stomach, and she rubbed her slick heat along it a couple of times, letting her wetness completely soak him. He tossed the pillow aside and grabbed her hips, his fingers bruising as he guided her up.

"Please tell me you're still on birth control. I don't want anything between us," he said, the words guttural.

"I am," she told him, barely able to talk.

"Then take me in your hand and bring me home," he growled.

She didn't even think about teasing him anymore. She wanted him. He pulled her up off the bed as she gripped his hard length and pressed it at her opening. She looked down at his wild eyes as he pulled her down. They cried out together as their bodies fit so perfectly as one.

She tried to move, but he held her in place as he shook beneath her. She tried moving again, and he still wouldn't let her move. She wiggled on top of him, and he groaned.

"Give me a second," he begged. He was trembling beneath her, and the power she felt in that moment was unlike anything she'd ever felt before. He was so over-the-top turned on, he wasn't able to control himself. She didn't want to give him the opportunity to pull back from her. She wanted him at her mercy.

She dug her nails into his chest, making him cry out in surprise, and then she lifted her hips and slammed back down on him. He called out her name, and she lifted up again and again as she lost control with him.

He reached forward and grabbed her hard nipples between his fingers, squeezing just enough to send an ache from her chest to her wet heat, and that's all it took to send her over the edge again. She squeezed him tightly as she continued pounding against him, and they cried out together as he released deep within her, his hot steel pumping against her walls.

They continued moving together as they both found satisfaction. Exhausted, Roxie collapsed on top of him, their flesh wet with the heat of their coming. He ran his hands up and down her back before he gripped her butt and squeezed. He was still hard inside her, and he pulsed as his fingers ran down the seam of her ass and slid along her wetness where they were still connected.

She should be done. He should certainly be finished, but she felt him pulse inside her as that beautiful ache began again. She wiggled on top of him as she lifted her head and kissed his jaw.

So quickly she barely registered it was happening, Kian grabbed her ass and flipped them over, never losing his connection inside her body. He pressed his torso up as he remained buried inside her, and she cried out at the pleasure of it.

"Now I get to make love to you the way I've wanted to from the very first moment I laid eyes on you," he said.

Too emotional. This was too emotional. She wanted to pull back from him, but he leaned down and kissed her, his lips soft and hungry as he gripped her thigh and opened her fully to him.

He slowly pushed inside her before pulling out to the tip and doing it all over again. His tight sack rubbed along the sensitive flesh below her wet slit, and his pelvic bone hit her bundle of nerves. It was all too much, and she once again got lost in him. His chest rubbed her nipples, and his lips caressed hers.

He didn't stop. He made love to her for an endless amount of time and built the ache up and up as she shattered in his arms, her body receiving unending pleasure. She was his, completely and utterly his. Anything he wanted from her, he could have. She didn't have the will to deny him.

Then he sped up again, and together they came in the most intense explosion of the night. She saw colors flashing behind her eyelids as she gave herself over to him. And when it was finished with his weight on top of her, his body protecting hers, she felt safe and cared for.

She closed her eyes and let herself go.

Chapter Twenty-Three

Thank you for an incredible night. Coffee's in the fridge, you just need to heat it, and fresh doughnuts are on the table. I got called in to work or I would have woken you up with a very satisfying morning. I plan on helping you sleep tonight.

Love, Kian

Roxie read the note and couldn't help but smile. Her entire body ached in the best way possible, and even though she didn't think it was feasible, she felt a stirring of hunger at the thought of doing that all over again.

She knew this was a dangerous path the two of them were taking, but maybe she should just admit they were on a runaway train and there was absolutely nothing they could do to stop it.

They hadn't talked about what was going to happen with Lily; they hadn't talked about if Roxie would even stay in this town. They hadn't made a commitment to each other. For all she knew, he could be seeing other women. But she was afraid to talk about any of that. She was afraid of becoming the woman she'd been when she'd left him.

It would be so easy to lean on him, to get lost in him. But then she feared she would never find herself again. She couldn't allow that to happen. She had to stay strong, especially for Lily's sake.

She heard the squeak of the door and realized Lily was up. She quickly grabbed her nightshirt, which Kian had thankfully left on the pillow next to her, and shoved it on about three seconds before Lily bounded into her room.

"Good morning, beautiful," Roxie said.

"Mornin'," Lily replied as she climbed into the bed and snuggled into Roxie's arms. This was their morning routine, and Roxie felt a bit of panic at the thought that Lily could have come in and seen Kian lying there in her spot. Would that traumatize her niece? Roxie couldn't believe she'd been so irresponsible. She hadn't even thought about it. Thankfully, he'd been called in to work, and she didn't have to face that quite yet.

"Did you dream good dreams?" Roxie asked, pushing out her guilt and focusing on their routine.

"I dreamed about unicorns," Lily said.

"Mmm, I like unicorns. I dreamed about piglets," she said. She actually had dreamed of the cute little things.

"Piggies?" Lily said, looking up with bright eyes.

"Yep, cute little pink ones," Roxie told her.

"I want a piggy," Lily said, her eyes getting that stubborn look that Roxie was beginning to count on.

"We'll have to visit Doc Evan again and play with them," Roxie told her, afraid to commit to getting any animals. Lily didn't look appeased, but she snugged against Roxie again, and Roxie rubbed her silky hair.

"I think we have doughnuts in the kitchen," Roxie told her niece. She needed to use the bathroom, and Lily was resting right on her bladder.

"Doughnuts?" Lily squeaked. She jumped out of the bed and rushed from the room. Roxie found her pajama pants, slipped them on, and ran to the bathroom. She quickly brushed her teeth and joined Lily in the kitchen, where she was shoving a powdered doughnut in her face.

Roxie looked at the box suspiciously. "How many did you eat in the five minutes that took me?" she asked. There were five in there now.

Lily shrugged as she took another bite, white sugar all over her flushed cheeks. She should try to monitor this a little better, but she was too sated to care much about anything right now.

There were three coffee cups in the fridge, and she wondered if he still remembered what she liked. She warmed a cup in the microwave, then sat down next to Lily, who'd already grabbed another doughnut. Taking a sip of the coffee, she sighed in satisfaction. Yep, a caramel mocha. It was perfection.

She drank half the cup before grabbing a bear claw and taking a bite. This was the best breakfast ever. Lily finally filled up and sat back to drink the milk Roxie had placed before her, then the two of them made their way into the small living room with Roxie's second cup of coffee, where they snuggled up on the couch and watched a cartoon.

Roxie couldn't help but smile at how right all of this felt. Her body ached in the best way, her tummy was pleasantly full, and her arms were filled with a happy child. She couldn't imagine it getting much better.

After the second cup of coffee was down, she left Lily with a coloring book and took a quick shower before she got dressed. Then she helped Lily get ready for the day. She had no plans this afternoon, as she wasn't working. The day was overcast but not too cold, so maybe they'd go to the park. First, she had to check her mail.

Opening the box, she found an envelope inside. There was no return address, no postage, just her name scrawled on it, almost unrecognizable. Her curiosity was certainly piqued.

She turned it over in her hands and wondered who it could be from. She hadn't been out much since she'd moved home and hadn't visited nearly enough people. It had been a long time since she'd wanted to establish roots, and she was almost afraid to do it now. Because, if she got too attached to being here again and things went really south when it came to her and Kian, she'd have to leave. Having friends here would make her realize how alone she truly was in the rest of the world. Roxie wasn't sure she could handle that right now, not in the fragile state she was allowing herself to get into.

Walking back into her kitchen, she checked on Lily, who was happily scribbling in her coloring book, and then she sat at the table and picked up another doughnut, not even feeling guilty about consuming so many calories. She'd definitely burned enough the night before. Her thighs were burning from all the exertion. Sex really should be listed as a form of exercise, as she'd never been as sore from a workout at the gym as she was from a rowdy night of sex.

Opening the envelope, she pulled out a single piece of paper. There was a short note:

Meet me at the bakery at three for a date. Wear sexy panties I can imagine ripping off you.

With love,

Kian

Heat suffused Roxie's cheeks as she looked over her shoulder where Lily was still in her own little world. Even if her niece had been there looking at the note, it wasn't as if she could read yet. Still, after reading it one more time, Roxie tucked the note away.

It was silly, really. It didn't mean anything. They'd sent sex messages the night before. But this was different. This was a . . . well, sort of a date. He hadn't said whether or not to bring Lily, but she was assuming she should. But would Roxie go?

She wanted to go. She found she really wanted to go. Before she could stop it, she found a girlish giggle escaping her mouth. The sound was so foreign, it shocked her into instant silence. Then she found herself giggling again. Lily looked up from the couch and walked over to her, a big smile on her face.

"What's funny?" she asked. She spotted the doughnut in her aunt's hand and climbed back up into a chair and grabbed one for herself.

"Oh, I just got a silly note," Roxie said.

"Note?" Lily repeated.

"Yep, a note," she said.

Lily quickly lost interest after she took a bite of her doughnut. Roxie was grateful they were on the last two, because had there been more in there, she feared the two of them would have polished off another half dozen. Then she realized Kian wanted to take her back to the bakery later that afternoon. Was the man trying to make her gain twenty pounds? Maybe. That way, she wouldn't be able to run away from him.

Before she was able to think about it too much, her phone rang. She didn't recognize the number on her caller ID and thought about letting it go to voice mail, but she could really use a distraction right about now, so she answered.

"Roxie?" the person said after only a second. She hadn't had time to give a greeting.

"This is Roxie," she said, not recognizing the voice.

"Oh, good, this is Sal," the man said, and now she recognized his voice clearly.

"Hi, Sal, how can I help you?" She searched her memory but didn't think she was missing an appointment.

"I wanted to see if you could come out to the doc's a little early and help out," Sal said.

"What do you mean?"

"We're having a thank-you for the volunteers on Saturday, and there's a lot of work involved. Wanna come help?" He might be posing it as a question, but Roxie knew why people had Sal calling for volunteers. His voice demanded an assent.

"I guess I don't have anything going on," she said hesitantly. "But I do have Lily."

"Perfect. We have lots of people that can't do any heavy lifting but love to hang with the kiddos."

The phone went dead. Roxie looked at it and wondered if they'd been disconnected, or if Sal had just finished with the call and moved on to the next one. She shrugged and guessed she was going out to Evan's house.

As soon as she told Lily, the child lit up. She was going to get to see the piglets again, and she was all for that. At least she'd be able to burn off all the sugar she'd consumed for breakfast. She hoped her niece didn't think that was going to be a morning ritual from now on. It was normally eggs and toast or cereal. Never sugar goodness, though Roxie wouldn't mind that too much.

It didn't take her long to drive out to Evan's, and she was barely out of her car before Eden was rushing up to her.

"I'm so glad you're here," she said, her cheeks flushed as she practically bounced on her toes.

"Why?" Roxie asked.

Eden rolled her eyes. "Because the old ladies are driving me nuts with their meddling, and I need someone else for them to focus their attention on," Eden answered honestly. Roxie felt the blood run from her face. She didn't need anyone trying to match her up with someone. That would be a nightmare.

Before Roxie could blink, Martha was there at her side and easily talked Lily into going with her to the barn to see the animals. Then Eden was dragging Roxie in another direction. She so wasn't used to all this. She was thinking it might be safer to stick with her niece than with the adults.

She was pulled into the house, where a bunch of people were arguing about how the party should go, and since Roxie had no idea what was going on, she felt like a fish out of water. She simply sat back and tried to be invisible. Maybe it would have been better if she had made excuses and not come.

Time was escaping her as she sat around the house planning and making decorations. She didn't realize three was approaching quickly. When she finally did look at her phone, she realized she was going to be late, if she chose to go.

She should at least text him, but she honestly had no idea what to say, so she sat there biting her lip as she continued to stress.

"Okay, tell me right now what you're thinking about. It looks pretty intense," Eden said, pulling Roxie from her thoughts.

She found her cheeks heating, giving away that she was indeed thinking of something. But she honestly didn't know what to say. She and Eden hadn't been in communication for a long time, and this was a lot to take in.

"It has to do with Kian, doesn't it?" Eden guessed accurately.

Now her cheeks flushed even more. She hated that her skin gave her away so easily. She never had been one of those people who could so easily lie. She was a little jealous about that fact.

"No," Roxie said, but even the sound of her voice betrayed her. It was shaky and deceptive. Eden laughed.

"Come on, everyone in this town knows Kian is crazy about you," Eden said. "He's been in such a better mood since you've come home."

"That's not true," Roxie said. Then she sighed. She had to share her secret with someone. It was killing her. Maybe it would be a mistake, but she didn't care. "Lily is Kian's daughter," she blurted.

"I figured," Eden said, not at all surprised.

"What? How?" She stopped trying to speak as she looked at her friend.

"You forget I was there with you at the park when you and Kian ran into each other again. The sparks were flying, and something was going on. Besides that, Lily looks just like Kian's little sister. It's pretty obvious."

"Well, now you know why he's been around so much. He wants Lily," Roxie said, feeling unusually depressed.

"You can't possibly think that's the only reason he wants to be around," Eden said as if she were a fool.

"Why? Did you talk to him?" Roxie asked, feeling a bit of hope. It was ridiculous how much her emotions were going up and down at the speed of sound. She was the one who'd walked away from him. She'd been the one to betray him. Sure, they had shared a couple of great rounds of sex, but that in no way solved the issues between them, and she shouldn't want to fix the issues, anyway. This was only about Lily, not about her and Kian.

"He doesn't have to talk to me for me to see the way he looks at you. The man has always been obsessed. You two are like two comets on a collision course for each other, and anyone with any good sense at all knows to stay the heck out of your path," Eden said.

"No. We've had our time together, and it didn't work out," Roxie said. Then she leaned in. "I got completely consumed by him. I didn't even know who I was anymore."

She felt so selfish saying this, but she had to talk about how she felt. If she didn't, she'd never be able to work it out in her own mind.

"Don't you think you can still be yourself and be in love?" Eden asked. She wasn't in any way berating her, which made it possible for Roxie to continue speaking.

"I wasn't able to do it before," she admitted.

"You've also had some time on your own to grow up and figure out who you are away from him. Do you like yourself more or less when he isn't a part of your life?"

Roxie had an immediate answer, but she closed her lips instead of spouting it out as she truly thought about the question. It wasn't something she'd ever taken time to consider.

"I don't know," she said. "When I moved away, I was running. I didn't even know who I was anymore, let alone what I wanted. I still don't really know. My sister died, and I've been taking care of Lily now, and it seems that my identity is now wrapped up in my niece. But I love being with her. I don't look at her as a burden at all," she quickly added.

"I understand that," Eden said. "But, honestly, it's okay to think about yourself, too. You have to be happy and fulfilled in order to be a good aunt or mother or wife."

"When in the heck did you become so knowledgeable?" Roxie asked.

A sad light entered Eden's eyes as she leaned back. "I've had my own heartbreak to deal with, and it caused me to do some soul-searching. I don't know that much, honestly, and it's much easier to analyze other people than myself. I just know that you and Kian are meant to be."

"Have you ever thought about talking to Owen, telling him how you feel?" Roxie asked.

Eden looked around the room to make sure no one was listening before she leaned in even closer and whispered quickly, "No. Don't say his name. He moved to New York to be this badass fireman and didn't even blink as he left me behind. It's over between us, and I hope I never see him again."

There was so much pain in her eyes and her words, and it broke Roxie's heart because she knew how her friend was feeling. The difference was that Roxie had seen Eden and Owen together, and she would have sworn the two of them would have happily gone off into the sunset together.

"When is the last time you talked to him?" Roxie asked.

"We're talking about you, not me," Eden pointed out.

"I know, but when?" Roxie asked. She found she liked focusing on someone other than herself as much as her friend did.

Finally, Eden sighed. "It's been two years."

"Have you tried calling, or has he?"

"No. He did try calling a couple of times in the beginning, and then I didn't hear from him again, and I was glad. It's over. I even dated another guy for all of five seconds, but it was too soon," Eden admitted.

"I'm sorry," Roxie said. She meant it. There truly was nothing like the pain of heartbreak.

"Maybe we are both better off just being on our own," Eden told her with a pout.

"I can agree to that," Roxie said.

Three o'clock had come and gone, and she hadn't texted Kian. He'd been stood up and was probably furious with her now. Maybe that was for the best, too. They really couldn't start something up. It wouldn't be wise.

The sun was starting to get lower in the sky, and the clouds were rolling in. Time was quickly fading, and Roxie knew she should probably be heading home. She'd checked her phone several times and hadn't heard from Kian at all. Maybe he hadn't shown up at the doughnut shop, either.

The thought of that made her cheeks heat again. She was just on such unsure footing where he was concerned, she didn't know what to think or feel.

"I should check on Lily now that we're pretty much done here," she told Eden.

"Yeah, I guess it's time to head out. I've noticed several people leaving," Eden replied.

The two of them walked outside, and half the vehicles were gone already, with more pulling out by the second. Eden told her goodbye, and Roxie headed toward the barn, where she heard Lily giggling so much, it made her smile.

She stepped inside and found Doc Evan and Lily sitting in the pigpen with all the little piglets climbing all over them.

"Well, this looks like fun," she said, leaning against the rail and smiling at them.

"I like the piggies," Lily said with a huge grin as one crawled up her leg and rested its tiny head on her.

"I know you do," she told Lily, who quickly turned her attention back to the small animals. Lily was so gentle with them, Roxie couldn't be more proud.

"How did you get roped into babysitting duty?" Roxie asked.

Evan looked up with a conspiratorial grin. "I avoid the meddlers as much as possible. I felt safer out here. The other kids took off a little bit ago, so I agreed to let Lily have some uninterrupted playtime. Come in and join us," he told her.

"I can't resist that invitation," she said, and quickly climbed inside and sat down near Evan.

For the next fifteen minutes, she was swarmed with baby piglets that couldn't seem to get enough attention. Roxie found herself laughing more than she had in the past four years.

"You're a natural with animals. You should have gone to vet school instead of becoming a nurse." Evan patted her shoulder.

She'd always enjoyed Evan's company. He was such a good guy. She was comfortable with him. Why couldn't she feel just as easy around Kian? Maybe because around Kian, she felt hot and bothered and never knew quite how to react. Would she have fallen in love with him if she'd never had such highs and lows? She wasn't sure of that answer.

With Evan, she was comfortable, thinking of him almost like a brother. There weren't any sparks, but what would it be like to be with a man whom she was simply comfortable with? No excitement, but no devastation. She wasn't sure.

"I might have to think about doing that. I'm finding that I do enjoy animals more than a lot of people," she told him, laughing again.

"Well, this looks nice and cozy."

Roxie froze at the cold fury in the voice above her. She didn't want to turn and look up, didn't want to see Kian's face, but almost as if she had no will to stop it, she looked anyway, and though he wasn't exactly glaring, he didn't appear to be a happy camper at all.

"Hey, Kian, want to join us in the pigpen?" Evan asked, seeming oblivious to Kian's bad mood.

Roxie decided to look away from him, afraid if she continued to stare, his eyes were going to shoot fire at her and burn her alive. This was the reason the two of them would never have a relationship. It was too intense, too much for her to handle.

"No, I was worried about Roxie and Lily when they didn't show up for our date," Kian said.

Roxie gasped as she turned and glared at the man. "We didn't have a date," she told him through clenched teeth. She might not want to cause a scene, but she wasn't going to allow him to make her look like some flighty girl in front of her friend.

"Yes, we did, for doughnuts," he told her, refusing to back down.

"I received a note from you. I didn't respond, and then I got busy," she said. Her own voice was growing colder by the second, and Lily seemed to be picking up on it because she looked at Roxie with wide eyes.

"It *was* a date," Kian said. "And last night was more than a date." But right after he said that with a smug look, he seemed to notice Lily's distress, and he calmed the tone of his voice. "Hey, Lily Bear, we're all good."

"Well, I'm definitely not getting in the middle of this," Evan said with a laugh as he jumped to his feet and quickly climbed from the pigpen. "You guys take your time, and make sure the gate is latched when you leave."

With that, Evan took off, his chuckle easily heard as he left the barn. Roxie was furious at the way Kian had just behaved, and because of that, she sat right where she was for the next ten minutes, ignoring the man. She felt his gaze on the back of her neck the entire time.

"I'm hungry," Lily said as she tugged on Roxie's arm.

"Oh, I guess it's past dinnertime, isn't it?" she said, feeling again like a terrible guardian since she'd forgotten to feed the child.

"We'll get pizza," Kian said.

"Yeah, pizza," Lily said before Roxie could correct him. Lily jumped up, startling a few of the piglets, who squealed and ran back toward their mama to hide. She ran to the fence and held her arms up for Kian to pick her up, then snuggled against his chest as they both looked over at Roxie, who was slowly rising.

"I'm just going to make some dinner at home," she said to Lily, refusing to look at Kian.

"I want pizza," Lily told her stubbornly.

Roxie had to take in several deep breaths. This kind of thing wasn't going to work with her. Kian couldn't paint her into a corner.

"It's been a long day, and you haven't even had a nap. We need to go home," she firmly told Lily.

The little girl's lip began to quiver, and a couple of big tears slipped down her cheeks, making Roxie feel about two inches tall and making her want to punch Kian square in the jaw. She probably would have if he hadn't been holding Lily at that very moment.

"I'll pick up pizza and bring it to your house," Kian told Lily.

"Promise?" Lily said, her eyes still watery.

"Yep, I promise. You ride home with your mama, and I'll get pizza."

She wrapped her hands around his neck and gave him a wet kiss on his cheek in her gratitude. Roxie wanted to tell him he couldn't just invite himself over, but he wasn't asking her permission. She was beyond frustrated now.

Lily wouldn't let her take her, so she stomped after both of them as Kian approached her car, once again grumbling about how unsafe it was. She was likely to punch him yet. Because she didn't want Lily to see that happen, she quickly dived into the driver's seat and locked the door. When the click went into place, Kian paused in buckling up Lily, and she felt his heated gaze on the back of her neck. She didn't turn around, but she heard his sarcastic *really* as if it were louder than a gunshot.

"I'll see you in about thirty minutes," he said. The words certainly were a threat. Maybe Lily would be passed out and she could turn all the lights off and pretend they'd both gone to bed. Roxie was really hoping.

She got home and gave Lily the shortest bath the kid had ever had, then brushed her hair and offered her some toast with jam, one of her favorite treats, but her darling child refused. Though she was hungry, her mind was set on pizza, and almost to the minute, Kian showed up at the door with a hot box and a smile.

Begrudgingly, she let him in, not happy at all about the situation. He had a smirk on his lips she would absolutely love to wipe off. Roxie was pretty silent as Kian and Lily talked all about their days with each other. He told her about a little girl he'd seen as a patient, and she listened as if she could understand any of it. She told him about playing with the other kids and all the tiny animals.

Roxie felt as if she wasn't needed in this conversation at all, and she didn't appreciate the feeling. It was in that moment that she knew she truly was the one out of place. She hadn't had a relationship with her niece until recently, and she'd wanted nothing to do with her sister. She was simply the aunt, nothing special. Sure, Lily was calling her Mama more and more, but she wasn't her mama. And the reality was that Kian *was* her dad.

The weight of sadness that suddenly rested on her shoulders was almost too much for her to take. She had to get away from the table. Her appetite completely gone, she jumped up and went to the bathroom. Looking at herself in the mirror, she barely recognized the woman gazing back at her. Who was she? She had no idea. She felt as if she were living on the outside of reality, just a stranger who was the only one out of place in this perfect little world.

She knew she had to pull it together for Lily's sake, but right in this moment, she couldn't seem to do it. She felt so unwanted, so out of place. She felt as if she had nowhere to go and no one who'd miss her if she were gone. It was like the first time she'd left this town. No one had come after her. She'd been able to slip away without anyone truly caring.

Tears streamed down her cheeks as she faced her own worthlessness. It wasn't a feeling she would wish on anyone. There was no one she disliked so much she'd want them to face the emptiness she was feeling.

Lily needed to go to bed. She truly should pull it together enough to get her there, but she couldn't face Kian right now; she couldn't even face Lily, who was perfectly happy to be with her father. They might not have told the little girl yet that he was her daddy, but she was drawn to him, anyway. She seemed to instinctively know it.

Roxie cracked the bathroom door open and called out to Kian. "Do you think you could help Lily with her jammies and tuck her in? I have a terrible headache, and I'm going to take a bath. You can see yourself out after," she said.

There was dead silence for a few seconds, and she wondered if he was going to refuse. He'd told her he wanted to know his daughter's nighttime routine, and this was the perfect way to be immerged into it.

"Yes, I've got it," he called back. She couldn't tell from his tone what he thought about her request, but she was too emotionally wrecked to focus on it. She closed and locked the bathroom door, then turned on the night-light so it was dark, and then she filled the tub.

She sat there for well over an hour, adding hot water when it began to cool. When she heard no more sound coming from the house, she decided it was safe to come out. She knew she was going to have to face Kian again soon, but at least it wasn't going to be tonight.

She deserved a small reprieve because she hadn't allowed herself to let everything sink in over the past couple of months, and now it seemed to be doing so with the force of a perfect storm.

Chapter Twenty-Four

Kian couldn't help but smile as he stretched out on Roxie's bed. If she seriously thought he was so easy to dismiss, then she truly had forgotten all about him in their years apart. That thought didn't bode so well for him.

He hadn't forgotten a single thing about her—not the way her body felt, not the sound of her laughter, or the way her cheeks would give her away every single time. He had been in love with her, and he was coming to the conclusion that no matter how hard he'd tried to forget her, he still was in love with her.

He truly had no idea how she felt about him, though. Kian didn't like this uncertainty, but he had never been a person to run from his problems. When he'd found her and Lily all cozy in the barn with the vet, he'd wanted to punch Evan in the face, then put Roxie over his shoulder and smack her ass a few times before taking her home and proving to her over and over again who she belonged to.

The second he'd had Lily in his arms, he'd calmed down. Of course Evan wouldn't try anything with his woman. That would never happen. But it was much easier to be rational when he wasn't filled with jealousy. He'd waited at that damn bakery for a half hour before realizing she wasn't showing up. It hadn't taken much investigative work to figure out where she was.

He'd been jealous all the way out there, and, well, it had piqued. But tonight had been ideal for him. He'd been able to have dinner with the two most important ladies in his life, and then he'd gotten to read a story to his daughter before tucking her into bed. She'd fallen asleep almost instantly.

Now, he'd been waiting in Roxie's room for a half hour. He was glad she was taking her time. It allowed him to calm himself and to think. Roxie was scared. He wasn't sure of what exactly, but she was scared.

When that happened, she tended to want to run. Kian just had to be strong enough for the both of them to not allow her to do that. He could certainly hold the burden of their problems on his wide shoulders. He'd be more than willing to do so. He just had to know what they were, first.

She should trust him a little bit by now. He had the power to take Lily anytime he wanted, and he hadn't attempted to do that. He didn't want Lily not to have Roxie. He wanted them all to be a family. He just wasn't sure how to make it happen. He didn't want to come on too strong and cause her to run again, but he didn't want to move too slowly, either.

He wished life could be just a little bit simpler at times. But then where would the fun be in that? He heard the bathroom door open, and his heart skipped a beat. The lamp was on the lowest setting, and the moment she walked into the bedroom, she'd know she wasn't alone. His eyes were fixed on the door.

Kian's breath was literally stolen from his body when she stepped into the room. Her head was down as she ruffled a towel through her long, dark tresses, her freshly bathed scent drifting to him, making him hard as a boulder.

His arousal poked up through his boxers, which were all he was wearing, and his stomach twitched. He curled his fingers into fists to keep from launching himself through the air toward her.

She had nothing on but a skimpy towel that was barely covering the top of her thighs, and her generous cleavage was about to spill out as she leaned forward. She still hadn't noticed him when she moved forward and sat on the edge of the bed, her head down as she scrubbed the top of her head.

Her smell was intoxicating, and though Kian had hoped the two of them would be making love this night, it hadn't been his main objective when he'd gotten comfortable on her bed. He'd wanted the two of them to talk first. He wasn't sure he had the willpower to make that happen now, though, not when she was so unwittingly tempting him.

"Damn," he growled, startling her, and she twisted. The action caused the towel around her body to open and fall away, revealing the undeniable beauty of her flesh.

Within seconds, he had her beneath him, and his lips were on hers. His hunger was nearly uncontrollable as he plunged his tongue into her mouth, his hands smoothing down her sides. She whimpered against him as she reached for him, her own need catching fire as quickly as his.

"I wanted to talk," he said as he wrenched his lips from hers, then dived into the crook of her neck and sucked her sweet skin. "But then you came in here looking like this, and I've lost my mind."

She whimpered as she arched her back into him. Her hard nipples were pressing against his chest, her legs spread wide beneath him.

"Take me. Make me stop thinking," she demanded.

The pain of her words nearly brought him back to reality, but she arched her back again and rubbed her hot core against him, and he lost his mind before rationality could seep through. She opened her lips and begged for a kiss, and he gladly obliged, sealing their mouths together.

They tore at each other's skin as if they couldn't get close enough, and Kian reached between their bodies and freed himself just enough to plunge inside her. He swallowed her cry of pleasure and pounded against her in a frenzy of movement.

He felt her clench around him, and he had to fight not to let go with her. This was too fast. He should have been sated enough to love her for hours. But he desired her so much, he couldn't get enough. And looking down at her flushed face was making him come undone.

Her thighs gripped him tightly, and he stopped moving for a moment to catch his breath. "More, I want more," she demanded.

Kian smiled down at her. "You're a greedy little thing, aren't you?" he said. He leaned down and sucked the curve of her shoulder, leaving his mark there.

"Yes, I want more," she demanded.

There was a new urgency in her tone he couldn't possibly deny. Kian jumped up and shed his shorts, his erection wet and ready for more. He looked down at her flushed body and nearly came.

"You better be damn glad I didn't leave when you so easily dismissed me," he growled.

Her eyes widened, and then she looked at him defiantly. That only turned him on more. He reached down and flipped her over, causing a squeal to escape her pretty little lips. He reached out and smacked her once on her perfect little cheek, making an outraged squeal escape from her throat.

She wrenched her head around to give him a piece of her mind, but he climbed on the bed, grasped her luscious hips, and slammed himself inside her again, buried so deep he didn't want to ever stop making love.

Any protests she might have been ready to give him evaporated, and she faced forward and called out his name, demanding more. His hips surged forward, his body making a perfect sound as it slapped against hers. Her ass turned a sweet pink as he pounded against her over and over again. His fingers dug into her skin, and he couldn't stop loving her.

She called out for more and more, and he gave her what she needed, what they both needed. He climbed on top of her, grabbing her hair with one hand as he pounded against her tight flesh while he reached around her sweet body and gripped her full breast with the other. Her nipple stabbed into his palm, and he felt a massive explosion building.

She bit into the pillow in front of her and screamed as her body convulsed around his, and that's all it took for him to let go and release with her. His pleasure shot deep within her, and in a few more pumps, he had nothing left to give.

Both of them collapsed on the bed, and Roxie tried crawling away from him, tried putting some distance between them. "No," he told her, his voice harsh.

She stiffened as he pulled her back to him, her back flush with his chest, her butt cradled in the safety of his thighs. She was tense for several moments, but finally she relaxed. Neither of them had gotten their breathing under control yet.

He didn't say a word. He knew she needed to process whatever it was she was feeling. She would talk when she felt she could. He wasn't going anywhere, and he had the luxury of giving her the time she had to take.

This was right where Kian belonged. He was done with letting her push him away, done with accepting her rejection. She was his, and it was damn time she knew it. They were a family, whether they'd chosen it or not, and it was time they started acting like one.

Kian's hand rested against her chest, and it comforted him to feel her heartbeat begin to slow. He wanted her, still. He would always want her. But for now, he was sated enough to talk to her; then he was going to make slow, sweet love to her, was going to show her with his body and mouth how much she meant.

"I want you and Lily to move in with me."

The words escaped him before he could stop himself. Well, his good intentions of letting her speak first flew right out the damn window. He felt her stiffen again and her heart rate increase. She twitched against him, but he refused to let her go. It was what he wanted, and at one time, what she'd wanted. He didn't see why it should have changed. They now had a daughter to think about.

"I don't want to talk about this right now," she finally said. She was trying to pull away from him, physically and emotionally, and he wasn't having it.

He flipped her over on her back and trapped her with his body, forcing her to look into his eyes. The mellow light cast shadows all around them, but she couldn't escape him like this. He could see into her very soul. He could see she was scared, but he knew it wasn't of him.

"Why did you leave four years ago?" he asked.

She blinked, refusing to look him in the eyes. It infuriated him, but he wasn't going anywhere, and it was damn time she knew it.

"I don't want to talk about this," she told him. "It's been a long day, my body is sated, and now I just want to sleep."

He smiled down at her, loving the crisp forcefulness of her voice as she tried to put her foot down. She'd been stubborn when he'd first met her, and it had made him want her all that much more. It helped that Kian knew exactly who he was and what he wanted. It gave him the confidence and strength to handle a woman as spirited and feisty as Roxie.

"I've been giving you time, and that doesn't seem to do me a hell of a lot of good, so I figure, time's up. You will talk to me," he said casually, as if he had all the time in the world.

He leaned down and licked the top of her breasts, lazily circling his tongue over the soft orbs before he circled her nipple. It instantly hardened, straining for his mouth. Her hands were both clasped in one of his, being held over her head, and he loved having her at his mercy. He licked her nipple and her back arched. He looked up and smiled at her. She gave him a withering glare.

"I hate you, Kian Forbes," she said, but the words ended on a sigh as he sucked her nipple into his mouth and ran his tongue over it.

"No, you don't," he said before switching to the other breast and repeating what he'd just done.

"I can desire you and still hate you," she gasped, her body arching again.

"No, you can't. It's not in you," he said.

He released her hands, and she fisted them in his hair and tugged hard. She was trying to hurt him, but she was only turning him on that much more. He tugged on her nipple with his teeth, just enough to give her a little jolt. She moaned.

"Why did you leave?" he asked again.

She closed her eyes and refused to answer him, but her fingers wrenched at his hair again.

"You're a dangerous little thing, aren't you?" he said with a laugh. She opened her eyes and glared at him.

Kian jumped from the bed, and she gazed at him in surprise. He was still hard and standing proud as he walked over to her dresser, and he didn't miss the light in her eyes as she caressed him with her look.

He opened a drawer and shut it, and she gasped at him.

"Stay out of my stuff," she said. She sat up as he opened the next drawer, finding what he wanted. He pulled them out, and her eyes narrowed as she tried to scramble from the bed, but he pounced and had her pinned again.

He grinned down at her and within seconds had her hands tightly secured to her bedpost with her own stockings. He sat on her legs and looked at his handiwork. Not too bad.

"You will pay for this," she spat at him, tugging against her hands.

"I'm not too worried," he told her. He leaned down and gave her a kiss that had him completely worked up again and left her panting. He had to be careful, because he wanted information from her, and he got distracted too easily by her perfect body.

He jumped up again and found another set of stockings. It didn't take long for him to have her feet secured. If looks could kill, he'd be a dead man.

"Now this is better," he told her with a smile. He lay on his side and ran his hands across her skin, enjoying how she quivered with each stroke of his fingers.

"Why did you leave four years ago?" he asked again.

He grabbed a pillow and held her body up, putting it beneath her ass to hold her up a little. She shook her head and then turned away, giving him a cold shoulder. He ran his hand down her stomach, then slid his fingers along her wet folds. She was soaked, which had his own arousal twitching. He easily slid two fingers inside her, then lazily moved them in and out as he sucked on her ripe nipple.

She groaned low in her throat as she struggled against her restraints. He kept stroking his fingers inside her hot body as he moved up the bed so he could see into her slatted eyes.

"Why did you leave four years ago?" he asked again before kissing her lips.

Finally, he was getting somewhere. Tears popped into her eyes, and she tried to glare at him, but emotions were coming to the surface. She was too vulnerable, completely open to him, completely at his mercy. He hated how much she was hurting, but the two of them didn't have a chance if she didn't face whatever it was she was running from.

"Why did you leave?" he asked again, gently kissing her as her tears began to spill. He continued gently stroking his fingers inside her body, keeping her languid and vulnerable. He wanted her, he always wanted her, but this wasn't about sex. This was about her letting go, giving herself to him.

"Tell me," he commanded, his voice gentle. He kissed her again, while continuing to stroke her body. Her tears fell in waves as she tried to fight the emotion. She opened her mouth to speak and closed it again. He kissed her softly once, twice, a third time. Then he rested his head against her breast, his fingers gently stroking her. He waited.

"I had to go," she finally whispered, the sound of her broken voice nearly undoing him.

"Why?" he asked. There was no judgment in his tone. He was her friend, he was her lover, he was her soul mate. He kept her vulnerable, kept her flame going, but he was gentle, loving, right beside her. His face rested in the cradle of her chest, where he could listen to her heartbeat.

"Because . . ." She hiccupped as sob after sob released. He waited. She continued to cry while he loved her and waited.

"I was lost," she finally said.

"I have always found you," he told her.

"But you didn't find me," she said.

He wanted to stop this. He wanted to end her pain, but he knew he couldn't. She wouldn't be free until she let it all out. He moved over her and slowly eased his body into hers, keeping their eyes connected. He fit so perfectly within her. How could she not feel it, see it, focus on it?

Gently, his fingers caressed her face as he slowly moved his hips, filling her, touching her, loving her with all he had.

"I will always find you," he promised. "I also know that sometimes you need to be free." He kissed her again and then leaned back, not moving, just allowing their bodies to be one, their hearts to beat in a perfect rhythm.

"I got so lost in you, I didn't know who I was anymore," she said.

This was it. This was the heart of the matter. Kian didn't know what to think about her words. She was looking him in the eyes, reaching for him, though she couldn't break the bonds he'd secured her with. He gazed at her as he shifted his body, letting her feel their connection.

"Don't you realize I'm just as lost in you?" he asked. He wasn't holding anything back in this moment. He was allowing her to see into his soul. He was giving her the gift of his vulnerability, something he'd never given another living soul.

"I don't want to be consumed," she said.

"I don't think we get a choice about that," he told her. "But we can respect each other enough to try our hardest to have boundaries."

"I don't think I know how to walk that line," she admitted.

He gazed at this beautiful woman and realized he didn't have an answer for her. He didn't know how to solve her problem. He just knew that he loved her, that he was willing to give her the space she needed to figure it out.

"I love you," he told her. Her eyes widened, and he watched as she tried to bring down the shutters.

Kian pulled out of her and felt an indescribable emptiness. He untied her feet, then her hands. Then he climbed back on the bed and offered himself to her. It was her choice to take him or not.

She sat there for a moment and then she crawled over him, connecting their bodies again. But she didn't want slow and sweet anymore. Now she wanted the pain to go away, she wanted to push it to the farthest places of her mind.

Kian could give her that because he'd made progress with her. He didn't know if they were going to have a happy ending or not, but he'd opened the door. It was her choice if she wanted to walk through it.

Their lovemaking grew more and more frenzied, and when she lay sated in his arms, he held her as she drifted to sleep. Before he allowed himself to drift off, he let her go and got up.

Kian gazed down at her for a long period of time, and then he dressed and walked out the door. He wasn't sure what would happen next, but he'd opened himself up to her. Now it was her turn to decide if she could accept what he was willing to give, or if she would choose darkness forever.

Chapter Twenty-Five

Roxie's nerves were exposed, and she felt more raw than she ever had before. She still didn't know what to think about the other night with Kian. It had been too much for her, and he hadn't relented. What did that mean?

Now, she had to go to this party at Evan's house, and she knew Kian would be there. She'd refused to ride with him, and he would have to deal with that. She wasn't going to allow him to control her, and she was more than capable of arriving at a place by herself, even if the man didn't think her car was suitable. He could deal with that. But she still didn't know what it was going to be like to see him, especially in public.

Her emotions were raw, her body felt foreign, and her mind was spinning. This was one of the reasons she'd run from him in the first place. She couldn't handle how he made her feel. It was too much. All of it was just too much.

Roxie took her time arriving, not wanting to be one of the first ones there. She figured if there was a crowd, it would be much more difficult for Kian to try to corner her. She might have blonde moments once in a while, but most of the time she could think, she thought a little too smugly.

When she arrived, she had a difficult time parking, as there were so many vehicles. She had to find a space what felt like a hundred miles from the main house. She'd been wanting to have a crowd there so she wouldn't be even close to being alone with Kian, but this number of people was quite overwhelming.

As soon as she opened her car door, she heard the noise coming from Evan's house. There were bright lights shooting up into the sky from what she assumed was a party area in the back. Her heart was thudding as she pulled Lily from her car seat. Her niece grinned at her, but she wanted to walk, so the trip to the house took twice as long as it normally would, but Roxie didn't mind that. It gave her more time to pull herself together.

There was a sign on the door that told people to come on in and go straight to the back. She walked into the house, though it felt strange to do so without knocking. There were people milling all about the house, and several said hello to her as she passed through. She recognized some people, and others she didn't know at all.

She really could use a drink, but she'd driven herself, so that was off the table. Maybe she hadn't been thinking enough about this, darn it. When she stepped out the back door, she realized there were a few hundred people milling about. A live band was playing a country tune, and teens and adults were having a great time, dancing and talking, and there was so much laughter all around her, it was impossible not to smile.

Lily was tugging on her hand as she spotted a group of children over at a giant bounce house. "Hold on, sweetie," Roxie told her, but Lily wasn't being patient at all.

"I'll take her to play."

Roxie turned to find Juliana Forbes standing next to her with a sweet smile on her lips. Kian's family had always been good to her, and they treated Lily with such adoration it was impossible for Roxie to try to pull from them.

"How are you?" Roxie asked.

"I'm wonderful, darling. How about you? We need to spend some real time together because I truly miss you," Juliana said. She didn't hesitate as she reached in and wrapped her arms around Roxie.

Without thinking twice about it, Roxie released Lily's hand and grabbed on to Juliana as if she were a lifeline. A tear fell, and she found herself shaking as she accepted the woman's embrace. If she could have ever dreamed of the perfect mother, it would be this woman with eyes so kind, they made a person instantly feel warm and taken care of.

Juliana held Roxie a long time before she released her. Her own eyes were shining as she looked at Roxie with a smile.

"I miss you, too," Roxie admitted as she wiped away tears. "I'm sorry I'm such a mess right now. I don't know what's wrong with me." She tried to laugh, but she was slightly mortified at how she was behaving.

"You have nothing to apologize for," Juliana told her.

"I've never apologized for not telling you goodbye four years ago," Roxie said. This was long overdue.

Juliana cupped Roxie's cheek in her small hand. "You had your reasons. And you don't have to explain yourself. I'm just happy to see you've found your way home," she told her.

Roxie had to fight new tears that wanted so desperately to fall. She'd never felt good enough to be a part of the Forbes family, but it wasn't because of the way they treated her. No, it was all inside her own head. Anyone who was lucky enough to become a part of their family should embrace their fate.

"Let me take Lily to play with the other children while you relax for a while. You can have some much-needed time to yourself," Juliana said.

Lily was bouncing up and down beside them as she gazed over at the kids. "Thank you," Roxie said. Though it felt good to finally apologize, Roxie didn't want to keep thinking about the past.

Juliana gave her one more hug before she offered her hand to Lily, who gladly took it and practically dragged Juliana away. Roxie had to take several calming breaths to pull herself together. She looked around and was grateful no one had seemed to notice their interaction. She moved over to the drink table and grabbed some iced tea, then found a nice little corner of the yard where she could stand back and observe.

"I see my mother's found her granddaughter."

Roxie felt tears again and pushed them down as she turned to see Kian beside her. He'd sneaked up from somewhere without her awareness. She really was all off-kilter. She'd been hoping to avoid any intimate moments, but it didn't appear as if fate was on her side at the moment.

"Yes, it's as if they never were apart," Roxie said.

Juliana was laughing with joy as Lily climbed a giant slide and bounced her way down. There were at least a dozen children playing, ranging in ages from two to what appeared about ten. The tweens were mostly in a group over at a set of picnic tables, and the teens were dancing. All the children seemed to be paired off.

"I hate that she missed out on so much time, but I'm glad they've connected now," Kian said as he watched his mother and Lily.

"I'm just grateful Lily has so many people who love her," Roxie said. There was a part of her that feared Lily being taken from her, but she pushed it down. It wasn't about her, it was about her niece.

"Me too," he said. He rested his hand on her shoulder, and the touch reached all the way into her soul. She was bound to this man in ways she had no understanding of, but they were tied together. If she could figure out what that meant, she might be a happier person.

"What are you two doing standing off by yourselves?" Evan asked as he approached with a pink drink in his hand.

"What are you drinking there, girlie man?" Kian quickly replied.

Evan laughed. "I have no idea. Someone handed it to me, and I have to admit it might look girlie, but it's damn good," he said as he took a deep swallow.

Roxie laughed, grateful for the distraction. She truly did enjoy Evan's company.

"I think I'll stick with the beer," Kian told him.

"Maybe 'cause you have to prove your manliness. I have nothing to prove, so I can drink pink drinks all night long," Evan taunted him.

Kian glared at the man as he took a step closer to Roxie. She rolled her eyes. Macho posturing never had been a turn-on for her.

"Do you want to dance, beautiful?" Evan asked.

Roxie felt Kian tense beside her, and she was about to accept the invite when Kian spoke for her.

"No, she's dancing with me," he said.

Evan wasn't at all offended. He just laughed as he moved away.

"That was rude, Kian," she told him.

"I don't care. You don't need to be dancing with Evan," Kian said.

Then he took her hand and began pulling her to the dance floor. She refused to cause a scene, so she reluctantly allowed him to drag her there. Right as they reached the edges, the tune changed to a slow song, and the overhanging lights above dimmed.

Roxie wondered if Evan had something to do with that. It seemed everyone she knew was trying to push her and Kian together. They didn't know all the baggage standing between the two of them.

And if Roxie allowed herself to fall for this man again, would she end up losing everything? That was her greatest fear. She'd not only lose herself again, but now she would lose Lily as well. Her heart squeezed at the thought.

"Relax and enjoy this," Kian said. They were at the edge of the dance floor, and she was practically shaking.

"This isn't a good idea," she told him. They could still turn away, and no one would notice a thing.

"Dance with me," he said in a seductive drawl that went straight to her core. By the expression in his eyes, he knew exactly what his voice was doing to her, and she hated the power he held over her.

She didn't know what else she could say to him. She didn't have the will to fight him, and there were people all around, so even if she wanted to, she couldn't deny him. She was sure it would be the talk of the town if she ran off screaming. Then again, it might be the talk of the town if she did fall into his arms.

"I wouldn't mind dragging you over my shoulder," he said with a wicked smile that sent flutters to her stomach. She wouldn't mind being locked in his arms. Dang it, she truly was losing her mind.

Roxie didn't give him a confirmation, but she allowed him to bring her the rest of the way onto the floor. The second he pulled her in close and she felt her body pressed to his, the feel of his hand resting in the curve of her back and his thigh brushing between her thighs, she lost all sense of doubt. This was where she always belonged, where she always felt the safest.

It was so turbulent with Kian, but at the same time, it felt as if she were in the eye of the storm, that he was her anchor, her safety net. How could she think he was the cause of her problems, and then, on the other hand, believe he was the only one who could fix them? She had problems—real problems.

"Look at me," Kian told her in a throaty whisper.

She couldn't refuse him and looked up, their gazes locking together, their warm breaths mingling. He pulled her even closer, and she was trapped, trapped in his embrace, in his eyes, in his very existence. She found she didn't want to escape. At least she didn't in this moment.

She forgot about the people surrounding them, forgot they had unresolved issues. She couldn't think of anything other than how it felt to be in this man's arms. He had once been everything to her, and it seemed like he might be that man again. Whether she wanted him to be or not, she'd let him consume her again.

The soft pulse of the music seemed to wash right through her, and she felt like the two of them were floating on clouds. No matter how she tried telling herself it was just a dance, she knew it was so much more than that. It was a seduction.

Her hand drifted from his shoulder and rested against his heart, which was beating strong and steady. She felt comfort in his strength, in his very presence. He truly was her haven in the storm.

She couldn't look away from his gaze, from the heat in his eyes, the softness of his lips or the pulse in his neck. His gaze caressed her face, and she could feel it all the way through her body. His eyes rested on her lips, and they tingled with the need to connect to his. She licked them, and a low moan escaped his mouth, the sound shooting straight to her core.

"You look beautiful tonight," he murmured, pulling her even closer. There was no mistaking the bulge pressing against her. It didn't matter how many times they made love, she'd never have enough of him. His desire for her was beyond arousing.

He leaned lower and caressed her ear with his lips. "Actually, *beautiful* is too mellow a word to describe how you look," he said, his hot breath sending shivers down her spine. She was going to melt in front of every person in this room.

Roxie tried to push him away, but he wasn't letting her go.

"People are watching us," she warned.

"Let them. I'm sure every man in this room wants to be me right now," he told her.

His hand slid over the curve of her ass before coming back up, and though she knew this was wrong, so very wrong, she couldn't seem to stop it from happening. It felt too good.

She shut down the doubts in her mind and simply enjoyed the moment with this man. She wasn't sure how many more times like this she would allow herself, so she had to take it all in, because, if she wasn't brave enough, she would walk away from this man again, and memories would be all she'd have left.

She closed her eyes and rested her cheek against his chest, the beating of his heart mellowing her even more. He tucked her against him, and it was only him and her. No one else existed; no one else could come between them, not in this perfect moment.

"I hope you're all having a good time!"

The boisterous voice came over the loudspeaker as the music stopped. Roxie's head jerked up as she looked to the stage, where Evan was standing with a microphone. He called some people up onstage, including Kian, who pulled away from her with reluctance.

She wanted to hold him tight, but she had to let him go. He gave her an intense look before walking away, a look that told her he had something to say. She decided she didn't want to hear whatever it was.

So, like a thief in the night, she went and collected a very unhappy Lily, and she slipped away from the party—away from Kian. She wasn't ready for that conversation yet. She just didn't know what she was going to think or say. So, she ran away again.

Chapter Twenty-Six

It was dark when Roxie got home, and though her heart felt as if it was breaking, she was at least grateful Lily had fallen asleep on the drive. Her niece had been ticked off Roxie was pulling her away from her friends. Roxie hadn't allowed her to play long enough, but she couldn't face all the Forbes family members, and she certainly couldn't face Kian anymore that night.

She was afraid he might show up later, so she planned on removing her spare key and turning out all the lights. She knew if he was determined, that wouldn't stop him, but maybe he would understand she needed a little bit of time. That wasn't asking too much, in her honest opinion.

Once more she'd forgotten to leave her porch light on and to set her alarm system, which was sure to tick Kian off. Then again, she often pissed the man off. Tonight seemed off, though, and a shiver traveled down her spine as she carried Lily while she fumbled in her purse to pull out her key.

As Roxie walked into the house, another shudder passed through her, and she couldn't figure out what was wrong with her. She was grateful when Lily stayed asleep and decided to let her sleep in her clothes that night. She didn't want to take a chance of waking her. Roxie needed a few minutes to herself. Maybe a nice hot bath.

The moment she sank down into the tub, she couldn't help but think of what had happened after her last bath when she'd walked into her bedroom. A shudder passed through her when she realized she hadn't grabbed the key on the front porch yet. But did she really want to? Would it be so awful if Kian showed up and took her mind off her worries for a single night?

The bathroom door was open, and there wasn't a sound in the house, so she knew Kian hadn't shown up. She'd left the party almost two hours earlier. If he'd been planning on stopping by, he would have done it by now.

Maybe she just couldn't make up her mind about what in the world she wanted. When her bathwater began cooling, she decided to get out instead of adding more water. She hadn't eaten anything at the party, and her stomach was growling. Slipping on her robe, she decided to dress later, and she headed straight for the kitchen.

When she walked into the small area, her heart began thundering in her chest. She'd never been afraid before in this house. It was in a quiet neighborhood, and in this town, in general, there wasn't a lot of crime. But sitting on her butcher's block was a knife she didn't remember putting there, and crumbs. Roxie was sort of emphatic about cleaning her messes up, and though she was racking her mind to try to remember if she'd been in a hurry and left a mess, she couldn't remember doing so. She would have taken a moment to clean up.

Maybe Kian had shown up. But he'd never before made himself at home like this. She had to be growing paranoid, that was all. Still, she walked through her house, first checking her bedroom to see if she was going to find him lying on her bed. Then she walked to Lily's room. For some reason, her stomach was tight as she neared the door and pushed it open.

When she did, Roxie's heart lodged up into her throat, and she found herself so terrified, she now understood what people meant when they said they were frozen in fear. Her limbs were unbending, her heart stalled in her chest, and her skin ran cold as a chill froze her entire body.

A man was sitting on Lily's bed, holding her in his arms as he rocked back and forth. The only light in the room was a castle night-light, casting eerie shadows across the man's demonic face. He looked away from Lily's sleeping pink cheeks and straight into Roxie's terrified gaze. There was something so evil about the look in this man's eyes, Roxie knew if she survived this, she would never forget that manic stare.

He raised a finger to his lips as he continued rocking, and though only seconds had passed, it felt like an eternity before Roxie was able to take in a breath. She had to remain calm so she could at least try to save Lily. She had to get the man away from her niece—from her little girl.

"Wh-what do you want?" she asked, her voice barely audible in her utter fear.

"Shh," he said before the most evil laughter spilled from his filthy lips. "You don't want to wake the child, do you?" he said.

"No. Why don't you lay her down and we'll go to the living room and talk?" Roxie said, trying to keep the terror from her voice as she forced herself to keep a calm tone.

He smiled as he looked down at Lily and then ran one of his filthy hands across her forehead. He leaned over and licked Lily's cheek, and Roxie's bile rose in her throat. She couldn't throw up now. She had to keep her wits.

"Pretty, pretty girl," he said as he leaned back. Thankfully, Lily was sleeping through all of this. If she woke up, she would scream bloody murder, and Roxie had no idea what this man would do to her.

Roxie was searching around her for a weapon, but she was in a child's room. She had nothing she could grab. This was every parent's worst nightmare, but something Roxie hadn't even considered happening. She should have, especially with the way her sister had died.

"I failed," the man said, an evil smile lifting his lips. "But don't worry, I've come back to finish the job."

He stood, Lily hanging limply in his arms, and Roxie was terrified he'd already killed the child. But she groaned as she tried to get more comfortable, and Roxie let out a relieved breath. She still had a chance to save her.

He set Lily down, not taking his eyes off Roxie as he whispered, "I'll come back to you soon, child."

The way he said those words would give Roxie nightmares for the rest of her life. He leaned over and picked up a giant knife from the foot of Lily's bed, and what little color was left in Roxie's body completely disappeared. She was going to die tonight. There was nothing she could do to stop this huge man from killing her, and what was worse, she wouldn't be able to save Lily.

She wondered if she could run back to the kitchen and grab that knife before he had a chance to hurt Lily. She didn't want to leave her niece, though. She couldn't take that chance. Tears poured down her face as she faced this monster, who began to move toward her.

She backed up. She had to get him out of the room. She didn't know what she would do beyond that, but she had to get him out of Lily's room. He followed her, that evil smile on his face as he lifted his knife and ran the back of the blade across his neck, showing her what he planned on doing to her.

"Pamela deserved to die nice and slow, and so did her bastard brat," the man said with another chuckle. Roxie froze in front of him. This was the man who'd killed her sister and unborn baby. This was the man who'd attacked Lily once already. He was back to finish the job.

"Why?" Roxie asked. She was hoping someone would pass by, someone would see something. Her curtains were open. She backed her way into the living room, praying a neighbor was walking their dog. He seemed oblivious to what she was doing. That was good. He was focused only on her. Even if he got her, she would scream and someone would come; someone would save her niece.

"She's a slut who had to die," he said as he cocked his head to the side. He was speaking in a matter-of-fact way, as if it were his duty to kill.

"Please don't hurt Lily," Roxie begged.

"What will you do for me to ensure I don't?" he asked with evil delight.

"Anything," Roxie said. "Let's leave the house. You can take me." She opened her arms, showing him she had nothing. She was his to do with as he pleased.

His lips turned up even more as he eyed her from head to toe.

"I like this house," he told her. "You even left me a key to get in. That was so very nice of you."

Roxie wanted to kick her own ass now. She knew a locked door wouldn't have stopped a man like this, but if she hadn't left the key out, then maybe she would have had a clue he was in the place; maybe she could have gotten away. If she'd listened to her instinct when she'd felt nervous at walking in the house, then maybe Lily wouldn't be in mortal danger right now. This was in her hands now.

"Please, just take me," she said, unable to control her tears now.

"Don't move," he commanded, his voice dropping, not a trace of humor there anymore.

Her body shook as he stepped toward her. She didn't try to run. She wouldn't leave this man alone with Lily. She couldn't. He came and stood before her and ran the tip of his blade down her neck, scratching the skin. She didn't make a sound.

He ran the blade down the V of her robe and nicked the top of her breast. She continued to shake, but she knew she was no match for this man.

"Open your robe," he said, his voice husky as he gazed at her chest.

Roxie was definitely going to be sick. There was no doubt about it. She was about to get raped and murdered. She couldn't think of a worse way to go. Her eyes burning, she reached for the sash of her robe.

Maybe, just maybe, she could use the robe to grab the deadly knife and then fight him. Yes, he could overpower her, but if he wasn't holding the knife, she could scream and pray her neighbors heard.

Just as she was beginning to undo the robe, her front door was smashed open against the wall, the wood shattering with the force. Roxie flew backward as someone yanked her arm and tossed her behind, causing her to land with a hard thump against her couch. Her head slammed against the cushioned armrest, and she saw spots of color for a moment and heard a thunderous roar.

Somewhere in the middle of the chaos, she heard Lily scream, and all she could think of was her niece. She jumped from the couch and ran to her niece, who was now standing in the hallway. She scooped her into her arms and ran for the front door.

She felt fingers try to grip her ankle, but she managed to slip free and ran outside, not stopping as she took off down the road. She heard sirens in the distance and prayed they were coming to her. And they did.

She made it a block down the street, Lily screaming at the top of her lungs, when the first police car screeched around the corner. It headed straight to her house. Another car shot past her, and then one stopped right in front of her. She stopped, shaking where she stood as a man climbed from the car, his hand on his weapon as he approached.

"Ma'am, are you okay?" he asked as he looked around.

She opened her mouth but couldn't speak. The fear was so real, so great.

"Ma'am, the ambulance is on the way. Do you need me to take the child?"

Roxie's eyes were wide; she was shaking. She knew she was in shock, and she probably should release Lily, but she couldn't loosen her grip. Lily's head was buried in her shoulder as she uncontrollably sobbed.

"It's okay, Roxie. I'm here. It's okay."

Roxie turned and found Kian beside her. The officer knew him and seemed to relax. "Is the house secure, Kian?" he asked.

"It's secure. They have the bastard," Kian said. "I've got Roxie."

The officer nodded, climbed into his car, and drove down to her house.

"Let me take Lily before you fall to the ground," Kian said, his voice soothing. His shirt was ripped, and there was blood oozing from his arm, but he was so calm.

"It's okay, Roxie, let me take Lily," he said again.

"I c-can't," she finally managed to say on a terrified sob.

"Okay, I understand," he told her. "Let's go back to the house," he suggested, and terror-filled shakes racked her body.

"Okay, we'll just sit right here," he compromised.

She allowed him to help her to the ground. Her neighbors were all out of their houses, looking to see what all the commotion was about, and someone placed a blanket over her and Lily. Kian sat next to her, his arm around her.

They didn't speak. They just sat there as he rubbed her shoulder. Soon the ambulance showed up, and she still couldn't release Lily, not even when she was placed on a stretcher and lifted inside the ambulance. She was still in fight-or-flight mode, and all she knew was that she had to save her niece. She must save her niece—her daughter. Lily was her daughter now. She was hers, and she had to save her.

Chapter Twenty-Seven

There were times in a man's life when basic instinct was all that kept you alive. There were times when you shut off everything except adrenaline and rage. When Kian had pulled up to Roxie's house, intent on giving her a piece of his mind for leaving, he'd realized exactly what that meant.

Her curtains were open, and a man was standing in front of her holding a knife. He'd taken about five seconds to call 911, to tell them a murder was about to happen, then he'd left his phone on, dropped on the front seat of his pickup truck, and he'd charged the front door.

In his rage, he'd kicked it in without a moment's hesitation, and then he'd lunged. He'd had the advantage on the attacker, as he'd come out of nowhere, but the man had been big, and he'd managed to get a couple of swipes of his blade into Kian. But there had been no way Kian was allowing that man to harm his family.

He'd subdued the man, and he'd seriously planned on ending his life so he could never be a threat to anyone again, but the cops showed up damn fast when he didn't want them to. Before he could strangle the man, he'd been pulled off him. It hadn't taken the cops, who just so happened to be family friends, to figure out who the attacker was in the situation. As soon as they had the man cuffed and secured in the police car, Kian had found Roxie. She was in shock and holding on to Lily for dear life.

And he loved her. She'd done everything within her power to save their daughter. He had been able to tell what was happening when he'd glanced in that window, and he knew she was trying to keep the man from Lily. Kian couldn't love her any more than he already did.

She would sacrifice herself for Lily, and that was something a lot of women couldn't say or wouldn't do. There were many people out there who would say that they would die for those they loved. But Kian knew they were empty words. Most people had a basic survival instinct, and when it came down to it, they wouldn't make the ultimate sacrifice.

A shudder passed through his body, and he was terrified to think about what could have happened if he hadn't come over. He'd taken his time, as if to prove to her he didn't have to chase her right away. What a foolish man he'd been. His stubborn pride could have cost him the life of the woman he loved, and his precious daughter who'd now been attacked twice before she was even four years old. That was so incredibly sick, it made him want to find the man again and beat him into a bloody pulp.

He'd begged the chief of police for two minutes alone with the attacker, and though his friend had told him he'd love to give Kian that time, he couldn't do it. Then Kian would become the guilty party, and he wasn't going to do that to him. For Kian to get his hands around that man's neck, he'd be willing to pay the price.

As he looked across the room at his beautiful daughter, he realized instantly that wasn't true. He would die for her, he'd even go to prison for her, but he wouldn't do something foolish that would prevent him from spending more time with his baby girl.

Roxie hadn't needed stiches. The cuts were superficial, thankfully, and Lily hadn't been touched this time. Well, she hadn't been hurt, he clarified. When Roxie had calmed down enough to tell him what she'd found when she'd opened Lily's bedroom door, he completely understood her terror and shock. He was so grateful that she'd been able to maintain a cool head. He wasn't sure he'd have reacted the same way. He was just glad he wasn't the one to open that door.

"Lily Bear, how are you feeling?" Roxie asked. Her voice was a little hoarse from her screams, but it was now calm. She was almost back to normal.

"Good," she said as she clung to Roxie's side. The need to hold his daughter was overwhelming. It was taking all the power he had to stay in the chair. His arm was patched, and he'd been given a drug to calm him, though he hadn't wanted that. The doc in charge had said it was better than him smashing things up. Maybe his friend was right.

"Can I tell you something special?" Roxie asked Lily.

She looked up at Roxie with her trusting dark eyes and nodded.

"You see Kian over there?" Roxie asked. Kian smiled as Lily looked at him and waved.

"Yeah," she said. Damn, he loved her so much.

"He's your daddy, baby girl, and that means he loves you to the moon and back," Roxie said, choking up on the last words.

Kian's heart lodged in his throat as she finally told his daughter who he was. He couldn't imagine the heartbreak he'd feel if she didn't accept him as such.

Lily turned her head as she gazed at him, maybe seeing if he was worthy of being her daddy. He found himself holding his breath as he waited for her verdict. Then she smiled the most innocent and beautiful smile he'd ever seen.

"Daddy," she said. She held up her arms, and he didn't hesitate to rush to her, lifting her up and kissing her cheek. "Daddy," she repeated before laying her sweet cheek against his chest.

Kian couldn't control the tear that slipped from his eye. He blamed the damn drug the doctor had forced on him, because there was no way it was an actual, emotional tear. He hadn't cried since he was five years old. He'd swear to that in a court of law.

He sniffed as he closed his eyes and pulled himself together. "Yes, I'm your daddy, baby girl," he said, his voice gruff.

She leaned back and looked at him, then raised her sweet little hand and rested it on his cheek, and his damn broken eyes stung again as he gazed into the innocent depths of his little girl's eyes.

"And Mommy," she said before she pointed at Roxie.

"Yeah, and Mommy," he confirmed as he looked at Roxie, who wasn't even trying to hide her own tears. She wouldn't even need the excuse of medication.

Kian sat down next to Roxie, his daughter safely held in his good arm, his cut arm wrapped around Roxie. "We're a family," he said.

Roxie stiffened the slightest bit next to him, and he found his heart breaking a little. She might not be ready for this. He knew he couldn't rush it, knew he had to be patient. But after a night like the one he'd just had, patient wasn't something he wanted to be. He wanted to protect and care for them both, and he wanted to do it starting right this minute.

"Yes, we're always going to be a family," Roxie said. But there was a bit of distance in her voice. Kian wanted to push the issue, but he knew he couldn't do that right now. He knew he had to let her figure it all out. She shouldn't make a decision when she'd just had such a traumatic night, anyway.

"Why don't you both come home with me tonight?" Kian suggested.

"Thank you, but I think I need to go to my house tonight," she told him. There was fear in her voice, like she was afraid of him getting mad at her over the request.

"I understand," he said. But he forced her to look at him as he said the next words. She needed to hear him. "I love you, Roxie, and I'm a somewhat patient man. But tonight scared me more than I've ever been scared before. I need you to make a decision."

She gazed at him with confusion in her eyes, and then finally she nodded. He leaned in and kissed her lips gently before backing up.

"Do you want to take Lily with you?" she asked with so much pain he knew the request was killing her.

"I always want Lily with me," he said and felt her body flinch. "But tonight, she needs her mama."

He felt the relief flood through her, and he knew he'd made the right call. He wanted both his girls home with him, and he had a feeling it was going to happen very soon. With that knowledge, he could give Roxie the space she needed to come to the decision on her own.

Chapter Twenty-Eight

Roxie wiped her eyes as she walked to the break room and poured what had to be her tenth cup of coffee in only four hours' time. She was more than grateful the hospital was slow today. She truly feared she'd make a wrong call, and a patient would be the one to pay the price.

She hadn't seen Kian in three days. Now, that might not seem a long time to the average person, but after all of their ups and downs, it might as well be an eternity. She'd been at work all three days, and Kian had been in the hospital, but he'd been on another floor, and she couldn't find a reason to go there.

She knew he'd stopped at the day care many times to visit with Lily, who was always more than happy to see him and had to tell Roxie all about their special time together. So, it was only Roxie he appeared to be avoiding. That was good, she tried to convince herself. He'd told her he was giving her time to figure it out.

But she was a wreck, an utter and complete wreck. She wasn't sure what she wanted or needed. But she did know for sure after that night a week ago when he'd pushed her to the breaking point, she hadn't been the same again. Then the attack had happened, and she'd been in even more turmoil. She couldn't sleep, she picked up her phone constantly to see if he'd called or texted, and she walked slowly through the hospital hoping to run into him. She wanted to see him, but her damn pride wouldn't allow her to call him and admit to that.

Though emotionally, she wasn't at all ready to face this man again, she also knew that he was a wonderful father, and she would have to get used to him being in her life. She just wasn't sure if he was going to be an intimate part or not.

Roxie couldn't even imagine how it would feel to see him with another woman, but she knew she either had to give him all of her or nothing. Kian wouldn't accept anything less than . . . well, everything. That's how she'd gotten lost in him the first time around. And it was so much more intense now than it had been back then.

"How's everything going, Roxie?"

She turned to find one of the new young nurses standing there with far too much perk in her step and eyes. Roxie hated the woman just the tiniest bit in that moment. She would love to feel carefree with no burdens on her shoulders. It didn't even matter if she was placing half of them on her own shoulders.

With an unusual attitude, Roxie found herself wanting to throw a kicking, screaming, downright three-year-old tantrum. She found herself wanting to throw her perfectly good cup across the room and enjoy it as it slid down the wall. Her lips twitched as she pictured the poor nurse's expression. It was almost worth it just for that. Instead, she sipped her coffee and smiled.

"It's great. How are you, Jeanette?"

"Wonderful. My boyfriend is taking me out to a romantic dinner tonight."

Ah, that's why the girl was being all social. She wanted to brag. Well, goodie for her, Roxie thought snidely.

"I shouldn't jinx it, but I think he's gonna propose," she added with a sigh.

"How old are you?" Roxie asked. She looked twelve but obviously had to be older than that.

"I just turned twenty-one. I graduated high school early," she said with a giggle.

Oh, the things Roxie wanted to tell this girl. She wanted to explain how much she would change in the next few years, wanted to warn her not to jump too quickly into marriage, wanted to tell her to run. But then that would be putting Roxie's own burdens on her. So, she just smiled and said what she was supposed to say.

"That's wonderful, I can't wait to hear what happens."

Jeanette beamed as she literally bounced out of the room. Roxie downed her coffee and refilled her mug before heading out to the floor again. Her shift wasn't even halfway over, and it felt as if the day had only just begun. Normally she loved her job, but Kian had her mind and emotions all screwed up, and maybe, just maybe, she was going to find him and give him a real piece of her mind. That made an actual smile pop up on her face.

Without her consent, or even being in her right mind, Roxie found herself heading to the elevators and pushing the "Up" button. She waited impatiently for the doors to open, and when they did, she stepped on with determination. She *was* going to give him a piece of her mind.

It didn't take her long to find him, and she was all worked up when she did. He was talking to another doctor, and she stood in his peripheral vision and tapped her foot impatiently. The other doctor eyed her for a moment before turning back to Kian, who didn't acknowledge her presence. That only infuriated her all the more.

She was about to scream when the doctor Kian had been talking to gave her one more weary glance then scooted away. She wanted to yell at the man that the hospital only ran so efficiently because of the nursing staff, and maybe he should give them a lot more respect. Somehow, she managed not to do just that.

Kian turned to her and really pissed her off when he gave her that same damn smile he gave rowdy patients, that calm-down-and-trust-me smile. She heard a low growl escape her lips and was shocked enough by it that she took a step back.

"We need to talk," she told him, her voice raw with emotion.

"Okay," he said, not attempting to argue with her. He was being perfectly reasonable, and that should have calmed her, but it only infuriated her all the more. If she was being even a little bit rational, then maybe she would realize how insane she was acting, but she was too far gone for that.

"We need to talk about the other night," she said, trying desperately to keep her voice down as people passed by them.

He seemed utterly relaxed, without a care in the world if people heard them or not. That wasn't helping her blood pressure at all. She was trembling; she was getting herself so worked up, and he was just calm, that damn patient-calming smile on his perfect too-handsome face.

"What about it?" he asked. He then had the gall to glance down at the chart in his hand. Roxie then did something she never thought she'd be capable of doing. She stepped up to him and slapped the file from underneath. The papers flew up in the air and then fluttered to the ground. Several people were passing by and stared, obviously trying to assess if they needed to call security or not.

She might have calmed down at that point if she hadn't looked into Kian's eyes and seen laughter in them. The corners of his eyes were crinkling, and his lips were twitching. He was trying desperately not to laugh at her.

The rest of Roxie's cool evaporated as she launched herself forward, more determined than ever to wipe that smugness from his face. She wasn't even sure who in the hell she was anymore; she just knew she had to damage him.

The chuckle that escaped him as he easily lifted her up, placing her over his shoulder, vibrated through her body, and she pounded her hands against his back. When she heard his next words, she felt her face go scarlet as she tried to sink within herself.

"Sorry about this, folks, we just have a patient who needs to be returned to the fourth floor," he said.

"Ah," came the response. The fourth floor was the damn psych ward! She was so spitting angry, she could kill him.

He carried her down the hallway over his shoulder, and Roxie continued to beat against his back as he laughed. He didn't stop until he went through a doorway and shut a door, the lock going firmly in place. Then, as if she were a sack of potatoes, he shifted her from his shoulders and tossed her on the bed.

The bright light was shining as he stood above her. The wretched man had the gall to lean against the bunk beds across from her, his arms folded as he gazed at her with a smile, as if he hadn't just humiliated her.

"Carry on," he said.

"Carry on?" she screeched. She didn't even recognize her own voice anymore.

"You were saying?" he prompted.

Roxie jumped from the bed, her limbs tangling, tripping her up, certainly slowing her momentum. Then she was finally on her feet and coming after him. He didn't budge. Just stood there as she pounded her fists against his chest. His expression never changed as she wore herself out. Finally, her anger dimmed, and then she was absolutely horrified at what she'd become, of what she'd just done.

Her eyes widened, and she took a step back, her hands going over her mouth. "I-I-I . . ." She closed her mouth. "I don't know what happened," she said.

Her knees gave out, and she flopped down on the bed as her head dropped. "I don't know what happened. I don't know why I was so mad."

She was close to sobbing, but she couldn't fall apart. She was in the middle of a shift. She had to get back out on the floor. As if Kian could read her mind, he lifted his phone, pressing it to his ear.

"This is Dr. Forbes," he said, his voice filled with professionalism and authority. "Nurse Gilbert will need to be replaced. I'm having a consultation with her that will take the rest of the shift." There was a pause. "Thank you."

He turned the phone off and faced her again. She stared up at him, waiting for an explosion, for some emotion other than humor to cross his face. She didn't know what to do or say. She wanted to run, but she knew there was no chance of that happening. He still said nothing, just gazed down at her.

"You can't keep standing there looking at me like that," she finally said. She was so close to falling apart, she wasn't sure she knew which way was up or down anymore.

"I'm waiting," he said. There was so much understanding and humor in his face, she didn't know what to think.

"You're waiting for what?" she snapped. She felt her anger rise again and tried desperately to push it down. She'd already humiliated herself enough for one day. She didn't need to add to the mess she was making of her life.

He smiled, his face almost serene, and she felt a sense of calm pass through her. She didn't understand it at all. What in the world was happening?

"I'm waiting for you to put it all together," he told her.

"Put what together?" she snapped. She wanted to pace, jump up, and shake him. She wanted action, but didn't understand what action. This was too overwhelming. It was all too much, and she felt as if she were going crazy.

"I love you," he simply said.

She gaped at him. How could he even say those words to her when she'd been acting like a crazy woman? Was there something wrong with him? Maybe she was perfectly fine, and he was the mental one.

"I love you," he repeated.

This time, the words sank in slowly and began drifting through her like a slow molasses warming her blood and easing her stress. She stared at him, not knowing what to think, what to say, what to do.

"I love you, Roxie Gilbert. I always have, and I always will." His words came out with such surety, such devotion. She felt her body sag, her mind let go and . . . and her heart open. It opened so wide, so painfully, that she clutched her chest. It hurt; it physically hurt as it beat erratically in her chest.

She stared at him as he continued to give her that serene smile as if he had all the answers. And suddenly she felt as if he did. She felt as if he'd known all along what was in her heart, in her soul, and he'd simply been waiting for her to figure it out. She couldn't find words to say as she gripped her chest, the ache turning into a warmth that radiated through her.

"I love you," she whispered. It was almost a question. But she did. She loved this man in an all-consuming, passionate way. But for some reason, she wasn't frightened by it anymore. She wasn't filled with the need to run away from him; she was filled with the desire to run straight into his arms, to let him hold her, to share the burdens and joys with her.

"I won't lose myself in you," she said, her voice awed. He looked at her, joy in his eyes as she figured it all out. He'd forgiven her for fleeing because he knew she hadn't known who she was. He'd forgiven her in the hopes she could forgive him. That's how it worked, didn't it? You loved someone in spite of the bad; you loved them in good times and in disasters. You couldn't choose which emotion to feel; you could only choose how to handle each situation.

But Roxie knew she couldn't run anymore. She had run in the wrong direction, and she'd almost lost the man she truly loved. But by some miracle, she'd been called back home, and now she had received a second chance.

Slowly, afraid her limbs wouldn't hold her up, she stood, her legs trembling. Kian didn't move. He stood right where he was, but he uncrossed his arms and opened them, showing her she had nothing to fear.

She moved quickly, pressing herself to him, finally accepting what he'd wanted to give her all along—himself. His love for her had survived it all, and now she could accept him and give him all of her. She had never had anything to fear but herself, and now that she was letting him, he would help carry that burden.

"I love you," she said. She said it again and again, and he rubbed her back and held her as she sobbed in his arms. He loved her. He truly loved her, and with that knowledge, she felt invincible.

Kian picked her up and carried her to the bed. He lay down and enfolded her. He didn't strip them bare, didn't make love to her, he just held her, and it was absolutely perfect. They would soon pick up their daughter, and their family would be complete.

"I'm going to marry you as soon as I can get the license," he said, his voice casual, as if there wasn't a chance of letting her escape.

"What makes you think I'll say yes?" she joked, joy in her voice.

He reached into his pocket and pulled out a small black box. He was leaning against the back of the bed with her resting between his legs, her back against his chest. She looked at the box in shock as he opened it, and a brilliant square diamond sparkled against the velvet.

Her fingers shook as she lifted them and traced the sparkling rock. She snatched her hand away as if she were stung. Tears fell down her face. How long had he been carrying this? She wanted to ask, but she didn't think it was possible to get words past the tightness of her throat.

"I carried this for two months before you left four years ago. I'm not telling you that to hurt you; I just want you to know how long I've loved you," he said. "I've now had it in my pocket again since the day after I saw you in that park."

His voice choked on the last word, and she felt her own heart break all over again at how much she'd hurt this man and how truly strong he'd been for the both of them. She twisted on the bed so she was on her knees before him.

She carefully cradled his face in her hands and leaned in, running her lips across his before she backed away, not trying to hide her tears from him anymore.

"Thank you for loving me. I will never be able to apologize enough for the pain I've caused you, but you need to know I will do my best to be your everything from here on out," she said, the words difficult to speak past the lump in her throat.

His eyes sparkled as he gazed at her, and then he pulled the ring out and took her left hand, slipping it on her finger. It was a perfect fit. He then cupped her cheek in his large hand as he smiled at her.

"For time and all eternity," he whispered.

"Yes, Kian, a thousand times, yes."

They stopped talking as his lips took hers. They sealed their promise to each other, and then, hand in hand, they went and picked up their daughter so they could start the rest of their lives together.

Epilogue

Why was it that sometimes it took a terrible tragedy to wake a person up? Roxie would never understand it, but she also wasn't a person who didn't learn from mistakes. She'd made too many of them in her life, and now she had been given a second chance, and she vowed not to waste it.

Kian held Lily in his arms, and the sound of her laughter was about the most beautiful music in the universe to Roxie. She rubbed her bulky stomach as she glided across the dance floor, her eyes focused on the two most important people in her life.

"There's my beautiful wife," Kian said as she leaned in and kissed him before giggling.

"With my stomach out so far, I'm having a much more difficult time reaching you," she said.

"I love this belly. I'm going to miss it," Kian told her as he ran his fingers across her protruding stomach.

"I'm going to miss it, too," Roxie admitted. "I love Lily as if she truly were mine. I also love this experience of carrying a child within me and getting to be there for every moment."

"Lily is both of ours," Kian said, and Roxie had no doubt of the truth in his words.

"We're blessed more than words could ever say," Roxie told him.

"Yes, we are, and we're a family," Kian told her.

"Dance with me," Roxie insisted.

She chuckled as he held Lily in one arm and wrapped the other around Roxie's waist. She leaned her head into his shoulder and smiled at Lily as the three, soon to be four, of them swayed to the music playing.

"Happy anniversary, Mrs. Forbes," Kian whispered.

"Happy anniversary, my love," Roxie replied.

He leaned in and kissed her, and she knew every single day would bring more and more joy to her life. It truly didn't get any better than it was right now. She'd been afraid of losing herself. Now she realized how foolish that was. She couldn't get lost in another person when she knew exactly who she was. It wasn't until she'd realized that that she'd actually found herself, and now she had the rest of her life to continue to grow into the person she was always meant to be.

"Joseph Anderson, I sure have to say I'm more than grateful you're my friend," Lucian said with a wide grin as he patted Joseph on the back.

"Hey, I'm not chopped liver," Sherman grumbled before he gobbled down the rest of a pastry that was so buttery, he couldn't help but moan in delight.

"Of course not," Lucian said with a chuckle. "I've been waiting for my children to pull their heads out for a long time, and it seems they just needed a little pushing to get the ball rolling."

"Well, you're not even halfway there yet," Joseph pointed out as the three men turned and looked to where three of Lucian's sons were standing off in a corner, away from the rest of the crowd.

"I wonder what they're discussing over there," Sherman said. "We should just put bugs on all of them, and then we'd know."

He would most likely do that if he could get away with it. The sad thing was, Lucian wasn't too against the idea himself, and he knew for sure Joseph would be on board.

"They are probably jealous their oldest brother is celebrating his one-year wedding anniversary with such a beautiful and sweet bride," Joseph said with a chuckle.

"Yeah, I somehow doubt that," Lucian said.

Lucian and his wife were thrilled that both their daughter and their eldest son had found spouses who not only made them shine, but who Lucian could truly say were their perfect matches. But he still had three sons who had darkness in their lives. If only they'd open their hearts, they'd find joy unlike anything they could ever imagine.

Owen was his most relaxed son, always ready to laugh with you or lend a hand. He would make a fine husband if he'd just settle down. Chasing fires was honorable and all, but it didn't keep you warm at night. That thought had Lucian smiling. It might keep him mighty hot if he was in a burning building. Lucian wasn't as worried about him as he was about Declan, though.

There was something his youngest son wasn't talking to them about. He wasn't sure what it was, but Declan had secrets he didn't share with anyone. He wore his emotions close to the chest, and he never made a mistake and exposed them.

Sure, his son was a fine man—all of his children were—but Declan had secrets, and he needed a strong woman who could help carry whatever burdens he felt he needed to carry alone.

Now, Arden, on the other hand, was primed and ready for love. That boy had been a miracle worker at the high school where he taught. He'd changed many lives of his students, and Lucian couldn't be prouder of the profession he'd chosen. He might not have his name shining in lights, but he was making more of a difference than most people in his position would choose to make. He was creating leaders and saving those the rest of the world had given up on.

"I think Arden is ready," Lucian said aloud, and Joseph and Sherman turned to gaze at the man in question. Just then he looked up, and his eyes narrowed in suspicion as he caught all eyes on him. Then he shifted uncomfortably and looked away.

"Oh yes, I think he's certainly ready," Joseph agreed.

Before they could speak further, a commotion broke out. The three men turned and found Lily dancing on her father's shoes as he slowly moved across the floor. Roxie was slowly approaching them, her cheeks glowing, her rounded stomach just beginning to show in her fourth month of pregnancy. She was already Lily's mother now, and soon she'd add one more child to their family.

Lucian couldn't be happier with his growing family. His daughter had given him a beautiful baby boy who'd just turned a year old a month earlier, and Lily was a fresh breath of air Lucian couldn't get enough of. He had to push back his sorrow at missing her first few years of life. That was a hard lesson he'd certainly learned from. Hopefully his kids had paid attention and were a lot more careful after that.

In about five months, he'd have another grandchild. He didn't want to be greedy, but he'd be satisfied if he had about twenty of the babies running around his place in five years on Christmas morning. Maybe he'd keep that thought to himself—at least for now.

Turning in the opposite direction from the dance floor, Lucian spotted where the noise was coming from. One of Arden's students was in a fistfight. Arden moved quickly, breaking the two boys up, Owen and Declan right behind him.

"Wonder what that's all about?" Sherman said.

"Arden will get it worked out," Lucian said, not at all worried.

Kian watched as his brothers marched the kids from the room, but he knew the situation was secure, so he went back to dancing with his bride and daughter, looking happier than he'd ever looked.

"Yes, today is a day of celebration," Joseph said with a beaming smile.

The three men quickly grew quiet as their wives approached, but not before Joseph winked. They'd never grow bored of helping to find happiness for those they loved. It was selfless, after all, Lucian thought before he wrapped his arm around his wife and led her to the dance floor. He'd also never get tired of holding his own perfect bride, who was just as beautiful today as she'd been the moment he'd met her.

ACKNOWLEDGMENTS

This book is the most emotional journey I have taken with the beginning of a new series. I always mix my personal life into my writing, and without a doubt, this book doesn't offer an exception. Kian and Roxie go through some heart-wrenching moments in this story, and it's because of the people around me that I'm able to write with such passion, happiness, anger, and laughter. I can't write alone, and I don't ever want to. Sometimes I hide away and pretend there isn't an outside world, but when I do that, my writing fails me. It's when I'm around friends and family that I'm at my best.

Thank you so much to the continued support from my fans, who I can't do the job I love without. Thank you to my family, who always support me no matter how crazy I get. Thank you to my friends, who make me laugh and get me to spread my wings and fly. Thank you to my Montlake family. You took a chance on me, have always believed in me, and make me feel like anything is possible, and I enjoy our visits so much. Thank you to Lauren, who is the best editor I've ever had. I don't say that lightly. You push me, motivate me, don't allow me to be lazy, and make my writing so much better, and you do it in a way that makes me want to be better.

ABOUT THE AUTHOR

Photo © John Evanston

Melody Anne is a *New York Times* and *USA Today* bestselling author who has written a number of popular series, including Billionaire Bachelors, Surrender, Baby for the Billionaire, and Billionaire Aviators. Along with romance and young adult novels, Melody has also recently collaborated with fellow authors J.S. Scott and Ruth Cardello for *Taken by a Trillionaire*. *Kian* is the first book in Melody's new Undercover Billionaire series.

A country girl at heart, Melody loves the small town and strong community she lives in. When she's not writing, she enjoys spending time with her family, friends, and beloved pets. Most of all, she loves being able to do what makes her happiest . . . living in a fantasy world (for at least 95 percent of the time).